Wolf pulled her to him. "You dislike me. Why? Is my kiss so different from that of the young Van der Rhys? Or is it the wealth that makes his kisses more bearable?"

"Your kisses make me ill."

The iciness of fear made her voice sound frigid with disdain. "I do not believe you," he said slowly, his anger bubbling just below the surface like lava before a volcanic eruption. He lowered his head and claimed her lips with his. Even as she trembled, so did he. He smelled the sweet wine on her breath and wanted to taste it on her tongue.

He crushed his mouth against hers until her lips surrendered and parted. His tongue, like a conquering warrior, swept inside to plunder every virgin area. She gasped, and he felt the last barrier of resistance drain from her body...

Another Fawcett Gold Medal Book
by Parris Afton Bonds

DEEP PURPLE

PARRIS AFTON BONDS
STARDUST

FAWCETT GOLD MEDAL • NEW YORK

A Fawcett Gold Medal Book
Published by Ballantine Books

Library of Congress Catalog Card Number: 82-91036

ISBN 0-449-12539-4

Manufactured in the United States of America

First Ballantine Books Edition: June 1983

A RARE FRIEND, A SPECIAL PERSON,

IRENE MALLAM,

THIS ONE'S FOR YOU

My gratitude to Gorka Aulestia, the University of Nevada, for his assistance in knowledge of the Basque culture; to James Laird, Research Historian, Wyoming State Archives; to Marge Sacsko, Lewisville Public Library; and to Dana Terrill.

stardust n: a feeling or impression of romance, magic or ethereality

*Webster's New
Collegiate Dictionary*

CHAPTER

one

*The scream stirred the cloying air in the straw-*thatched cottage. A brown-robed priest smoothed the damp, straggly hair back from the young woman's forehead. The mounded stomach beneath the woman's course, homespun skirt heaved with its effort to eject the fetus. The aged priest sighed. Another child to cramp the already crowded hut. What was this, Mary's fourth child? Nay; her fifth.

There were some things about his faith he would never be able to reconcile. It wasn't just the burden of unplanned-for children that he questioned. Somehow it seemed to the priest—and he knew it was blasphemous—that God too often overlooked the plight of Ireland.

For hundreds of years the Irish had suffered beneath their own burden: the burden of being tenants under the English landlords, the burden of being Catholic under Protestant rule, the burden of plowing a land already too overworked.

Another scream burst from her pain-contorted mouth, and the priest worried how much longer she could endure the agony of her labor. "The child," she moaned. "It won't come."

"Ahh, yes," he consoled in his priest's soothing voice. "The wee one will come soon. Only a little while longer, Mary, and your child will arrive on the first day of a new century.

"January first, nineteen hundred," he mused, more to himself now. "Surely a most propitious time. Like the new century, the child will be strong of mind and heart. And this one shall be a lassie for a change, to lend you help, Mary."

But the mother did not seem to hear him. Her knees jerked up again and she emitted a high-pitched, animal howl.

It was just as well she did not hear him, he thought sadly, for most likely, as quite often happened these days, the wee one would be born dead.

The old Tartar gypsy hesitated outside the timbered hut roofed with straw. She knew that the young farmer, Josef Zhdanov, frowned upon her profession. A White Russian and of the Greek Orthodox Church, he set himself above the likes of her, for all that he and his wife lived in a hut not much better than her own horse-drawn van.

Yet it was the young wife who had summoned her. The gypsy knocked on the dilapidated wooden door and, at the weak call of the voice within, entered. Fortunately the husband was still at work, threshing flax in the fields. The young woman lay stretched out on the straw-packed mattress. In the hut's dimness her stomach bulged like the high dome of the mosque of Saint Sophia. She patted it now with both hands, whispering, "Please, I wish to know of the baby's future."

The gypsy rubbed her horny hands together and advanced closer to the mattress. Alas, she had not brought her tarot cards, fearing to incur the wrath of the husband. But for a few rubles—yes, she could manage to see into the future.

She knelt and placed her hands over the stomach so that her fingers overlapped that of the young farm woman's.

Intently she stared at the mound as if it were the crystal globe used by some of the members of her ancient profession. After a long moment she said, "Your first born will be a male child." (Wasn't that what all mothers wanted to hear?) She heard a cart roll up before the hut. "A strong, healthy boy with a will to match," she added hurriedly.

The young woman, for all her frailty, would not release the gypsy's hands. "But what of his future?"

The gypsy panicked. If she did not get her rubles now, she might not get them at all. "A few hours hence, your son will make his appearance, on the first day of the new century. A most favorable omen, I assure you! The rubles now," she urged.

Gratified, the young woman blissfully dug into the pocket of her drab linsey-woolsey skirt and held forth a handful of carefully hoarded coins. The mound of santimes barely equalled one ruble, but the gypsy scooped the coins into her own palm. At the last moment remorse overcame her, and with an uncharacteristic gesture she thrust several santimes back into the young woman's hand.

The child would probably not live, she justified as she scurried from the hut. The woman was far too delicate. And if the baby did survive the birthing, the times were too bad for it to live past the first few days or weeks at best. The few santimes would be needed to bury the urchin.

CHAPTER
two

The slight child, clad in the long woolen skirt and threadbare boy's tweed jacket, looked more an eight-year-old than her full twelve years. She cast an anxious glance around her as she hurried through the hamlet's cobbled streets with her precious package clutched beneath one rail-thin arm.

The old apothecary had assured her the medicine he sold her was good for stopping bleeding. The sixpence she had spent was the last of the money her father had allotted her for the month's housekeeping expenses, and her father would no doubt be enraged. But she had been frantic that morning at the sight of the blood that trickled between her legs.

Through the morning hours, as she swept the earth-packed floor and cleaned the two-room cottage, she weighed in her mind the decision of approaching her father with the problem of her bleeding. But the memory of his brooding actions over the past months deterred her.

He was drinking more of the dark stout these days—that was understandable, what with the tension mounting between the Anglo seat of government in Dublin and the Irish revolutionists, the Sinn Fein. For more than a year now Maggie had known her father and brothers were part of that secret movement rebelling against British rule.

Maggie suspected that she must be growing up—that like the women from the hamlet of Celbridge she was getting cabbages, as she called the budding mounds on her chest. She wished her mother had lived, to explain to her these changes. Maggie considered going to the parish priest, yet shyness forbade her.

Still, Father Patrick had always been kind and understanding. He had taught her the Anglo letters and her numbers when her father made it clear she would not be going to school with the children from the hamlet. And though she could read precious little and she wrote with labored concentration, it was more than her father or four brothers could do. Unlike her, they weren't hungry for knowledge. They had no curiosity for any of the events that went on "beyond the pale," which was at one time the area extending slightly outside of Dublin and ruled by English law, or the Pale.

She thought now about the bottle of medicine. Some of the words on the label she could understand. Yet the others—perhaps she should stop by the abbey and see Father Patrick. He would be able to tell her the larger words. But, no, she would be late getting dinner. She did not want to incur her father's wrath again.

The way he had spanked her backside three days ago when she had dropped the bucket of milk, her pain had not been nearly as great as her humiliation. Only the entrance of her oldest brother, Seamus, caused her father's hand to halt. When her father released her from his knee, she ran into the one bedroom and, blinded by tears, almost knocked over her spinning wheel. She feared her father, his oxlike size, his black moods.

Her steps slowed through the evening's soft mist, which

lent a magical aura to the small sapphire lakes, the *loughs*, that quilted glens of yellow gorse. In the distance patches of clouds, rolled in by the Gulf Stream that warmed the Irish shores, muffled the great heather-clad Wicklow Mountains. Tucked into the oak-shrouded foothills were white-washed stone cottages much bigger than the one inhabited by her family.

Only as the vivid green of the landscape gave way to the raw umber-brown bogland, the marsh or *carcaighe*, as it was called in Gaelic, did Maggie's footsteps quicken. No Irish mist could camouflage the bleak, barren land. But it was their land. After generations of working the land as lowly tenants, her father had finally managed to pay off the British landlords.

She hurried past the low stone walls, stopping to gather tuffs of peat, the dried turf of the boglands. Once inside the thatched-roof cottage she hid the medicine bottle in the loft beneath her blanket, then set about fueling the fire with the peat. When the men entered, she was dicing leeks for the *brotchan foltchep*, a soup with milk and oatmeal added.

"Well now, how be your day, Maggie, me darling?" Mick, the first one through the door, called out. He was the second born, and her favorite. The sixteen-year-old's jocular, irrepressive spirit brought what little pleasure Maggie found in her life. Since the day she was five and tall enough to stand on the cart to hang the laundry on the line, she had left behind her childhood frolic and assumed the role that had once been her mother's in the Moran household.

Mick tossed his cap on one of the pegs and grabbed the small girl about the waist, lifting her so that her fair hair mingled with the yellow straw of the low roof. "Mickey," she giggled, "put me down!"

Her brother chuckled with delight, his mind's eye recalling his sister as a tot: the wide, laughing mouth, the

dancing shamrock green eyes, the wildly curling hair that
variated from flaxen wheat in the summer to silver frost in
the winter. A leprechaun that diminished as the tot grew.

"Put her down." Dermott Moran dwarfed the doorway.
The father's ruddy face was set in dark, stern lines. Maggie
often imagined that the King Lear, whom Father Patrick
had told her about, must have looked just so. It was the
black Irish in their father, Mick would explain.

The same dour nature, though diluted by a touch of
melancholy, ran through the blood of her brother, Roe, who
was the middle child. She thought that Roe missed their
mother more than the rest of the children. She and Hugh
were too young to remember their mother, her death coming
so shortly after Maggie's birth.

Mick slowly lowered Maggie. Like the rest of the children, he obeyed his father implicitly. Maggie began to shape
the potato patties. Roe, Seamus, and Hugh filed past their
father's baleful eye to hang their caps and sweaters on the
pegs, then followed Mick into the bedroom to change their
clothing and wash up. Dermott Moran settled his hefty bulk
into the rocker before the peat fire and lit the clay pipe. "Ye
be late with the dinner, Margaret."

"I, I had trouble with Tildy." Maggie's small hands fu-
riously patted the cakes. "The old cow refuses to share her
milk, father. But there still be enough cream left in the
crock," she added hurriedly. What if someone told him
they'd seen her in Celbridge today?

She moved past her father to drop the patties into the
lard that sizzled in the cast iron skillet over the fire. She
could feel her father's gaze boring into her back, and she
wished her brothers would finish washing up. It was something her father seldom bothered to do. Father Patrick had
instilled in her the necessity of cleanliness, and she had
managed to convince her family of the necessity. All but
her father. No one had the power to sway him, not the
parish priest nor the British parliament.

"Ye getting old enough now to put your braids up," her father said, breaking into her thoughts.

She jumped, but continued to flip the patties. "Father, some of the girls in Celbridge are cutting their hair short."

"Unbecoming for a female it is."

"'Tis a dozen years into the twentieth century. Things have changed since you were young."

The man's stubby-lashed eyes narrowed. His large, hair-speckled hand reached out to jerk Maggie's tumbling wealth of sun-gold braids. "You don't be talking back to your father, Margaret."

"Aye." She moved away and turned her attention back to the potato patties. Fortunately, her brothers lumbered back into the main room. The usual dinner confusion settled over the small, smoke-blackened room, until Dermott Moran called for silence as he led the blessing over the meager spread of food. Then Maggie began the chore of waiting on the menfolk, who expected her servitude as their due.

Though Mick might be her favorite, it was always Hugh, the youngest, she served after her father's plate was filled with the potato patties, thick leek soup, and soda bread marked with the traditional cross. To her, Hugh was the baby of the family, although he was a full year older than her twelve.

Bending near him, their fair heads almost blended into one. The two were the only blondes in the auburn-haired family. "There now, Hugh, my babe," she said gently as she rationed out the last of the milk to the boy, "you must drink all of it. 'Tis a grown man it'll make of yourself."

She wrinkled a patrician nose at Roe, who was cutting the foam from his stout with his knife. "Roe, be minding your manners, now."

The fifteen-year-old grumbled. "It's not Dublin Castle we're dining at, Little Mother."

Only when the last of the male Morans had eaten and retired from the table to make their weekly trek to the Celbridge pub did Maggie allow herself to sit down and eat the little left of the now-cold food. She knew her father and brothers would drink in the murky pub and plot rebellion for another two hours—long enough for her to take her weekly bath.

The bath water was, as always, cold, for the peat needed for fuel could not be wasted on such luxuries as bathing but was to be sold in Celbridge with the rest of the farm produce. The girl washed her saffron-streaked hair with the rose soap, a gift from Father Patrick that she hoarded. When she finished, her skin glowed a dusky rose from the abrasive scrubbing, which was necessary to remove the week's encrusted dirt.

Her hair lathered and rinsed, the child stepped from the tub. Her thin body cast a wavering shadow against the fire's light, a light that wavered suddenly with a draft of air that swept into the room. She whirled with the opening of the door to see two British soldiers. They were dressed in the standard khaki uniform with the trousers tucked into canvas-gaitered boots. They wore on the front of their peaked caps the metal badge that distinguished them as serving in Ireland.

She tried to shield her nudity with her arms, though she did not understand why she should suddenly feel ashamed. Their leering gazes frightened her, and she began to tremble.

"The rest of your family," the large, beefy soldier demanded, "Where are they?"

"My father and brothers," her tongue stammered, "they're in Celbridge. They'll be back soon," she said, forcing a confidence into her voice she did not feel. "You had best be gone."

The other soldier, as big but with a weasellike face, slid a glance at the one who had questioned her. They both smiled and edged into the room. The beefy soldier shut the door behind him. "The Irish lass needs to be taught more respect for men."

It seemed to Maggie that her bones froze, and she stared helplessly as the soldier passed his rifle to the weasel-faced one and advanced toward her. A sick, quivering feeling erupted in her stomach. The soldier's hand shot out now and jerked her arms away from her body. A lewd grin erupted as his pale eyes beheld the breasts that burgeoned like rosebuds. His breath, smelling sourly of stout, sucked in.

The child jerked back to life. "No!" she pleaded.

What happened after that seemed to happen too rapidly for Maggie to later distinguish in her mind. The sudden scuffling between her and the one soldier; the other soldier calling out, "Hurry!" Hands grabbed at her as she tried to twist away. A knee gouged apart the coltish legs that still lacked the curves of a mature girl. Her mouth opened to scream, and the soldier cuffed her across the jaw.

The ringing in her ears distracted her momentarily from the hideous thing happening to her. But when the searing, crucifying pain ripped through her, her body bucked spasmodically beneath his locking hold on her. She felt the tender tissues tear with the continuous plunges of the soldier's heaving, foul-smelling body.

The soldier rose, wiping at himself. "Your turn," she heard him pant. A scream of terror and pain gurgled in her throat. It reached her lips only to be silenced abruptly by another sharp stab of pain between her legs. After that her perception of time was warped. She was not certain when the two soldiers finally left. But it seemed only a little while until she heard the noise of drunken singing outside the hut. Her father and brothers entered the room, and their voices broke off. "Oh, my God!" Mickey called.

"Two soldiers," she murmured. "British soldiers."

The towel she had laid out was swiftly wrapped around her. She felt herself being carried up the ladder to the loft and laid on the molded straw. Mickey patted her cheek, as if not knowing what to do. "'Tis all right, me darling," he murmured, then stole away.

She lay on the molded straw and listened to the sound of her father and brothers in the room below as they discussed what to do. "We must go to Dublin and inform the British headquarters what happened," Mick said—or was it Roe's voice?

"Don't be a fool!" her father exploded. "They would investigate. They would find out about our activities. Besides, 'tis the way of a man with a woman since time began."

Hugh interrupted. "But she's just a—"

"Child?" her father scoffed. "Have you not been noticing her? She's ripe for womanhood."

"Father's right," Seamus said. "We've worked too hard to take a chance that the British might find out about the Sinn Fein."

Maggie listened. She felt the terrible pain that ravaged her childish body and clawed at her soul. At first her small hands wiped with frenzied scrubbing motions at the chaffed, hairless mound. But she could not wipe away the debasement and degradation, the feeling that she had been dehumanized. She did not know whom she hated worse: the men who had violated her, or her father for his callousness. She felt betrayed. Her helplessness, her confusion, took root inside her in the form of a small seed of fright and bitterness and fury.

After a few moments, when lucidity returned, when she realized her efforts were ineffectual and that she was changed forever, her fists pressed against her mouth to stifle the sobs that choked her. "Mother, mother. Please, dear God. Please, mother." Her bewildered voice pleaded for more than an hour before it trailed off to nothing in the night's musty darkness.

CHAPTER
three

*F*or twelve the youth was tall and well built, so much so that the young women in the St. Petersburg iron and steel works factory mistook him for fifteen or sixteen. The Russo-Japanese war eight years earlier, in 1904, had depleted a large portion of the male population, and the hungry eyes of the female workers followed the lanky figure with the muscle-ridged shoulders as it moved back and forth along the open-hearth furnaces.

The intermittent flare of the furnaces' orange-red flames highlighted the youth's sable-brown hair and swarthy skin. His dark coloring, so different from the Slavic fairness of his family, had often prompted his father to comment that Wolfram was a throwback to an Armenian ancestor who served under Peter the Great as a cavalryman in the Cossacks, which was from *Kazak* or adventurer. And above all else, Wolfram was an adventurer.

Wolfram Nikolai Zhdanov, naked to the waist, shoveled the last of the coal into the coking oven. The sudden flare illuminated his sweat-sheened torso. The factory's whistle blew, and he wiped the perspiration from his forehead with the back of his arm before he thrust the shovel in the coal car and headed for the exit along with the rest of the workers.

Among the younger workers, the children, there were always new faces. Children did not possess the stamina to survive the heat and heavy labor required in the steel mill. At least, Wolfram thought wryly, they did not survive on the little food purchased with the meager 300 rubles, or $150, a worker received for a whole year's labor. But besides being an adventurer, Wolfram also was a survivor.

At the mill's wide, sliding corrugated door he grabbed from his stall the too-small burlap shirt with the still-legible words "Ukranian potatoes" printed across the back. He shrugged into it before striding out into the hot and sultry August evening. Though it was still a good five hours until midnight, soon would come the flush of dawn.

He did not join the others, most of whom drifted toward the workers' barracks. Instead he set off for the Admiralty Quay, the city's center, and the Narodny Dom, which was a combination restaurant, bar, and meeting place of the working class. His fists jammed into his pockets, his long legs covered in a swift, smooth gait the wide, dirty wooden boulevard along the bank of the Neva River.

He made the same journey every day. The handsome public buildings and large private residences and palaces no longer awed him as they first had when his family came to St. Petersburg the year he turned five. Now only one thing impressed him: the political talk that was whispered among the vodka house tables like the wind's low sigh before a storm.

Wolfram had first visited the vodka houses when he began to follow his father, demented with grief, from one vodka house to another. He would sit, watching his father drink away his life, as a great many did during those depressing times. Then, when his father was too drunk to care, he would help the rapidly aging man back to the barracks. Why he looked after his father, he did not know. For as long as Wolfram could remember his father had seemed stern and uncaring—uncaring, that is, except for the love he and his son shared for the slender, blond woman and fair-haired girl who had been Wolfram's mother and sister.

It was during the lonely hours of vigil over his father that a new breed of intellectuals who frequented these vodka houses introduced Wolfram to chess and Chekhov, to Tolstoi and Dostoevski, to Rimski-Korsakov and Tchaikovsky. Few could afford the vodka, but always there were the thought-provoking conversations. Yet now the intellectuals talked of other things, of injustices and inequities, abstractions that Wolfram's quick mind absorbed but did not quite understand.

With the first of the strange uncertain light that heralded each summer night that seeped into the dusk, he strode more quickly across the bridge spanning one of the many canals that laced the city, which two hundred years earlier Czar Peter the Great had ordered built on the Neva's muddy marshes by driving over 1200 piles into the bogs.

On the other side of the Fontanka Canal Wolfram passed a beer and sandwich kiosk, and to ignore the hunger pangs that attacked his stomach he turned his thoughts on the chess game he hoped to finish with Lev, the nineteen-year-old who neither had a job nor wanted one. It seemed a much more adventuresome life to Wolfram, and he would have opted for Lev's vagabond life-style were it not for his father, bedded in the workers' barracks by consumption.

Instead there faced Wolfram that terrible necessity of their survival, the necessity of every so often selling himself. It had been Lev, in fact, who had suggested it. "Everything in this poverty-beseiged city's for sale, including sex for a loaf of bread. Why not get paid by some titled lady for your first time in bed? With your devilish looks, my friend, your twelve years will make little difference. Who knows, your youth may even be an enticement."

That first time, arranged by Lev six months earlier, Wolf-

ram's curiosity overcame his lack of experience, and with
the seductive stroking by the dark, stocky woman, a wife
of a *Pomeschik*, or landowner, he managed to accomplish
that for which she had generously paid.

But this means for keeping his father and himself scarcely
equalled as a diversion his interest in chess and politics.
The things he did for the women who bought his youth, he
forgot as promptly as he forgot the nameless female faces.

A soft, low whistle distracted Wolfram's thoughts from
his planned series of moves in the forthcoming chess games.
His gangly legs halted their long strides, and he looked up.
He was in an older part of the city now, where the streets
were narrower and winding and the gothic apartments were
crowded elbow to elbow. On the steps of the nearest apartment stood a girl whom Wolfram judged could not be much
older than himself, maybe fourteen or fifteen at the most.
But then, he reminded himself, he was only a few months
away from thirteen.

"Boy," she called softly. "Come here."

Normally he would have laughed and shrugged off the
obvious invitation from the streetwalker. But this one, this
young girl who watched him with a clown's theatrical smile—
she captured his interest. It wasn't just the bright red-painted
mouth in the face almost hidden by the plaid head scarf,
nor the slender body enveloped by the too tight cotton tunic
and flimsy skirt.

He sensed in her that same desperate will to survive that
ran through his own veins. But her lips, her eyes, were
tempered by a vulnerability that doomed her efforts. Boldly
he walked to the first step. Although she stood a step up
from him, his height put him on eye level with her. "You
wanted something?" he asked, a grin carving his lips.

The girl, though already accustomed to all sorts of men,
shrank from the boy's deceptively lazy smile. It was the
grin of a cub predator. But the girl was hungry, and she
said brazenly, "I want to give you an hour of pleasure."

Fascinated, his eyes fastened on her carmined lips. "Give, or sell?"

Her laugh was forced, the smile pasted. "Come inside, and we will talk about it."

"And suppose I tell you I have not a ruble? Am I still invited inside?"

The girl needed the money. There would be others along, when the night deepened. And she was afraid of this boy. The sand brown eyes, so pale they were almost yellow, were hard and feral despite the curved lips. Yet she unaccountably could only manage to nod her acquiescence.

He followed the girl down a hallway that probably once had been graced by Persian runners and tall gilt mirrors reflecting blazing crystal chandeliers but now was dingy with age and smelly with the odors of human habitation, of cooking cabbage, sweat, and, yes, excrement. At least it was warm. The room she entered was dimly lit by a gaslight. It was a bare room but for the mattress on the floor and an old brass samovar for making tea. Yet it was much larger than the quarters inhabited by his father and himself. "You live here?" he asked, incredulous.

Her sky blue eyes fastened on him. "There are others." She knew he correctly guessed the identity of those "others" she shared the apartment with. They were out soliciting as she had been.

Before his face drawn taut with what seemed an animal lust, she turned away and nervously began to divest herself of her tunic and the scarf knotted behind her head. The wash-yellowed cotton blouse and long, woolen skirt dropped about her thin ankles. She turned to face the youth—and was paralyzed by the awful flames that leaped into his eyes.

A wave of red washed over Wolfram. It had happened only in dreams, this fierce, agonizing weakness. As his glazed eyes slowly moved over the streetwalker, he grappled in the throes of his dreams.

The girl's body was small and delicately slender with

high taut breasts. Her hair, pulled back in braids from her tense face, was the color of cornsilk. She was so similar to ... The knowledge was shattering. So shattering that he was unaware as he spun away and fled the apartment with a memory, a nightmare, fast on his heels ...

They were peacefully marching through St. Petersburg's streets, the peasants and factory workers, to protest the hardships the nation was suffering under the Russo-Japanese war. This particularly quiet Sunday would later be called Bloody Sunday. Wolfram walked between his father and mother, who carried his two-year-old sister, Aija, on her hip. Only the year before, in 1904, Wolfram's family had migrated from the mir, a collective farm near the Baltic Sea, and Wolfram was still unaccustomed to the St. Petersburg's bitter cold winters.

His father's lot in the mir, as most of the other farmers, was small and did not include grazing land for cattle nor trees enough for firewood. And the peasants, the Dark People, were not allowed to move away from the village until the Baltic barons had been paid for the land of the whole community. Life was hard and unhappy, and thousands of peasants flocked to the cities. They were herded like sheep into the factories and slums and were in constant fear of losing their jobs.

On this icy Sunday in January they marched to the Winter Palace hoping they could persuade the Czar to do something for them. Father Gapon, the Orthodox priest, bore a petition to the "Little Father," as the Czar was affectionately called. The hopeful 1500 workers were grim but quiet; the only noise was the soughing of the frigid wind through the wide boulevard. Aija sniffled, and Wolfram's mother gently hushed the tot, shifting Aija to the other hip with care not to drop the sacred ikon that she, like many others, carried.

Wolfram's cheeks burned with the cold, but he was afraid

*to complain. Suddenly the silence that enveloped the march-
ers was broken when the sound of horse hooves rumbled
through the boulevard. The Czar's famous Cossacks! Wolfram tried to turn around, to wrench free so he could see
the horsemen. At the same time someone shouted the name
of the Grand Duke Vladimir. Hundreds of heads jerked
upward to the Winter Palace's balcony. There, a man in a
white, medal-spangled jacket pointed to the marchers and
called out something to the royal guard immediately below
him.*

*Wolfram did not exactly understand what happened after
that. The thunder of the horses bearing down on the marchers seemed to be echoed by the booming of the royal guards'
rifles and the sudden screaming of the people around him.
Then he was torn from his father's grasp by the surge of
the panic-stricken men, women, and children. "Papa!" he
called.*

*But now horsemen rode down the marchers, their scim-
itars swinging to the left and right, and Wolfram's father
was lost to the boy's view. People scattered everywhere.
Wolfram whirled to his mother for protection—in time to
see the silver flash of steel. His mother's head toppled like
that of a broken statue, while her warm hand still clutched
his. At the same moment he screamed, his crying sister
tumbled from their mother's grasp; a small, neat red hole
pierced just below the little girl's left eye.*

*Horror filled the boy's lungs. His short legs buckled. He
pitched to his knees between the two people he loved best.
His mother's head lay just beyond him. Her honey-gold hair
splayed across the snow to tangle with the golden locks of
his sister's. The clouded blue eyes of his sister and mother
stared blindly up at the gray sky.*

*Wolfram threw back his head and howled, the long,
strangling cry of a beast in absolute agony. He flung himself
across his mother's slim decapitated torso and buried his*

head between the motionless breasts. When his father found him, the blood from his mother's severed neck was coagulated on his cheeks, as it was coagulated in his sister and mother's fair hair.

CHAPTER
four

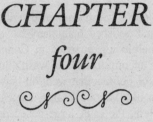

"*Hey, luv, bananas only thirty pence a bunch.*"

"Me jewel-and-darlin', 'tis a grand day, isn't it!"

"T'anks, dearie. Ta-ta!"

Maggie loved to close her eyes as the horse pulled the dray through Dublin's Moore Street Market. The distinctive Dublin brogue of the vendors and the lilting conversations of the visitors delighted her ears, just as the sweet pungent odor of the pyramided vegetables and fruits and the briny ocean scent of the oysters and mackerel tempted her always hungry stomach.

For the past two years, since 1914, when Maggie had turned fourteen and Great Britain had declared war on Germany, the Moran family had been bringing their produce every Saturday to sell in *Bail Atha Cliath*, as the Irish called their capital city. But lately, after the barley and oats and beets were sold, when friends and acquaintances adjourned to Madigan's Pub there at the market for the famed Guinness stout, or journeyed over to nearby Ballsbridge to attend the horse races, Dermott Moran and his sons sought out the bastion of white stucco, black trim, and bottle-glass windows that was known as Brazen Head.

During this time Maggie usually wandered the market, browsing through the other open-air stalls or peeking in the gaudy shops whose facia boards were painted to give a three-dimensional effect. But on this Saturday the Moran produce took longer to sell, and with the other stalls closed already, she was forced to accompany her father and brothers to the Brazen Head.

Despite the pub's warm ambience, with its Tudor-timbered ceiling and polished mahogany bar that boasted the red-speckled marble top quarried in Connemara, Maggie was extremely uncomfortable. It wasn't just the constant low, tense talk of politics that went on between the Moran males and men like Padraic Pearse, James Connolly, and Eamon De Valera, the thin, large-nosed man who'd been born in America. The talk of sedition, as the British would have termed it, Maggie had endured for years.

No, what was unbearable was being forced to sit with all the men crowding in on her. Her lungs felt deflated, as if her oxygen supply were rapidly depleting. That claustrophobic feeling had been eating at her for three years, since the night the soldiers raped her.

Since then she had been careful to never let herself be alone for long in the cottage. She kept a butcher knife with her when she slept at night. She almost had come to hope that perhaps a sense of morality had restored some sanity to her father's behavior. She wanted desperately to believe that she was as important to him as were his sons. But daughters could not fight revolutions. Daughters could not carry on family names.

Now the hulking presence of the male sex overshadowed her life, so much so that she found herself wishing to be a man, a man strong enough to defend himself—a man strong enough to kill.

And, with a certain horror at her own thoughts, she

penitently applied herself all the more diligently to caring for her father and brothers, even while another part of her mind wondered that her brothers never took note of her father's overbearing attitude toward her. Was it so imperceptible? Were they, like herself, afraid to cross him? Or, like their father, did they simply regard her with the same status as that of a servant—or one of the farm animals to which one gave little thought of comfort or concern?

Even now, in the shadows of the smoky pub, her father and brothers drank with unconcern while she sat silent, waiting on them. "With England at war, luck'll be with us, gentlemen," the heavyset Padraic Pearse was saying lowly. "On Easter Monday we'll strike. We'll take the General Post Office first. And from there we'll declare the right of the people of Ireland to the ownership of Ireland!"

Eamon nudged James Connolly and Padraic, and the two men, their faces florid with patriotic enthusiasm, followed Eamon's nodding glance to Maggie.

"Oh, she won't be giving us away," Mick interjected, quick to catch the drift.

"We know she wouldn't mean to, lad," Eamon said, "or we wouldn't have let her listen in today. But now that we're laying the final plans, she could, without meaning to, let them out." He slanted a look at Dermott. "Perhaps she should join the women in the pub's snugs."

The women who wished to drink a cup of Irish coffee or sip sherry drawn from an ancient cask of Amontillado were usually relegated to a snug, or closed booth. But Dermott Moran set down his tankard of mead obstinately. "Me daughter stays with me."

Hugh and Roe looked bored by the discussion, and Seamus's attention had now turned to the buxom barmaid who refilled his pint-o'-porter. Maggie fought off the male intimidation that had hitherto kept her silent and said, "I'd prefer to return to our market stall."

"And what will you do with her Easter Monday?" James

Connolly shook his balding head dubiously. "Things could get out of control."

"Then she stays with my mother," Eamon said with an exasperated finality. For the first time Maggie was addressed as if what she thought were of importance. "For all that my mother has lived many years in America, you'll find her to your liking, Maggie Moran. A grand lady indeed."

Kate Coll De Valera, Eamon's mother, was a grand woman indeed. Born in County Limerick, she immigrated to the United States as a young girl. Now she was staying with her son in Dublin in one of the Georgian terrace houses that, like tightly woven Irish linen, ran row after row along Eccles Street.

With their caps held respectfully in their large hands the Moran men stood behind Eamon, dwarfing the Sinn Fein leader. Eamon introduced the tiny, snow-haired woman that morning before the men left for the rendezvouz with the other Fenians. "Dermott Moran is in Dublin on business, mother, and needs a respectable place for his daughter to wait."

Mrs. De Valera was warm and gracious, inviting Maggie back to the kitchen for a cup of hot tea, "while the menfolk be about their business."

Maggie wondered if Eamon's mother knew just what the business was, but she refrained from saying anything. Instead, as she followed the old woman through the house, her eye ran over the Axminster rugs on the wooden floor, the lead glass lamps, and the upholstered furniture, shabby but so comfortable looking. Draped on the wall behind the couch was a flag with red and white stripes and stars on a blue background. The flag—the United States flag, Maggie guessed, recalling Eamon's statement about his mother immigrating to America—seemed to dominate the room. But Maggie was more interested in the shelves of books lining one narrow wall.

Kate De Valera turned when she realized the thin girl was not following her, and saw the waif standing almost transfixed before the books. A beautiful child, really—or rather, a young woman, for Kate guessed the girl must be somewhere around fifteen or sixteen, though she was small for her age.

Only the girl's square-set jaw flawed the subtle delicacy of the features, features that evidenced an ancient aristocratic heritage. Hardly what one would expect in comparison to the girl's cloddish menfolk. A shame her father couldn't afford to dress the child more suitably: a smarter skirt that didn't swallow her and a modern jacket instead of the old black shawl—and, Holy Mother, would you look at those worn boots!

"Do you read much, lass?"

Maggie blinked and looked at the old woman who had come to stand at her side. How to confess she had barely gotten through the primer Father Patrick had given her? She took off her blue woolen scarf and her honey-streaked braids tumbled free. "No, but I would like to, mum."

"Call me Kate, child. Go ahead. Glance at the books while I get the tea. James Joyce's book is there somewhere. Grand book it is. Eamon just bought it last month. You know, lass, the man used to live on Eccles, just down the street, until several years ago. Well, now, be on about yourself, and I'll just be a moment."

Maggie did not know who James Joyce was, nor recognize the names of the other Irish authors she made out: William Butler Yeats, Oscar Wilde, Jonathan Swift, and Oliver Goldsmith. But her slender fingers trailed lovingly over the books' spines. The little she had been able to read from the primer had enabled her to escape for a few precious moments the drudgery of the cottage.

Kate returned bearing a tray with teacups and light yeast cakes sprinkled with currants and raisins. Noting the girl's hesitancy and puzzled frown as she leafed through one of the books, the old woman accurately guessed that Maggie had had little experience in reading other than the most elementary things. She set the tray on the old, smoothly worn table, saying, "Reading's a good thing for a person, lass. It was only after I got to America that I really learned how to read."

Maggie returned Yeats's book, *Cathleen ni Houlihan*, to the shelf and shyly took a seat at the table. "Cream, me dear?" Kate asked.

Maggie nodded, and Kate said, "You be welcome to take one of the books with you, if you want. You can return it your next trip into Dublin."

"Thank ye, mum." Imitating Kate's use of the flatware, Maggie tasted the yeast cake and found it delicious. Everything about the De Valera house was so much more appealing than the cottage that she hated the idea of going back.

For one tempting moment it crossed her mind that all she had to do was to find the nearest constable and report what she knew about the rebellion planned for sometime that day and she would never have to worry about her father tyrannizing her again.

But there were her brothers to consider. Yet had they ever considered her? For too long she had been forced to perform the menial tasks unfit for the men of the family! Still, how could she bear to see Mick imprisoned? And Hugh, whom she had mothered as her own, melancholy Roe, and Seamus, who had taken her on her first ponycart ride? The cake lodged in her throat with the conflict that raged inside her, and, half-choked, she began to cough.

She was spared the decision when the sound of a distant booming erupted. "Now, whatever can that be?" Kate asked, frowning. "It's a durty wind that's been a'stirring all morn, bringing thunderstorms most likely."

Maggie's teacup rattled in its saucer. The gunfire signaled the beginning of the revolution. By the time the two women finished their tea, the noise of the gunfire had faded. But then there followed a series of explosions that drew Kate and Maggie to the window. People were spilling out into the street. A hurried knock at the door brought a neighbor with the news that a rebellion was in progress.

"It's the Fenians," the toothless old man said. "They've declared us a Republic, that they have!"

Maggie watched Kate's ruddy face grow pale. Thanking the old man, she closed the door. "Holy Mother, it's Eamon! I should have guessed it." She turned to Maggie. "'Tis what your father and brothers were doing with Eamon, wasn't it now? Plotting the rebellion."

Maggie nodded, and Kate crossed to her and put her arms about the girl who was shorter than she by half a foot. "All we can do is wait. Pray the Virgin Mary, the fighting'll be over soon."

They waited, but the hours crept by with only occasional reports from friends and neighbors. "The British have landed additional troops in the bay." "No, the Prime Minister has recognized the Republic of Ireland."

Night came. The fighting continued with sporadic flares to light the sky. Kate put Maggie to bed in the back room. The bed was little more than an iron cot, but to Maggie, accustomed to the straw mattress in the loft, it was a luxury.

For three more days she and Kate kept vigil, Kate praying for her son's safety, Maggie wishing for her father's capture. Ironically, the memory of Father Patrick's recitation of a Bible verse encouraged her vengeful thoughts: "For freedom Christ has set us free; stand fast therefore, and do not submit again to a yoke of slavery."

With a burning sense of inferiority, she swore that one way or another she would never again be brought low by the male sex.

The fourth day brought an end to the siege. The main body of rebels, over a thousand men, had surrendered to the British. When Kate learned of the news, she said, her voice cracking and tears coursing down the funneled wrinkles of her cheeks, "Maggie, me dear, you can't stay here any longer. Within a few hours the British will be at our door. At best, we can expect house arrest. Is there nowhere you can go?"

Maggie paused. Behind the old woman, on the wall above the couch, was the flag. Maggie's chin came up, and in that instant old Kate realized that it was actually the square-set jaw that made the girl's beauty something out of the ordinary.

"Aye," Maggie said. "To America."

CHAPTER
five

ॐ◊◊ॐ

Grigori Effimovich Rasputin, *the half-mad peas-*
ant who posed as a holy man, or *starets*, and obviously
controlled the Czar through his seeming ability to help heal
the Czar's hemophiliac son, was said to be not only ignorant
but completely immoral.

While Wolfram Nikolai Zhandov could hardly be called
ignorant—consorting as he did with other intellectuals who
were forever organizing workers and peasants to protest
against low wages and bad working conditions—Rivkeh
would certainly call Wolfram immoral. Disgruntled nobles
claimed that Rasputin had some sort of mesmeric power
over the Czarina. The university girl suspected the same of
Wolfram's effect on the females with whom he chose to
amuse himself.

Her thoughtful gaze slid from the water-spotted ceiling
down to the young man stretched out next to her. The thick-
lashed eyes were closed now in sleep, but she was all too
familiar with their raffish, hypnotic quality—as familiar as
she was with the satanically handsome face and the muscle-
striated torso.

29

What she would never be familiar with was the intricate workings of the young man's mind. He was a paradox to her. He showed a complete lack of desire to conform to any code of morals but his own. His wild passions that brought a blush to her olive skin; his youthful excesses that matured him far beyond his sixteen years; his endless succession of women, though illogically he always returned to her... this unrestrained, reckless behavior contrasted with his fervent patriotism.

Even his patriotism was illogical, for while he loved the land, he hated the Little Father. "What you don't understand, Rivkeh," he had muttered impatiently before he had taken her earlier that night, "is that the Czar is the only remaining monarch with absolute power to sit on a major throne. Long before this his more enlightened colleagues, like Victoria of Great Britain and Louis Philippe of France, had to answer for their actions to their ministers and national legislatures."

What he said meant little to her. Her life was as she had always known it: pampered by a wealthy family, a childhood at boarding schools, and then the university—until Wolfram had entered it to change it drastically. Now she cared about nothing, neither her classes nor even Wolfram's precious politics, only the moments that brought him to the apartment and to her arms.

Her fingertip crept out to touch the deep line that clefted his chin. Wolfram's hand shot up to capture hers. Using the Latvian endearment for beloved, she said, "It's still too early to rise, *miluli*."

"It's too late," he mocked, moving her hand down to his groin, "I've already risen. Kneel over, Rivkeh."

Leaving Rivkeh's dingy apartment, Wolfram jammed on the hat of cheap lamb's wool and turned up the collar of the long belted khaki overcoat that fell to where his blousy pants tucked into the high peasant boots with the run-down heels. Even so, it seemed the cold penetrated to his very bones. He should have stayed inside with Rivkeh. She had pleaded with him to remain with her. Her attachment to him never ceased to amaze him, for there were times he glimpsed a small flicker of fear in her eyes when he took her.

Despite March's bitter cold winds and the early morning hour, sunlit by the North's long white nights, bread lines were already queuing in front of the bakery shops. To forestall further riots by the hungry women and children, Cossacks rode the streets of Petrograd—changed from its German name of St. Petersburg since the war began with Germany and Austria-Hungary. The riots were not just a result of the harvest that had failed the last two years. The war with the Central Powers was creating a shortage of medicine, clothing, and nearly everything. And thousands of Russian soldiers, some who had been armed with sticks instead of guns, were deserting and returning home.

In 1914 Wolfram had been old enough, at fourteen, to fight on the front, but he and the other very young and very old males had been needed to work the steel factories to turn out armaments. Now, two years later, he was more than just a worker. He was one of the members of Petrograd's Social Democratic Labor party and a leader at the factory's soviet, a small council of labor leaders.

His father should have been pleased, had he lived. But among his last words as he lay wasted on the hemp-thatched bed were those of condemnation. "For all your brave words and deeds," his alcoholic-roughened voice rasped, "you are afraid, my son. You are afraid to give to anyone the child's love you lost when your sister and mother died."

Wolf was in a hurry and considered catching the horse-drawn streetcar that had stopped one corner away, but the dwindling kopeks in his pockets convinced him otherwise. His brisk strides that had lost their lankiness of boyhood took him on past the Alexander Theater, where later that night fur-clad nobility would gather for a gala performance

of Massenet's "Elegie." And, if all went according to plan,
there would be a thousand angry striking workers to watch
the nobles' grand entrance.

Wolfram's lips stretched flat. He could only hope the
Petrograd Soviet of Workers would demonstrate peacefully.
Vivid memories of another demonstration eleven years earlier branded in his brain brilliant colors of blood red and
tawny gold.

Lev, who was waiting for Wolfram in one of the book-
shops that sold month-old English newspapers, did not share
Wolfram's pessimism about the strikers' demonstration. "It'll
work," he reassured Wolfram as he paid for a French newspaper.

"Have you ever participated in a demonstration?" Wolfram shot back, and without waiting for Lev's reply paid for
an obligatory purchase with the last of his kopeks.

He and Lev were to meet before the demonstration with
a Bolshevik radical, Alexander Kerensky, at the Bolshaia
Konnyushennyaia's officer store, which had a good restaurant and enough people coming and going that it was un-
likely they would be noticed.

The three spoke in low tones. "I understand your reluctance about a demonstration of this magnitude," Kerensky
assured Wolfram smoothly. "But you are still very young
and do not comprehend all that is about. If in order to have
a government run by the working people, we have to have
bloodshed, then so be it."

Unseeingly, Wolfram stared down at the English-Russian
dictionary he had bought in the bookstore. "Bloodshed accomplished nothing in 1905," he said, his tone harsh, his
lips set in an uncompromising line. He looked now at the
goateed Kerensky. "If bloodshed occurs tonight, Kerensky,
it will only deepen the division between the Mensheviks
and the Bolsheviks. And we want cohesion with the Mensheviks, not party disunity."

Lev, who was almost as tall as Wolfram but lacked the

frame of muscles his friend had built up shoveling coal at
the steel mill, studied the confrontation going on between
Kerensky, who was a leader of the Duma's left wing dep-
uties, and Wolfram. Wolfram had always intrigued Lev,
since that first meeting with the twelve-year-old in one of
the vodka houses, before the government had prohibited the
drinking of the alcoholic beverage.

For sixteen, the boy possessed a maturity of a twenty-
five-year-old—or maybe a seventy-five-year-old, Lev
thought, recalling the sometimes haunting look in the depth
of the boy's piercing eyes, like an old person who had seen
too much. And in the few years Lev had known Wolfram
the boy *had* seen too much, done too much.

Too much dissipation, too much debauchery for sixteen
years. But then when a young man was as darkly handsome
as Wolfram, without a person to care for, without a home
to return to... mentally Lev shrugged. There were many
wild, homeless souls roaming mother Russia's streets. But
they were either drifters or petty pillagers. They did not
have Wolfram's tireless drive, nor his leadership, so ably
demonstrated in the boy's ability to organize a soviet among
the other young workers and even many of the older ones
at the factory.

Yet it was a ruthless leadership. Remembering those
early chess games with Wolfram, Lev realized he should
have foreseen then the relentlessness. Wolfram permitted
no freeloaders in the factory soviet. Everyone served his
purpose, or the sixteen-year-old exiled the sluggard from
the soviet.

And Wolfram seemed to be just as relentless in his personal relationships. He never permitted himself to become
too familiar with one person, drifting from affair to affair
with the females and cooly detaching himself from the males.
Lev supposed he, and of course the university student Rivkeh, knew Wolfram the best—which was very little indeed.

Kerensky's narrow face remained bland, but Wolfram

noted the party leader's thumb rub agitatedly against the fingers. "We lose nothing by splitting with the Mensheviks. They would weaken the Social Democrats by opening the party to everyone, *Tvarish*," he said using the Russian for comrad.

"The party is for everyone," Wolfram corrected.

"Still . . . ," Kerensky conceded, smiling thinly, "now is not the time to push the point. And bloodshed will come as it will."

Wolfram waited for the troika carrying a fur-hooded couple to slide past before he crossed Nevsky Boulevard and made his way toward the Alexander Theater. Already a sea of protestors were gathering. He moved to stand on the fringe of the crowd.

Across the way he could see a bareheaded Lev urging leaflets on some of the people. Wolfram smiled grimly. Just how many of the peasants and workers did Lev think could read? Overhead waved a scarlet banner with the inscription in large white letters "All the Power to the Soviet." Farther toward the front of the crowd, Kerensky stood on the seat of an automobile, exhorting the people to revolt. "The proletarians have nothing to lose but their chains!" the man yelled, his fist clenched above his head.

Privately Wolfram thought the working class had a lot to lose, beginning with their lives. Something inside Wolfram always leapt at the conflict of challenge, of a snarling fight. It exorcised the dark beast that seemed to possess him. But this, this slaughtering of the helpless . . . Maybe Kerensky's implication that he was too weak in his ideals to make a good party member was right.

The army of serfs shuffled restlessly in the chill, raw evening, straining to see the jewel-bedecked men and women as they paraded from their elegant coaches into the theater. Angry mutterings went up from the impoverished spectators at the arrival of each new party of barons or generals or dukes.

As the meagerly clothed peasants and workers moved apart and came together like flotsam on a tossing ocean, Wolfram spotted a tall, beefy man and a smaller, stockier one grab Lev's arms. Instantly Wolfram guessed: police spies. The Czar's Third section sent to watch over the Social Democrat party's members. For days now he had felt them following him.

The dreaded purge was on!

He glanced around and sighted at least three more police spies. Their dress, warmer than that of the motley crowd, gave the men away. They shoved their way toward him. He glanced about for Kerensky. The man had disappeared.

Wolfram ducked his head to better blend his unusual height with that of the shorter men and women and threaded his way through the people toward the far side of the boulevard. Countless little open cabs, peasant carts, and army trucks impeded his progress. Once he reached the river, he halted, panting. An old droshky waited on the promenade beneath a winter-denuded elm as the even older driver watched the demonstration.

Wolfram bounded into the wagon and wedged himself between the bags of grain. "Get the wagon moving," he hissed at the old farmer. "Now, if you value your life."

An absurd threat, for he had no means of enforcing it. He heard the farmer's cackle. "You mean *your* life, don't you, son?"

Sweat beaded on Wolfram's forehead. Laboring on the Trans-Siberian Railway was not what he had planned for his life. Neither was being shot at the early age of sixteen. Then, mercifully, the droshky jerked forward as the horses plodded their way across the bridge.

The trip seemed to take hours. Wolfram discovered with disgust that he shared the droshky with not only bags of

grain but also carcasses of sheep and hogs. With fervent
thanks, he left the farmer on Vasilevsky Island and trotted
from there across to the Admiralty. His back felt awfully
broad and exposed as he made his way to Rivkeh's apartment. Without knocking, he entered—to find her sprawled
beneath a thick-set, balding man whose naked buttocks
flagged above her.

"What the cursed—" the man began, yanking away from
Rivkeh to face Wolfram.

An amused grin passed over Wolfram's sardonic features
at the sight of the man's rapidly shriveling member. "Take
you clothes and get out."

"See here!" the man protested, struggling to his feet. A
glance at Wolfram's larger, imposing physique quickly re-
duced his ire. "But it's cold out there in the hall, and the
tenants—"

Wolfram's brow raised. "It'll be worse in here."

The man grabbed for his pants and scurried for the door.
Rivkeh slid into a much-mended quilted wrapper and huddled on the mattress, waiting for Wolfram to turn his attention to her. It greatly irritated her that Wolfram never
displayed jealousy. But for that matter neither did he show
distaste for her means of earning the extra money needed
for her studies since her parents had disowned her for her
bohemian ways. He seemed to calmly accept it, as he expected her to accept his sometimes erratic, often bizarre
behavior.

"*Sasodits!*" she swore. "Wolfram, that was an admiral
you just booted out!"

He ignored her and crossed to the small closet where all
his worldly possessions were stored—another tunic, in much
worse condition than the one he wore, a pair of the full,
baggy pants, a forage cap, a few books, and the razor, its
strop and brush. "Get your things together, Rivkeh," he said
and thrust his own into a stained, shabby satchel. "You've
got to leave here. Now."

In spite of the dispassionate voice, she sensed the urgency. "Why?"

"The police spies. They'll no doubt be swarming around here soon."

A sharp rap at the door interrupted Wolfram's answer. He spun around. "It's me, Lev," came the anxious voice from the other side.

Wolfram swung open the door to confront his blood-smeared friend. The young man staggered inside. "The police spies?" Wolfram asked.

Lev collapsed on the mattress. "Hell, no." He paused to catch his breath. "The cossacks again. They opened fire on the protestors. I got caught in it. Just an arm wound." Wolfram felt the old sickness strike. Always the bloodshed and the innocent children. Was there an Aija out there lying lifeless in the snow, or a young mother silenced by death?

"The confusion helped," Lev continued weakly now. "It gave me the opportunity to escape the police spies."

"Delayed the spies," Wolfram corrected. "Not escaped. Not as long as we continue to stay here." He caught his friend under the arms and hoisted him up. "Can you make it as far as the Finland Station?"

"The railroad station?" Rivkeh asked. A tiny spasm of fear worked at the pulse of her throat. "Where are you going?"

He turned to face her. "To Latvia."

CHAPTER

six

"*Dia's Miure dhuit.*" *God and Mary be with you*—those were Kate De Valera's last words as she handed Maggie the bagful of pounds.

The bagful that Kate advanced Maggie barely equalled fifteen dollars—the amount needed for passage on one of the largest battleships in the world, the *U. S. S. Wyoming*, which had brought war supplies to Great Britain. Maggie's footsteps echoed along with the other three hundred and forty Irish emigrants who slowly moved up the metal boarding way to the steamship. On the deck the frightened and confused Croatian, Polish, Russian, and Italian refugees crowded to see the famed green of Eire. They were disappointed to find that a fine industrial haze of gray colored Dublin.

Upon reaching the deck, many of the Irish emigrants turned to look back at their homeland for one last glimpse. Families clung to each other with despair glistening in their eyes. But for others, like Maggie, there was nothing to look back upon but poverty, drudgery, and aching misery.

Within the mist she knew stood the hulking horror of the gray granite Kilmainham Jail, where executions of the revolutionaires were taking place daily. The day before, James Connolly had been shot seated in a chair because his gangrened legs could not hold him up. Padraic Pearse was shot at dawn in the bleak prison yard. Fortunately Eamon, because of his American citizenship through his mother, had escaped execution so far.

And Maggie's brothers and father—their fate, like that of many of the other revolutionaries, was still unknown. Her heart felt heavy, like the weight of a stone, for her brothers, especially the laughing Mick. To find that those dancing eyes were stilled ... it was an unbearable thought. Not so the image of her father's massive body wasting away in some cell. The knowledge that she herself might still be apprehended by British soldiers quickened her steps up the walkway.

"Down to the steerage," the uniformed crewman told her when it came her turn to pass him her ticket. His accent was gravelly, making it difficult for her to understand him. But she followed the stream of peasants down the narrow, steep stairway that was dark and slippery. Only then did she understand that steerage meant the basement of the steamship, the part kept for the passengers who paid the lowest fares.

And only then, as she passed the people lying in bunks stacked one on top of the other, did she realize that she was one of the few females aboard the ship. With the cost of the fare so high, the fathers and sons naturally went first, to get jobs and then later send for the families.

Her breath began to rise in her throat in short spurts; perspiration dotted her lip. She knew it had nothing to do with the heat, the lack of air, the insidious stench. It was the sudden press of men about her—the burly man to her left, the short, stout old man behind her, the pimply-faced youth on her other side whose sweaty hand brushed against hers.

She hurried to catch up with a young woman who plodded ahead of her with a baby balanced on one well-padded hip and an unwieldy clothing bag on the other. A boy who looked to be about five clutched at the woman's skirts. "Could I be helping you?" Maggie offered, shifting the sack of books Kate had given her to the arm that held the small wicker suitcase of clothes contributed by Kate's neighbors.

The woman grinned gratefully, and her freckles gathered across her nose and cheeks like clusters of grapes. She passed the baby to Maggie. "To be sure. Me name's Peg O'Connor. That's Brian 'oo have, and the tyke's Jamie. And 'oors?"

"Maggie," she answered, feeling her air-starved lungs expanding again.

"Come on along, Maggie, me girl. We'd best get us a berth 'fore they all be taken. Me husband wrote that those of them that don't lay their claims on bedding sleeps on the decking, ticket or no ticket."

Maggie followed the young woman, whose hair looked as if it had been caught in an eggbeater, as she elbowed and pushed her way through the crowd of men. "Your husband is already in America?" Maggie asked her when they reached the steerage compartments reserved for the few women and children passengers.

Peg dropped the clothing bag on the first lower berth they reached and arched her back, rubbing at it with stubby, nail-bitten hands. "Went over last year he did." She nodded at the baby, who still slept despite the noise and turmoil and heat. "Brian boy was his last good-bye."

The young woman grinned broadly at her jest. Maggie managed a small smile to hide her embarrassment and tried to set Brian on the bunk with his brother, but the tot clung to Maggie's fingers with one hand while he sucked on the thumb of his free hand. "With 'oor looks, me gal," Peg said, noting the girl's regal beauty despite the cheap clothing, "Brian isn't going to be the only male a'holding on to 'oo."

A male holding on to her was the last thing Maggie wanted. She took pains over the following days to stay clear of the male portion of the steerage deck. But the confining berths, barely eighteen inches wide and smelling of chlorate of lime and carbolic acid, forced her and other claustrophobic-stricken emigrants to seek the top deck. Out of necessity she had to pass through that portion of compartments to reach top deck and the daily fresh air, but she always made certain that she took Jamie with her. Peg, burdened by the demands of nursing Brian, was only too happy to relinquish the keeping of Jamie to Maggie.

Some days the weather made it impossible to go out on the top deck, so Maggie sat in a corner of the steerage's damp decking with Jamie and read to him throughout the long hours. He was a quiet child and seemed to be easily entertained by Maggie's melodious voice. Often the few other children and women, all of whom could not read, came to listen to the stories of Yeats and Wilde and Swift. And if Maggie mispronounced a word, no one was the wiser.

During the worst of the storms, dishes would fall out of the top berths, breaking on the decking. And while women screamed and babies cried, Maggie would lie in her berth. The bunks were stacked so closely that there was not room to sit upright. In the darkness of the hold she conjured up the fashionable worlds painted in the novels she read.

She knew such societies existed. She had glimpsed their elegance in Dublin's Merrion Square and outside the Abbey Theatre where the Anglo-Irish elite descended from elegant broughams and even an occasional motorcar. She knew how greatly they contrasted with the world she knew. She smelled her sweat and that of the emigrants about her. Her work-roughened hands were not the petal soft ones of *Ivanhoe*'s

Rowena. And, she acknowledged bitterly, she was not the genteel virgin of *Jane Eyre*. Somehow, in America she would rise above that.

Kate had warned her that not all Americans were millionaires and that the streets weren't paved with gold, as many hopeful but ignorant immigrants believed. Maggie was not ignorant, but she was hopeful. She *would* change her life.

To while away the two-week voyage, the passengers crowded the top decks on the evenings of fair weather. Accordians and harmonicas, balalaikas and mandolins were produced, and the music from the many countries represented aboard the steamship filled the salt-tanged air. With Jamie asleep, Maggie lost her excuse to avoid the evening affairs. Still, she managed to escape the other emigrants by secluding herself among the ventilators and rigging with a book. Neither Peg's cajoling nor the timid requests of the bashful young men to dance shook her resolve.

The ship was a community in itself, and word soon got around that the small, lovely, tawny blonde was aloof because she thought she was better than everyone else. And wasn't she? She was self-educated, which automatically put her far above the others in their eyes. Proud as a lioness she was.

Maggie chose to say nothing in her defense. And it was her defense. Her aloofness hid the near panic that struck her almost dumb when some young man, hat twisting between his hands, approached her. Sometimes the young men did not even speak the same language, but they were able to make known to the other females their wish to dance through sign language and the age-old use of a flirtatious eye. But no male had yet succeeded in receiving more than the merest glance from Maggie... until the fourth night out when the wind suddenly fluttered the page she read by lantern light and a tall frame cast a shadow over the page's words.

*   *   *

Wolfram could not complain of the quantity of the meals aboard the American steamship, but the quality of the soups of boiled meats, salt fish, and potatoes . . . They were placed on a large table in great, rusty-looking tins that needed scrubbing. When the other steerage passengers scrambled for the first choice, often using their dirty fingers instead of their forks, he found his appetite diminished.

He often wondered if he should not have thrown his lot in with Lev and remained in exile in Riga. But the Latvian capital and its pastoral countryside reminded him more than he realized of his early childhood years. He had sat with Lev in the old, once splendid Kaiserwald café, now cratered with shellfire and all but isolated by the various street barricades, and argued. "What has happened to your patriotism?" Lev had sneered, angry that his friend would not wait out the most recent purge.

Wolfram's eyes narrowed, staring out over the old city's many church spires, bathed in the sunset's gold. He should have been irritated by his friend's gibe, but he simply felt nothing. At sixteen he had already experienced a life-time. Neither the luxurious weeks he had been kept by the titled lady with the ungodly lorgnette the year before nor Rivkeh's impassioned pleas three days earlier not to leave her had made an impression on him.

"I guess I just don't give a damn," he had replied finally. The next night out, along with hundreds of other refugees, he had boarded a Finnish ship bound for Great Britain.

He watched now as a filthy ragpicker plunged his hands into the kettle of soup for a tender piece of meat. No longer hungry, Wolfram turned away to find in the line next to him the short, slender girl he had noticed several times before. With the gold-streaked hair and the dark-fringed green eyes set in a sculptured face, she was indeed good-looking. But he had seen beautiful women before, and normally she would have drawn no more than a dispassionate glance from him. Blondes he had never found appealing. And since that episode years before with the streetwalker he no longer needed to puzzle over the reason; he merely accepted the fact and left it at that.

Yet the glacial expression in the young girl's eyes, the haughty withdrawn set of the lips caused him to pause each time he saw her. And each time he set the momentary interest down to the usual female-male challenge, and passed it off. As he did this time, moving on past her down the line to return to his berth. He would eat later, when the crush was gone and his appetite returned.

Lids closed, his hands locked behind his head, Wolfram's lips moved silently as he mentally pronounced the English sentence. *Khan jou derek me tu Szekenevo?*

Somehow the intonation seemed all wrong, if the accents of the Britishers he consciously listened for were in any way similiar to that of Americans. He picked up the English-Russian dictionary he had purchased at the bookshop the day of the demonstration and looked at the sentence once more: "Can you direct me to Second Avenue?"

The strains of the Italian street song that the violin melodized drifted down to steerage to disrupt his concentration, and he tossed the book in the berth's corner and rolled from the bunk in the smooth movement of a natural sailor. Though the hot sun still danced above the waves of the western horizon, the top deck was already filled with emigrants anxious to partake of the evening's entertainments.

The older children played tag about the lifeboats and smokestacks while the younger ones hung to the skirts of their mothers, who, with faces turned to catch the light salty breeze, strolled about in twos and threes, gossiping. The old men sat in corners with chessboards propped on crates, and it was here that Wolfram considered going when a sultry voice called out to him in German, "Where have you been keeping yourself, Wolfram?"

Slowly, reluctantly, he pivoted. His German was not as fluent as his Russian or, of course, his native Latvian, but he could carry on an intelligent conversation in German if he had to. His glance flickered over the brunette sauntering toward him with a most provocative sway of her hips. The cheap flower-printed dress did nothing to hide her Junoesque proportions. A string of amber beads was twisted artlessly in her abundent hair. "Studying," he replied carelessly. He was not in the mood for a repeat of their last meeting, two evenings before.

Elsa was. Her gaze ran hungrily over the tall, powerfully built young man whose broad shoulders stretched the worn navy blue fisherman's sweater. A sudden tightening warmth in her loins reminded her of the prowess in lovemaking that he had demonstrated in the cargo hold. Her hand reached out possessively to touch his chest. "There are better things to do. Like dancing, for one."

His gaze strayed past her to fall again on the girl he had noticed several times before. She sat next to a ventilator, trying to read some book by the last of the rapidly vanishing sunlight. So she possessed a degree of intelligence as well as a ravishing beauty, a beauty that whispered that girl was untouched—and untouchable.

An olive-complected Italian boy with a red bandana around his neck and patched overalls tucked into his boots interrupted her. The hopeful swain ducked an awkward half bow and swept his hand in the direction of the dancing couples. The girl shook her head quickly, coldly, and dropped her gaze back to the book.

"*Ja*," Wolfram answered at last. "There is the dancing." He shrugged off her hand and strode past her toward the young Irish girl.

"You will dance?" It was put as a question, but because of his limited English vocabulary and the harsh, clipped tone natural to the Slavic language, the request came out sounding like an order.

Maggie's head snapped up. The same discomfort that had swept over her at the approach of the last boy and made casual speech difficult attacked her now, but a thousand times worse. This young man's towering height, his commanding presence, slammed home the memories of her father's hulking bulk and his tyrannical, domineering manner.

Her gaze locked with the young man's dark one. It was some seconds before she was able to speak, though it seemed like a hellish eternity. But to Wolfram the long deliberation appeared an act calculated to insult. And her terse "No" was almost a physical stinging slap.

His eyes narrowed. Then, swiftly, a grin eased the dark brooding face. A challenge. The next ten days would pass more quickly than he had anticipated.

He bowed low, a sweeping bow that would have held its own in St. James' Court. Rapidly his mind selected words and phrases of the dictionary. "Another time. But soon."

CHAPTER
seven

❦

The confinement of the battleship was much worse than that of the cottage. At least when her father's presence had become too overbearing or her brothers too demanding, Maggie could escape out into the fields. But now, there was nowhere to escape from the tall young man's mocking countenance. Even the darkness of her berth yielded up the image of the Russian—if what Peg was telling her about his nationality was true.

"A real rogue, the lad is," Peg continued as she let the infant Brian suckle at one sagging breast. She adjusted her back more comfortably against the lower berth's wall. "And brash as they come. Too cold and hard for the likes of me. Still, all in all, I'd let him give me a whirl around the deck— and maybe some other places," she added with a sly chuckle, "if me husband wouldna be a'finding out."

In the semi-darkness of the berth above, Maggie took a deep breath, wishing she could be as blasé about the young man. But the way he watched her when she went top deck for air, the way his eyes seemed to laugh at her—it was as if he knew her secret, her cowardice. She could only be thankful that he had not come near her since that first time two days earlier. Seeing him at meal times was enough of an exertion. The fear that he would approach her again as he had promised—"Soon," wasn't that what he had said in that raspy-deep voice?—it knotted her stomach so that eating was nigh impossible.

"Well, shall we be going top deck?" Peg asked, buttoning her blouse, which was damp with perspiration. "I imagine the evening fun is already beginning."

"I don't think I'll be going up tonight."

"What?" Peg stood up to peer at Maggie. "This is the second evening in a row 'oo've passed up."

Maggie held up a copy of *She Stoops to Conquer*. "It's too interesting to lay aside right now."

Peg snorted and bent to tuck the sleeping Jamie and Brian safely into the berth. "What's going on top deck is a lot more exciting than some old book. Stay down here long enough, me girl, and 'oo'll be a'smelling like this slimy hold."

Maggie knew she smelled bad enough as it was. Her fastidious nature resented going weeks without changing clothes, and her skin fairly crawled when it came in contact with the damp, musty bedding. But most of all she resented that through her cowardice she was permitting another human to dictate to her. How could she be so lacking in self-esteem as to grant someone else the right to dispose of her life? She waited until three women edged past the berth, then said, "I'll be coming up in a moment, Peg."

"Good for 'oo. The air'll put the roses back in 'oor cheeks."

Peg moved to catch up with the three giggling women, and Maggie slipped out of the berth to the decking. She smoothed the rumpled skirt over her still boyishly slim hips and straightened the frayed cuffs and collar of her blouse and tucked the wisps of stray hair into the golden-brown braid at the crown of her head.

The gestures seemed fully feminine ones, those of a young girl primping for a suitor. But for her the gestures were a means of composing the trembling inside her, as a soldier shines his brass, dons his helmet, and rechecks his rifle in the unnerving moments just before battle.

The yellow light of the porthole moon and the soft gleam of the ship's kerosene lanterns illuminated the crush of people on top deck. The boisterous laughter and gay music hid the anxiety that gnawed at each of the emigrants. The European peasants had heard stories of immigrants arriving in America only to be sent back. Would it happen to them? Had they saved their money for what seemed like a lifetime only to take a wasted voyage?

Just as Maggie had done on the previous evenings she had come top deck, she sought out the remotest section of the deck reserved for the steerage passengers. This time the spot was not near any of the ship's lanterns; neither was there a place to sit. She stood in the darkness with the book pressed against her chest. As she surreptitiously watched the dancing couples, her foot tapped restlessly to the Polish polka. If only she could dance alone, dipping and swaying to the lively music, with no one to watch.

Following the pattern of the couples who were now waltzing, her feet moved a few inches each way in the waltz's square pattern. And when the waltz crescendoed, she executed a small neat whirl—only to halt at the voice that spoke out of the dark. "We dance now?" Once again the question seemed issued as a statement rather than a request.

Without giving her a chance to refuse, Wolfram took the book and set it down next to the bulwark. But when he took the girl's resisting right hand and put his free hand about her waist to pull her out into the mainstream of dancing couples, he was jolted by the strange current that began to pass between them. Quickly his gaze sought hers, wondering if he would find the answer there to the incendiary effect she was having on him.

Unlike some men, who remain incomplete all their lives, never knowing the joy of responding fully to womanly charms, he had learned early to enjoy that feminine realm, a realm he had come to know intimately and understand completely. But he could not penetrate the mask of distance this young woman's eyes wore.

They faced each other, two young people made old beyond their years, two young people no longer innocent.

Desperately Maggie wanted to refuse him, but the words would not pass beyond a throat suddenly sealed tighter than a tomb. She went rigid in his arms as his hand, pressing at the small of her waist, maneuvered her through the maze of whirling couples. Her heart galloped like that of a stampeded horse. Unable to gracefully pull away, she stared frozenly into the shoulder of the wide-knit ribbed sweater.

His head bent near her own. "You dance often by yourself?"

The low voice held a hint of teasing. Her jaws clamped together to still their trembling. The male scent of the young man, the overwhelming closeness that seemed to press down upon her, was too much. Perspiration broke out on her lip. At his husky chuckle, her head jerked up. The words of contempt still would not come, but her eyes scorned his laughing gaze before her lids dropped to quickly shield her fear. "Go away," she finally managed, her own voice as husky with the old anxiety as his was with mocking.

"No," he said, taking great delight in the exchange. Why the girl should interest him he could not imagine. She was not at all the kind he favored. The fair coloring of her type, with the gold-kissed hair bound so tightly in the braids and the skin that was as pale as Russian snow, seemed washed out when compared with the darker young women he preferred, women who held warmth. Only the girl's voice had any warmth to it, a mellifluous quality despite the harshness she purposefully inflected in it.

Then her chin snapped up and her eyes blazed at him

with a rebellious heat that seemed to sear clear through to his soul. Why had he not noticed before how vivid a green her eyes were?

He pulled her closer so that the length of her body was pressed against his, so that it seemed he could actually feel an inner fire emanating from her. "We will finish the dance." He wished he had studied more of the English language so that he could prolong the conversation. Her reactions were far more piquant than anything that Elsa could provide.

With her breasts pressed against the young man's chest, Maggie felt that old stirring of revulsion. She trod down on his foot and quickly pulled away as, out of surprise, he loosened his grip about her waist.

As she wove her way through the people, she was afraid to turn around and see if he followed her. She retrieved her book, glanced around for sight of the disturbing young man, and then escaped below to the steerage.

Thereafter her days aboard the steamship were haunted ones. The one time she had looked up into that dark visage, she had seen the purposefulness etched there. He would torment her again if he had his way.

For the first time she began having nightmares. That hideous night the soldiers violated her she had shut away to the dungeons of her memory. Now those dungeons had been unlocked by the young Russian. She would awake in the dead of the night, perspiration drenching her clothes, her lips trembling with the unscreamed terror that clawed at her. Shadows, triggered by her sleep-disturbed nights, ringed her eyes. The docking in the New York harbor could not come quickly enough. There at last she would be free of the young Russian.

Wolfram would never forget the joy he felt when, after so many dark days on the crowded ship, he saw the tall buildings of New York and the Statue of Liberty. It was the symbol of all his dreams: freedom to start a new life.

Then came Ellis Island, the detention center for immigrants that he had heard called the "Island of Tears."

Lying about one mile south of Manhattan, the island had once been used by New York's early Dutch settlers as a picnic ground. The passengers told stories of immigrants who had been held there for many days, and of others who had been sent back to Europe. To what, Wolfram wondered? Europe was old and dying, suffocating in the decadent wallowing of the rich, the abysmal suffering of the poor, and the war's cruelties that would mar the face of its continent and its peoples forever.

Still, as the ferryboat jammed with immigrants drew near the island, Wolfram felt an unaccustomed sense of panic. The noise and commotion were unbelievable. So many languages, were being spoken at once. The shouting and pushing guards called out hard-to-hear instructions as the immigrants were herded off the ferries and into one of the red brick buildings.

The guards tied large tags to the backs of the immigrants' coats. Wolfram craned his neck to see his number: 3027. At the end of a long hallway these numbers were shouted out in Italian, Yiddish, Greek, Croatian, Polish, German, and other languages. After much pushing and yelling the newcomers were separated into groups of thirty and taken to Registry Hall. It was the largest room he had ever seen, larger even than Finland Station. A maze of aisles created by metal railings crisscrossed the room. The noise was a din of shouts, curses, and crying children. He thought that surely the Tower of Babel could not have been worse.

Long lines of people stood in these aisles waiting to be questioned by immigration officers or examined by doctors who would mark on the backs of the immigrants coats with chalk the letter "H" for heart, "Sc" for scalp infection, "K" for hernia, "R" for rash, and so on. The most dreaded letter of all was "X". People marked with an "X" were usually sent back where they came from.

Wolfram watched as the family ahead of him were examined. Three of the four children passed the examination, but for some medical reason the couple's daughter, who appeared to be about ten, was marked with the X, to be returned to Europe alone. The mother broke out in violent sobbing as their daughter was separated from the rest of the family, and the stoop-shouldered father held his wife against his chest when the girl was led away.

The impersonal, indifferent attention of the inspectors irritated Wolfram, and when the medical examiner looked at his face, hair, neck, and hands, it was all he could do to refrain from shrugging off the man's hands and walking away from the building. Only the fact that he was bound by the perimeters of the island restored some equanimity to his mind.

Instead, when he was directed toward a group of benches to await the final test, he found a vent for his irritation in the form of the young Irish girl, who sat on the last bench against the wall. Why he chose to torment the girl he had danced with he neither knew nor at that moment cared. He took the vacant space beside her and experienced the satisfaction of seeing the shock that widened her eyes when she realized who the man next to her was. With deliberate casualness he reached across her, letting his forearm brush against her small high breasts, and wiped the smudge of dirt that trailed up along her right cheekbone. His insides were jarred when a shocking wave of—was it pain?—swept over him, taking him unaware. What was it about her presence that strangely disturbed his peace of mind?

Following the path of his thumb, a flush crimsoned her skin. At the intake of her breath, he abruptly felt shamed. He knew what he was doing was an attempt to reduce his own fright at the strangeness of the country, the people, the language that overwhelmed him. His bravado was rapidly deserting him.

"We meet again." The anger directed at himself made

his voice sound more harsh than he intended. But he wanted to hear the girl's Irish way with English speech, the half-wild, half-majestic cadences. Looking into those remote eyes, he felt like he was sinking ninety fathoms deep.

When she bolted to her feet, his hand shot out to capture her wrist. It was an effort to make an apology, but the unexpected call of his number forced him to release her. Still, the face of the girl did not fade quickly from his mind as he prepared himself to answer the questions shot at him by a tired, stern-looking official.

"Can you read and write? Do you have a job waiting for you? Who paid your passage? Have you ever been in prison? How much money do you have? Let me see it now."

On and on went the questions, until Wolfram got more and more confused. Suddenly he was handed a Landing Card. It was difficult to believe the ordeal was over in an afternoon. His fears were unfounded. The statue in the harbor had not turned her back on him. America had accepted him.

And it mattered not to him that his Landing Card now listed Wolfram Nikolai Zhdanov as Wolf Nicholson.

CHAPTER
eight

*W*ith *repetitious boredom Maggie brought the* wheel knife down in accustomed precision and sliced the to-bacco leaf into six one-inch strips. The scraps of waste, along with the stems of the stripped tobacco leaves, she raked into the greasy, brown-stained bed-ticking pouch fastened to the front of her workbench. Dexterously her fingers rolled the leaves about the packed cigar and quickly pasted it.

"Here you go, Jamie," she said, managing a smile as she slid the finished product down the workbench to Peg's five-year-old. It was seven-thirty at night, and the child's lids kept closing in utter weariness as he packed the cigars into wooden boxes.

Maggie was tired too. She rubbed her arm across her forehead and glanced down the bench at Peg, who was at the bunch-maker rolling the packed tobacco into the cigar-shaped modes. How the woman managed and cared for the baby Brian, whom she kept in a crate at her feet, was beyond Maggie. But then Maggie wondered if Peg really was man-aging. The woman seemed to have aged fifteen years, looking an old forty, in the five months since they had arrived in New York City.

All Peg's carefully thought out plans had collapsed on that first day. Her husband was to have met her and the boys at the pier with the train tickets to Boston, tickets that should have been bought with money Peg had sent him. For two and a half days Maggie waited with Peg, dozing during the night on a bench beneath a tree in Battery Park's Bowling Green. But the husband never did come. It was known to have happened before, husbands deserting their families once they were separated by an ocean.

Maggie sighed and returned to slicing the leaves. It could be worse, she told herself. At least the owner of the factory tenement allowed Peg to keep the baby with her. True, she and Peg did the cheapest grade of work at the lowest wages, twenty-six cents an hour, for twelve hours a day, six days a week.

For the first time realizing that a man's wages could not fall below a limit, Maggie knew why women were forced to choose the paths of shame. Faced with the fifteen dollars monthly rent and the cost of food, how long before she and Peg might be forced to resort to such a path? Oh, God! That bread should be so dear, and flesh and blood so cheap!

At last eight o'clock came and she, Peg, and the children began the journey through the East Side's foul core of New York's slums. Once so fastidious, Maggie no longer was bothered by the stench from the hawkers' carts of rotting vegetables or the filth that accumulated in the narrow alleys. But she was not yet so inured to the squalor and degradation that the sight of street Arabs, homeless children sleeping in piles of such refuse, did not jerk at her heart.

The wonders of the city still amazed her: the steetcars on lines overhead called "els" driving above the horse-drawn trolleys; the Woolworth Building, the world's tallest structure, rising among the other skyscrapers that were named for the topmost ship's sail; the many cinematograph houses that were replacing the theaters and featured in moving pictures Mack Sennett's Keystone Kops or Pear White in *Perils of Pauline*.

Even the people, a human flood of immigrants that made up the city's population, amazed her. Incredibly, New York held more Irish than did Dublin—in addition to holding more Italians than Rome, more Germans than Bremen, and being the largest Jewish city in the world.

Usually the two women and two children made the journey in a silence born out of bone-weariness through trash-littered streets to their Mulberry Bend tenement, in the almost totally Irish Sixth Ward of the Bowery. Neither woman relished entering the old two-story and attic house that had been built for one family and now housed five.

October's wind drafted through the thin walls. Rags, malodorous bones, and musty old papers piled the hallway. Lines of wash suspended from fire escapes blotted out the sky. What wallpaper there was peeled in shreds from the walls of their small twelve-foot room. Such a hopelessness befouled the already fetid air of the slums of Mulberry Bend. To Maggie even the dirt-floor stone cottage outside the hamlet of Celbridge seemed infinitely preferable to their tenement. But she had only to recall the bondage she had served beneath her father and brothers and her steps would quicken toward the haven of the tenement.

But this night she was forced to slow her steps as Peg, her breath frosting the air, described eagerly her conversation with the Bohemian girl who worked one bench over and directly in front. "Svelta's cousin is an upstairs maid for one of those high society women, a Mrs. Van der Rhys, who is in that club for women's equality."

The excitement in her friend's voice caused Maggie to throw a quick sideways glance as she skirted the water hydrant in front of her. "The National Woman Suffrage Association?"

"Aye, that's it. Anyway, Mrs. Van der Rhys be planning

a demonst—a march for the women up Fifth Avenue Sunday. 'Tis been so long since we did something, and wouldn't it be fun now to watch the march and maybe take a peak in the windows of the grand stores?"

Brian began to fret and wimper, and Maggie reached over and took the babe from Peg's weary arms. "Seeing how much better others live doesn't brighten my day, Peg. I'd rather spend my one day off—"

"Reading!" Peg sniffed. With her hands free, she hugged Jamie, who stumbled along in half-sleep against her side. "Reading about how the other half outside the slums lives, am I not right, Maggie, me gal?"

Maggie pulled her woolen shawl around Brian's tiny body to further shield it from the biting wind, and the child momentarily ceased his crying. She thought about her brothers, especially the youngest, Hugh, whom she had babied like her own. She missed them terribly, but not the drudgery they expected and demanded. Perhaps someday she would gather the courage to write them. But then who would read the letter for them?

It was that lack of education that made life so hopeless. She knew it would take a lot of luck for her and Peg to escape the hopelessness of the slums. Lives, like clothes, were worn through and out before put aside. At the factory tenement people worked until they collapsed from the ravages of consumption due to the tobacco fumes. She knew that were she to miss two or three days due to illness her place at the bench would be rapidly taken by another.

"I don't plan to stay in the Bowery forever," she whispered fiercely against Brian's cheek.

Peg tossed her head, her red hair dull now. "We could be worse off. At least here in America a person can send his children to school and buy his own home, with a little luck. Here I won't be a'having to live in poverty all me life like me mother and her grandmothers afore her, with a little luck." She threw Maggie one of her old impish smiles. "And the right man."

That was something Maggie wanted no part of: a man. Waiting on men again—it was an old servitude that Maggie wanted to put behind her.

Suddenly Peg's suggestion to watch the suffrage parade did not seem like such a bad idea.

In the caravanseries that lined the slums of the Bowery, which had gotten its name from the Dutch word *bouwerie* for the farmland it once was, Wolf found a bed for a dime. The cheap lodging house offered no more than a time-yellowed, foul-smelling blanket and a room full of bunks that were merely strips of canvas strung between rough timbers. At least there was the questionable comfort of the red-hot stove he shared with thirty-two other men perched in the canvas bunks about and above him.

It was not the most secure perch. At intervals a restless sleeper would roll off and fall to the next tier of bunks. During the first weeks, Wolf awoke more than once to listen to the snoring of the men. It sounded like the regular strokes of a ship's engine. And the slow creaking of the beams under their restless weight added to the illusion of once more being aboard ship.

Restless as the sleeping men, Wolf would shift in his bunk as his thoughts drifted through the days he had spent on the *U. S. S. Wyoming*. And the Irish girl. Maggie, he had heard her called. Was she on her way to join a brother or cousin already in America? Or perhaps a fiancé?

The idea irritated him. He would have liked to reduce the girl's haughty demeanor before she dominated some poor helpless husband. He tried to tell himself it was only that his male ego had been afronted. But he sensed it was something else, something much more. "The damned fey quality of the Irish," he muttered. And, uncomfortable with the feeling, he would shift once again, positioning himself diagonally across the bunk to better accomodate his long frame.

More important things needed to be mulled over. Like finding work. Soon. The men who gravitated toward the Bowery were of the ilk who had sunk to the lowest level. The lazy, the shiftless, or the unfortunate. Unable to find work, they turned to begging, thievery, or, worse, the welcome nirvana of the stale beer dives.

He recalled one such nearby dive, off Chatham and Pearl streets. A cellar, really, with slimy walls and a floor hard-trodden with mud. A group of wretches, men and women, grouped about a beer keg that was propped on the wreck of a broken chair. They sat on apple crates and nail kegs, passing from hand to hand tomato cans filled at the keg. In the group's center a wrinkled hag dealt out the stale beer. A pile of copper coins rattled in her soiled apron.

Wolf shuddered at this picture of the life that lay before him. In Russia at least there had always been work, forced labor though it was. He resented going another day to the Bowery Mission; the small handout of hard rolls and weak coffee emasculated a man.

But the next day the Bowery Mission brought more than just the handout he waited in line for. He sat at the table with the tin mug of coffee, studying the now well thumbed through Russian/English dictionary in a determined attempt to master the language of his new homeland.

He had observed that it was the immigrants who refused to try to learn English and adapt to the American culture, who persisted instead in reading newspapers printed in their own language and shopping at stores that sold food from their old countries, who stayed only in the Little Italys or Little Polands, it was they who remained shackled to the dregs of poverty.

Absently his hand stroked the rough-shaven skin of his jaw while his lips silently pronounced the words, "legislative," "executive," and "judicial." When the mandatory five-year waiting period was up, he meant to have his citizenship. He meant to one day escape New York, which reminded him of St. Petersburg, though the American city was more advanced. But there still existed the same class distinction: the very rich, and the very poor.

A tap on his shoulder brought him back to the Mission's dingy room, in which he sat with nearly a hundred and fifty other "vagrants." He looked up into a kindly face of an old man in a priest's black garb.

The priest pointed toward the dictionary. "Son, do you speak English well?"

Wolf's eyes assessed the old man, trying to see what might lay behind the facade of the kindly expression. At last, he nodded. "I speak English."

The priest raised a grizzled eyebrow, noting the omission but also noting that the young man's pronunciation was impeccable, with only the slight trace of a foreign accent. The priest slid into the space on the bench beside Wolf. "One of the benefactresses of our mission is looking for a chauffeur," he told the young man. "Have you had any experience driving a motorcar?"

The word "chauffeur" Wolf did not recognize. But the word "motorcar" had been one of the first he had learned upon seeing the New York streets crowded with sedans, touring cars, limousines, and even electric broughams that edged out the horsecar lines and hansom cabs. He met the priest's wise eyes. "I could drive one," he hedged.

The priest slapped his knee with a conspiratorial smile. "Marvelous! You now have the chauffeur's job, son, for the Van der Rhys family."

CHAPTER

nine

᧬᧬᧬

"*We* *are demanding an American right denied* only to criminals, lunatics, idiots, and women: the right to vote!"

Flushing with her exhortation and the thunderous applause that followed, Mrs. O. H. P. Belmont, a *grande dame* of New York society, took her seat in the brownstone's parlor packed with women from every walk of life, from working women like Maggie to the renowned poetess Edna St. Vincent Millay and the actress Lillian Russell. Most of the women there wore the traditional yellow color of the cause; some sported corsages of yellow daisies, jonquils, and buttercups.

Maggie had watched the suffragette's parade the Sunday before. But she had not given serious consideration to the open invitation issued by one of the marchers to attend the next rally, to be held in Greenwich Village—a picturesque part slum, part shabby-genteel area curiously isolated from the roaring modern city that surrounded it.

Her decision to attend had come the night before when

she read to Jamie the creation according to Genesis. "Peg," she asked, after kissing Jamie good night, "has it ever occurred to you that on the authority of the Bible—which was written by men—woman was created as an afterthought of the Almighty, solely to relieve Adam's boredom?"

Peg, who was rinsing a diaper, laughed. "That only just came to 'oo? Do 'oo not realize that Queen Victoria's daughter, a firstborn mind 'oo, received a mere twenty-one-gun salute, while Edward got a whopping hundred and one?"

Maggie knew then that she would attend the suffragette's rally.

Following Mrs. Belmont, Marie Dressler rose. Maggie leaned forward to watch the almostugly, bulky woman, who was the current star of broadway, sing a parody of "Heaven Will Protect the Working Girl." Laughter and applause reigned until Vera Walden, in whose home the rally was being held, made her way to the front of the parlor to quiet the women. A plump, attractive woman, she smoked a cigar. "Sedalia Van der Rhys, who has graciously sponsored some of our rallies, will speak now."

The woman stood, a stately woman in her forties whose fading beauty was preserved in hair dyed the rich color of mahogany, and wearing clothes that whispered of elegance. Her lips formed a tight smile. "The Riverside Political Equality Association wishes to inform our sister suffragettes that it has ordered from England a specially designed tea service decorated with the slogan 'Votes for Women.'"

In the rippling applause that followed, Maggie wondered just how the tea service contributed to the cause of the women's rights movement. In fact, it seemed to her that the movement so far had not in any way bettered the woman's life.

"There has to be a better way," she muttered to Peg later that evening.

But Peg was too excited about her own piece of news.

"Svelta's cousin—the one that works for the Van der Rhyses—she is pregnant and will be a'quitting."

"Then Svelta should apply before the family finds someone else," Maggie said.

"Read this one for me," Jamie asked.

Maggie took the book the boy held out, Stevenson's *The Master of Ballentrae*. Peg said, "Svelta doesn't speak English good enough."

"Then why don't you apply?"

Peg held the fretting Brian to her sagging breast. "The family dinna be a'wanting a maid with children to rear. Why don't 'oo apply? The job pays twice as much as 'oo make now."

Domestic service was an old servitude that Maggie wanted to put behind her—as she would her corset. That, at least, had come out of the suffrage rally. No longer would she apologize for her figure.

She ignored Peg's suggestion and began to read to Jamie, who huddled close to her on the sagging, tattered couch.

Later that night, Brian suddenly began a helpless wail mixed with a hacking cough. A soaring temperature mottled the baby-fair skin. "What can it mean?" she asked Peg, who bent over the crate to stroke Brian's throbbing little body.

No bitterness etched Peg's voice as she said lowly, "It means that the dirty bow of white 'oo saw on the door downstairs today will have another story to tell. Brian's a'dying with the measles."

"No!" Maggie whispered. "We can get a doctor."

Peg looked up at her, her face rough and old. "What doctor would be coming out on charity at this time of night, and here, in the Bend?"

Maggie rushed from the room into the dark hallway. Her bare foot stepped into some decaying vegetable as she located the sinks used by all the tenants. The pump squeaked rebelliously when she turned on the faucet; the icy water,

smelling like a cesspool, dribbled into the sink. She wet the
hem of her nightshift and hurried back to the room. Kneeling
at the mother's side, she said, "Let's hope we can cool the
babe down, Peg."

Peg looked at her with blank eyes. "What right have we
got to hope, such as we?"

Such as we. The words flitted through Maggie's mind
like a worrisome fly.

When Brian was buried in Potter's Field the next day,
she knew she would apply for the maid's position.

The Van der Rhyses, she was to learn, were an old
Knickerbocker family whose wealth had been based on great
landholdings. Mrs. Van der Rhys made it clear from that
first day that the new-money families, the Whitneys, the
Morgans, and the Goulds, were social inferiors to the Schuy-
lers, the Livingstons, and the Van Rensselaers.

"Gone are those great days," Sedalia sighed, and set the
great Persian cat from her lap.

Maggie, dressed in an ankle-length black dress and
starched white apron and cap, put away the woman's discarded hobble skirt, and her boots and gaiters. "These days
one sees only the vulgar and showy at the Metropolitan
Opera House," the woman continued, talking more to herself as she inserted the pins in her piled hair. "Common
people with their newly acquired wealth, and eager to flaunt
it."

"Yes, madam." Since the Sunday before, when Sedalia
had interviewed and hired her (Maggie never mentioned the
suffrage rally), Maggie had quickly learned to repress her
thoughts behind an expressionless countenance.

Unraveling the labyrinth of halls and rooms of the Van
der Rhys house came more slowly. House? Maggie thought.
The Van der Rhys house in Riverdale, which was some
miles north of New York City along the Hudson River

palisades, was more like the great stone castle outside Dublin. Surrounded by a black wrought-iron fence with spikes, the Van der Rhys estate boasted massive tree-shaded grounds, a Romanesque pool, and a carriage house converted to a garage for the three motorcars.

The neo-classical villa contained opulent interiors—the Peacock Room, the Chinese Room, the Garden Room—with painted ceilings, highly polished period furniture, red damasks and velvets draping the high windows. Incredibly, a gymnasium shared the third floor with the maid's quarters.

Maggie began to lay out the evening clothes on the studio couch that was covered with a *kilim* spread; Sedalia's bedroom was the Turkish Room.

"No, no, Maggie," Sedalia turned from the dressing table's large gilt mirror that was sheltered by the draped *gobbah*. Her eyes, rimmed by a faint network of lines, swept over the dress with distaste. "Not the watered silk. It's a little too ostentatious for tonight. I believe the black charmeuse dinner gown will do admirably—and the embroidered heels with the large paste buckles."

The black charmeuse? What was charmeuse? Maggie went through the closet guessing, and hoping the dress she picked was the one the woman wanted. She noticed that the fishnet train had torn loose from the gown's right shoulder. While Mrs. Van der Rhys bathed, she slipped into the sewing room to get a needle and thread. As she stooped to light the Tiffany lamp beside the rocker, a pair of hands encircled her head to close over her eyes.

Her breath caught short at the male voice that said, "Guess who?" The darkness, the masculine scent, the hands—tremors rippled through her. "Come on, Greta," the gay voice teased, "you have to forfeit a kiss if you can't guess my identity."

The jocularity in the voice, reminding Maggie somewhat of her brother Mickey, caused her to relax, though only slightly. "I believe, sir, that you are Mr. and Mrs. Van der Rhys's son, Franklin." She drew another deep breath. "And I believe that you are the one with the mistaken identity."

"Oh my God," the voice breathed. He took his hands from her eyes and switched on the lamp. In the room's muted light, the two studied each other. Maggie saw a young man of medium height with a pair of dancing robin blue eyes and toffee brown hair center-parted in the Douglas Fairbanks movie-hero look. His lips formed a disarming smile. "How did you know who I was?"

"Your mother. She told me you were away at Princeton." Maggie did not add what the cook, Polly, had told her. "All of New York's debutantes are chasing Mr. Franklin— including some of the Van der Rhys' hired help." Winking, the roly-poly Polly added that Svelta's cousin, Greta, had been among the women chasing Franklin—until Mrs. Van der Rhys dismissed her. Another lascivious wink and a few aside remarks hinted that it was most likely Franklin's child that the former maid was carrying.

Franklin's gaze swept over Maggie's silvery gold hair beneath the starched cap, lingered on the bowlike upper lip above the full lower one, and swept down along the curves and indentations that the uniform did not completely hide. "Since you know who I am," he said, and caught her fingers to bring them to his lips, "won't you tell me who you are?"

She pulled her hand from his grasp. "That you shall have to ask of your mother. Good evening, sir."

She escaped from the room that evening, but Franklin did not let her off so easily over the days that followed. The next time he found her alone, she was cleaning his bedroom. She whirled from the bed when she heard the door close and saw Franklin leaning against it with his arms folded. "I'm home for the Thanksgiving holidays," he told her, "and I won't return without a kiss to be thankful for."

She straightened from smoothing out the bed's tufted coverlet and warily eyed the young man. His smile was infectious. "Do you always get what you want?" she asked, trying to keep her lips in a firm line.

He laughed aloud. "Always. Don't you know I'm an only child: overloved, overpraised, and overprotected."

"The poor little rich boy who always gets what he wants," she mocked.

"Hardly. Mother wants me to go into real estate, father wants me to go into banking, and I . . ."

"And you what?" she asked when he paused.

He laughed again. "And I want to be chosen Princeton's Master of Revels again this year. In other words, I really don't give a damn. Except maybe about winning a kiss from a very pretty young woman."

"If you touch me, I shall call your father."

Franklin's laughter held genuine amusement. "And I shall tell the old man that you sought me out. After all," he pointed out, "you *are* in my bedroom."

Real panic assailed her now. She did not want to lose the job. With the money she could save from her wages, she meant to find a way to become independent, perhaps even begin a business of her own. Somehow she meant to rise above her poverty, because poverty meant dependence on a man. And then there was Jamie and Peg to consider. She had hoped to send Peg a portion of her first month's wages.

Her obvious distress must have moved Franklin, for he said, not unkindly, "Blast it, Maggie, my mother has no consideration in choosing maids." He straightened from the door with a daring smile and moved toward her. "Greta practically chased me into the bed, yet you are too niggardly to bestow one kiss."

Maggie blushed at the reference to the bed, but before he reached her, his father's imperious voice halted him. "Franklin! Where the devil are you?" The door opened, and William Van der Rhys stood there, his glowering gaze going from his son to Maggie and back. He was a somewhat heavier version of his son, and dressed with the same male sartorial splendor in a fawn morning coat with matching striped cashmere trousers. Only the walrus mustache, pince-nez glasses, and the faint lines of three decades distinguished them apart.

"You wanted me, father?"

The older man seemed to quiz her behind the pince-nez lenses before saying, "I'm on my way to the bank. I'd like for you to spend the day with me."

"There's a good wind out of the southwest, and I planned to run the *Corsair* up the Hudson today. After all, I am on vacation."

"I see." The older man's blistering look swept in Maggie. She quietly and quickly excused herself.

But the man's tirade that his son would play away his life—and fortune—followed her down the hall. She was only relieved that the father had not followed her down the hall and dismissed her from her job.

Wolf raised from beneath the hood of the Pierce-Arrow and rested his elbows on the shiny fender as he studied the slender young woman, the newest maid, swatting the rug beater against the carpet suspended from the line. The high sweep of cheekbones glowed pink with either the exertion or the brisk November air, or perhaps both. The first time he had seen her, not quite a week before, he thought he had to be mistaken. It surely could not be the same young Irish girl he had crossed the Atlantic with. Fate wouldn't play the same trick twice.

Watching the way the gently rounded hips swayed with each swing of the rug beater, the way her breasts strained against the coarse material of the shawl, he felt himself hardening. Maggie. There were at least fifty other willing women in Riverdale. So why her? he asked himself for the hundredth time.

Obviously it had not been a fiancé she had come to

America to meet. Yet the lack of a fiancé did not seem to hinder her, he thought as he sighted young Van der Rhys approaching her, dressed in a wind slicker over a smart V-neck white sweater, gray flannel baggy knickers, and canvas shoes. The young man called out something as he crossed the dry winter grass, and the girl turned in that direction, smiling.

Wolf picked up the wrench and went back to working on the engine. Old Van der Rhys preferred the commuter train and the new IRT subway, but Mrs. Van der Rhys would want one of the cars, as she did every afternoon. As she no doubt wanted something else.

With a grimace, he finished tightening the hose clamp and made his way up the narrow stairs of the carriage house that had been converted to a garage. The chauffeur's quarters were small but comfortably furnished—at least as comfortably furnished as anything he had ever known. He had his own bed, a four-poster no less, though he still had to lay diagonally to accomodate his length.

Quickly he pumped the water into the sink and washed his grimy hands before donning the duster. The cap he pulled low over his eyes, but the goggles he left behind. Their restriction on his senses annoyed him. Mrs. Van der Rhys was already below waiting. If she was impatient, she concealed it beneath her carefully schooled expression of society's boredom.

He knew better. Even nearing a mere seventeen years he had experienced too much, intimately known too many females to miss the telltale signs. Sedalia had a little more finesse than some of the others, but the glitter in her eyes was unmistakable as she wrapped about her the fur-lined motoring coat, which was unnecessary on the cool but sunny afternoon.

Sedalia watched the young man crank the automobile. No paunch marred his physique as it did William's. "I'll be going to Sherry's for lunch, Wolf."

She liked the young man's given name. It had a hard
sound, like the young man's appearance. Just saying the
name made her shiver with anticipation. She had never
thought about taking a lover before. It had not mattered that
William had his mistresses. It relieved her of her "duty."
She was content with her luncheons and dinner parties, her
summers spent in Newport and her winters in Florida. But
this winter . . . perhaps this winter she'd stay at Riverdale.

CHAPTER

ten

⟪ ❧⟫

Maggie put down Shelley's Queen Mab *and sat* upright in the bed. Had she heard something? Her eyes were tired from so much reading, and maybe her mind was just tired also. No, there she heard it again. Someone was coming up the back stairs. Stumbling up the back stairs, it sounded more like. She slipped from the bed and crossed the first steps to the door, placing her ear against the wood. No one but the servants used the back stairs, and no one but herself at this time of night.

Her breath suspended as she listened for footsteps. Instead: "Ssssh, damn cat!"

She jerked upright from the door. A male voice. A drunken male voice. The butler, Malcolm, drank some, she knew. But he was nearly sixty; surely he wouldn't be coming up to accost her. There was the chauffeur. She had yet to meet Nicholson, so she doubted the intruder was he.

"Maggie, gal," came the sotto voce, almost at her ear. "Open up."

Franklin! She pressed her cheek closer to the door. "What is it?" she whispered.

"Damned bow tie won't give."

The cat screeched, and Franklin swore again. Lest he awaken the entire household, Maggie quickly opened the door. He almost fell in atop her. The cat hissed and shot behind Maggie. Between the two, the man and the cat, she toppled backwards onto the bed.

"Ahh, Maggie," Franklin said in a happy slur, "you want me, too."

The old image of the soldiers hovering over her, the putrid smell of alcohol. Her fingers dug into the sheets. Yet Franklin seemed so helpless, his expression so contented as he lay sprawled half on her. "You're drunk, Franklin Van der Rhys!" she reproved, but her lips twitched.

"Stinking drunk, madam." He flashed a silly smile. "Had to celebrate my last evening 'fore returning to the Halls of Learning." He struggled to sit up. "Can't go to bed with my bow tie on. Most improper."

She pushed herself up beside him. He reeked of a woman's perfume, and powder clung to one eyebrow and speckled the shoulder of his black dinner jacket. Her fingers began to work at the knot of the white bow tie. She could feel his eyes watching her. "Maggie, gal, you can't send me back without that kiss. Bad 'nuff going back anyway."

Beneath the warmth of his gaze, her fingers faltered at his tie. Nervous, her speech lapsed into the syntax of her homeland. "But 'tis good the schooling will be doing you, sir."

"For what, Maggie? For a life my parents want me to lead? To marry shum—some debutante on the Social Register and produce more unhappy Van der Rhys sons."

She pulled the bow tie free and pushed up and away from Franklin. "Then do whatever it is you want to," she said with some exasperation as she stood over him.

Franklin laughed and grabbed her waist. "I want to kiss you."

She twisted free and went to open the door. What if he

did not leave? Or what if Franklin became angry at the rebuff and saw to it she was dismissed? Dear God, she did not need any more trouble. Not now.

"Not going to shen—send me out into the cold, are you?" He shifted unsteadily to his feet and lurched toward her.

She dodged his hand and gently pushed his shoulder toward the doorway. "Come back at Christmas," she pacified. "Then we shall be seeing."

She shoved the door closed and leaned back against it, her eyes closed. One month until Christmas. One month to hope Franklin found someone else to turn his attentions to.

Wolf heard the light footsteps on the stone drive but did not bother to slide out from beneath the motorcar. He was not up to facing Mrs. Van der Rhys just yet. She was demanding more of his time, blaming it on all the last-minute Christmas shopping she needed to do. But he knew it wasn't shopping she wanted. All too often now her hand lingered at his shoulder as she directed him to a certain street or called his attention to something in a store window they passed.

He remembered the few women of wealth he had known in St. Petersburg. A woman scorned could be a very powerful enemy. Hell, why didn't he take her? It had been months since he had known the comfort and release to be found in a woman's arms. His resentment caused him to miss the bolt he was trying to dislodge with the hammer and hit his thumb instead. "Well, hell!"

He heard the shocked intake of breath. A feminine voice said with a prim Irish accent, "Mr. Nicholson, Mrs. Van der Rhys has asked me to tell you she shall be a half hour late."

His gaze swept out to see the pair of neatly turned, booted ankles. He groaned. *"Sasodits!"* he cursed, this time resorting to Russian. Maggie. His bad mood was not improving.

He shoved himself out from beneath the Bentley and grinned up into the young girl's startled face. With an almost malicious delight he saw her mouth drop open. "No!" she whispered.

He came to his feet to tower above her. The black uniform she wore made her seem even smaller, tinier, like a fragile porcelain doll. But there was nothing fragile about the glare she turned on him. Why did it suddenly seem as if the garage was charged with energy—an energy that arced between them?

He shifted his weight to one foot and planted his fists at his hips. "It appears we are fated to meet, Maggie Moran," he said in slow, distinct words that were like a clock's staccato beat.

She whirled, and something perverse made his arm shoot out against the garage's brick wall to block her way. The girl spun around to face him. Beneath the thick, lacy lashes her hazel eyes, no—they were as green as clover leaves—widened. His gaze dropped to the hollow at the base of her throat where her pulse hammered, then raised to fasten on her lips. It surprised him that they trembled. "You have never been kissed, have you?"

Wordlessly the girl shook her head in a negative gesture. He could almost smell the wariness that narrowed her eyes and flared her nostrils. It angered him. He was already foul-tempered that day. With slow deliberation, he bent his head over hers. Her eyes stared up at him as if she were in a trance. His lips ground against her soft, vulnerable ones.

Only then did she try to twist free, swerving her head away from him. He pressed his length against her, pinning her to the rough brick. His long fingers anchored in the hair at either side of her head, holding it immobile. There was something about her hair that was representative of the girl herself, the way the tawny tendrils fought to escape the constraining braids. When his lips descended this time, the girl opened her mouth to scream and he buried the scream in her throat with another dominating kiss. Against his stomach he could feel her heart thudding out its rebellion—and fear, too?

Slowly his anger ebbed. His mouth softened its assault, moving over hers with a feather-light touch. He felt her go still and sensed the slight change within her. His lips moved upward over the contours of her face to kiss first one eyelid, then the other, before slipping down to claim her lips again in a kiss that this time questioned.

Her almost inaudible moan reached him, and something inside him answered its call, answered her innocence and loneliness. His hands dropped to slide around her back and waist and crush her against him in a kiss that held only the terrible need that had ached within him for so long.

He knew when the girl's submission came by the way her strength deserted her, the way she almost sagged within his embrace. Shaken, he moved slightly away, though still holding her to support the two of them against the wall. His head raised. Her eyelids lay closed, her thick lashes dark half moons against her skin's pallor. "Maggie . . ."

Her square jaw snapped up in something akin to a queen's regal pride. Then her fist slashed out to impact with his jaw. Momentarily stunned, he shook his head to clear the ringing. He looked down at the girl struggling to free herself. Against his mass she was like a puppy yapping at his heels. But she was a scrapper. For the first time in a long time, he threw back his head and laughed.

"If ever," she drew a raging breath, "if ever you touch me again, I'll—"

"You will return the kiss next time," he laughed. It was a promise he'd see to it she kept, he told himself as he watched her stalk away, her delightful curve of hips enticing.

CHAPTER
eleven

"I believe that includes everyone." Mrs. Van der Rhys put down the list and her little gold pen on the cherry-wood secretary. "I shall send the invitations out tomorrow morning. Will you please tell your father to see to the wines and liqueurs, Franklin?"

Maggie set the tea service on the small inlaid Turkish table. From his mother's chaise lounge Franklin, who was home again for the Christmas holidays, flashed Maggie a wink. She ignored it and proceeded to pour the tea. Franklin said, "I really think you ought to invite Joe and Beth to the New Year's party, Mother."

"Franklin, we have been all through that. It is simply out of the question."

"But Christ, she's my cousin. And Joe is one of my best—"

"Franklin, please. Please do not say 'Christ.'" Mrs. Van der Rhys closed her eyes and rubbed her temples with ring-laden fingers. She was exhausted. And she was irritated: Wolf continued to ignore her.

Well, from now on she would treat him with the same

disdain reserved for all servants and put him in his place—
which she meant to be her bed, sooner or later. Then there
was the maid Maggie. When she had interviewed her, the
young girl had kept her head down, her eyes lowered. It
wasn't until recently that she had begun to perceive the
girl's beauty, an arrogant beauty that was out of keeping in
a servant. And her speech. Though colored with the Irish
cadence, the syntax was that of a literate person. It would
do well to watch her. She was no doubt far too easy with
her ways. And there was Franklin to consider. He was a
young man with an eye for the women now, and knew no
discretion.

Sedalia opened her eyes to find her son eyeing her sourly.
"I have explained to you about Beth and Joe a dozen times,"
she said in an attempt to pacify her son. "We can have them
for dinner sometime when no one else is going to be here."

"But Beth seldom gets a chance to see any of the people
she used to know and—"

"Beth," said Sedalia, "should have thought of that before
she married a mechanic. I cannot invite her and Joe here
when the Whitneys and Astors and people like that are going
to be here. What would they think? Be reasonable, Franklin."

"But he's perfectly—"

"Yes, yes, I know. He talks and dresses quite correctly,
if overconsciously. But it is not the same. After all, it is
background that counts. You cannot deny that blood will
always tell."

Maggie handed Franklin the teacup that rattled in the
saucer. Rage boiled inside her. The pomposity of people
like the Van der Rhyses!

She looked down just then and saw Franklin's face as
he accepted the tea. A stricken look of loathing, almost like
that of one suffocating, masked it. She felt the same suf-
focation, the wild need to escape the confines of the fur-
niture-congested mansion and breathe. To be free.

Instead, she escaped below to the butler's pantry, where Malcolm was taking the dirty breakfast dishes from the dumbwaiter. The small elevator that ascended to the master bedroom by electronic means never failed to amaze her, as did the steam heat that seeped from the brass wall pipes and the telephone that rang constantly. It had taken her days before she could pick up the earpiece and speak into the receiver without a breathless croak.

"I'll take care of the dishes," she told Malcolm.

The rheumy eyes in the old face smiled gratefully. "Why, thank you. Mr. Van der Rhys did want me to shine his patents this morning."

She was putting the blue and white English willowware into the glass cabinet when Franklin came up to stand directly behind her. "Go out with me tomorrow," he whispered in her ear.

"I can't." She continued putting up the dishes, wishing he would go away. What if his mother came down?

"You can. It's Sunday, you have the day off."

She whirled on him. "Can't you understand? I work for your family. And the upper and lower classes don't mix. Or didn't your mother make that plain enough just now?"

His jaw tightened. "Too plain. God, but it's stuffy in here." He caught her shoulders. "I'll take you up to Sagamore Hills, if you want. We can see Roosevelt's prized horse stables. Or ride out to Oyster Bay and watch the sloops come in."

She opened her mouth to say no, and he said, "If you don't go with me, I'll kiss those ripe lips of yours right here in front of Malcolm and Polly and the whole damn disapproving family."

With a sigh, Maggie relented, moved not just by Franklin's teasing threat but by a real desire to escape from the claustrophobic mansion and see the Long Island countryside.

She met him in the garage early Sunday morning, before
the house stirred. She had dreaded running into Wolf, but
either he had not yet arisen or he was already gone.

"Come on, my old-world girl," Franklin said and helped
Maggie into the Bentley.

He looked dashing in his Norfolk jacket with a tweed
cap. When he climbed into the far side, his glance took in
her threadbare jacket. Taking off his woolen ascot, he draped
it over her head and knotted it about her neck. All the while
his gaze roamed her sculpted face, studying the excitement
of the outing that was mirrored in her marvelous eyes.
"You'll get chilly," he explained, his voice suddenly lower,
warmer.

The December day was gloriously sunny, and the car
protected them from its raw wind. To Franklin's delight,
Maggie was more impressed with his car than she was with
the rows of the Sagamore stables. Afterwards, they drove
out to the bay. Maggie fell in love with the quaint little
shops—they reminded her of Dublin. The wind off the bay
stung her cheeks and whipped Franklin's ascot from her
head so that strands of her hair blew wild. Laughing, Franklin hurried her into the next establishment they came to,
The Old Pelican Restaurant. "Let's have something to eat,"
he suggested.

"Oh, no," she begged, glancing at the casually but well-
dressed people at the tables. She stood close to the door as
if ready to bolt. At his questioning glance, she raised her
chin, looking as haughty as some *grande dame*. "I've never
eaten in a restaurant before, in front of everyone." When
still the frown of puzzlement etched his face, she added
quietly but with great dignity, "I don't know the right utensils to—"

He laughed and grabbed her hand. "You've served those
old fuddy-duddies in my parents' home long enough to know
proper manners better than they do. Just follow my lead."

He pulled her to the nearest vacant table, where a young

plump girl about Maggie's age waited on them. Franklin did the ordering: delicious butter-broiled snapper, steaming carrots and peas, and a great loaf of freshly-baked bread...more food than Maggie had ever had set before her in her lifetime. The white wine added a glow to her cheeks, and she smiled readily as Franklin leaned back after the meal and told her of his experiences as a boy—of chasing his cousin Beth up the front stairs and down the servants' backstairs, of hiding in the dumbwaiter and scaring old Polly when it came down from the master bedroom and she opened its door.

The approach of evening reminded the two that they needed to be returning to the house. When he wheeled the Bentley into the garage and helped her from the automobile, she was only a little wary, as she always was when in the presence of a male. Perhaps it was the wine she drank that relaxed her caution.

He squeezed her hand. "You're good for me, Maggie," he said softly and kissed her on the nose. Then his lips descended toward hers, and she pulled away.

He laughed. "All right, Miss Prim, but I mean to have that kiss before I return to school this time." He released her then, saying, "I'll go on inside and keep my father busy with some handball and you can follow in a few minutes." His lips lost their curve. "I don't want them to discharge you, Maggie. And they would. They're just snobbish enough to."

He grabbed her and kissed her then, quickly, before she could protest. Whistling happily to himself, he left her alone in the garage.

Wolf lay with his hands clasped behind his head. He heard the car roll into the garage. Franklin was returning with Maggie. A vision of her came unbidden to his mind: her heavy unruly hair unbound to mantle her shoulders and back, the enchanting shape of her deeply curved mouth, a dangerously sensual mouth, yielding willingly to him one of those rare scintillant smiles he had seen her bestow on Franklin.

He rolled to a sitting position in the bed and ran his fingers through his thick dark hair that would not lay smoothly in a part. He told himself that Maggie was little more than a child, though he guessed they were of the same age more or less. He felt eons older. He had seen too much, done too much—things he wasn't proud of.

He felt stifled, jaded, weary. And he felt himself drawn too much to Maggie. She both baffled him and held an allure for him that he could not rid himself of. He should collect his wages and be on his way. Perhaps it was the cossack, the adventurer in him that made him restless.

Nude, he rose and stretched his muscle-roped frame. Reluctantly he drew on his trousers. He had not heard Franklin close the garage doors and knew he would have to. Mentally damning the pampered Van der Rhys scion, he padded down the cold, wooden steps and plunged into the darkness of the garage.

The sudden shimmering of gold to his left drew his attention, and he saw Maggie spin around to face him. "I—I am waiting for Franklin."

He could tell by the belligerent thrust of her jaw it was a lie. He came to stand before her, his hand on the Bentley's door. His frame blocked all outside light. "So, it is mistress of the house you wish to be."

"It's not like that." Her tone was blistering.

He took her small hand, roughened with work, and before she could jerk free, he pulled her to him. "You dislike me. Why? Is my kiss so different from that of young Van der Rhys'? Or is it the wealth that makes his kisses more bearable?"

"Your kisses make me ill."

The iciness of fear made her voice sound frigid with disdain. "I do not believe you," he said slowly, his anger bubbling just below the surface like lava before a volcanic eruption. He lowered his head and claimed her lips with his. Even as she trembled, so did he. He smelled the sweet wine on her breath and wanted to taste it on her tongue.

He crushed his mouth against hers until her lips surrendered and parted. His tongue, like a conquering warrior, swept inside to plunder every virgin area. She gasped, and he felt the last barrier of resistance drain from her body. The wild calling of his primitive nature overrode his veneer of civilization. He had the urgent need to find out what she was like when she let herself go.

He slid one arm under her knees and lifted her to cradle her against his bare chest. His mouth did not release hers despite the protest that stirred deep in her throat. He began to climb the dark stairs and ignored the hands that pushed against his chest in a feeble effort to gain freedom. All about them it seemed to him a strange light wavered. His garage apartment fairly crackled with a static electricity. But he was not interested in exploring the phenomenon at that moment. There was only one thing he was interested in exploring.

When he lowered her to the rumpled bed, she scrambled to the far side. Her long skirts got in her way, and his hand shot out in time to capture hers. He dragged her back to the bed's center and anchored her there beneath one leg. "You give freely to Van der Rhys but you have fought me all the way." His voice was level, but he could feel the pressure building beneath it. And he could feel the pressure building in her, expanding her ribcage and contracting it in tight, rapid throbbing. "Why?" he demanded. "I want to know why the hate?"

"You ask me why," she said. Her eyes burned a deep blue-green, like the hot core of a raging fire. "Because of men like you, men who suppress women with their authority, and with brute strength."

He sensed she spoke with great effort, with brave effort.

"Men like the British soldiers," she continued in a shaken rasp, "who mounted me when I was but twelve—as if I were an animal for their needs! A receptacle and nothing more!"

His eyes flared, then the lids quickly lowered to conceal his shock. She was trembling, and he knew she could not stop of her own free will. One swarthy hand came up to brush away the tendrils that had escaped from the knot of braids during her wild bid for freedom.

"Hush," he murmured. Gently his lips brushed her wet cheeks, brushed her long damp lashes, and came back to still her quivering lips with a warm, soft kiss. "The bitterest tears in the world are the tears of children," he said quietly, almost absently, recalling his own tears for his mother and sister. Then the sweet smell of lilac talcum drew him back to the girl who lay frozen half beneath him.

Her lips moved ever so slightly, as if welcoming the sensation his parted lips conveyed. He knew she was surprised by the pleasure that could be found in the kiss. She made no protest as he pulled her against him so that their bodies lay lengthwise.

Despite the desire that hammered inside him, he began to make love to her slowly, with great tenderness. His hands met no resistance as he pulled the pins from her hair, scattering them across the rumpled sheets. His fingers combed the braids loose so that her hair tumbled over the delicate curve of her shoulders like liquid gold frothing, cascading, and foaming in eddies about her arms, waist, breasts.

"It blinds the eye," he whispered and entwined his fingers in the brilliant wisps that seemed to curl of their own volition, as if they had a life of their own. "Your hair is as I knew it would be."

His fingers slipped down to pull aside her coat and work at the buttons of her blouse. She began to shake violently. He sensed her instinctive withdrawal. "No," she cried out, shrinking from his embrace.

His eyes narrowed. "I think you are a coward, Maggie," he said softly, dangerously.

She pushed away from him. Her breast heaved, drawing his gaze to their ripeness despite his anger. "What you want I shall never give you freely," she spat. She pulled her shabby coat about her as if it were a queen's robe. "You shall have to take me as the soldiers did."

It was like a slap in the face. With a tremendous effort he restrained himself from picking up the thrown gauntlet, from jerking her against him and taking her then and there. He smiled, but his eyes were impersonal and cold from his lacerated pride. "But I am not one of those soldiers."

"Every man is one of those soldiers!"

"The time will come when you will give yourself to me just as passionately as you wanted to only moments before."

He saw she wanted to hurl herself on him and scratch and bite him like some proud lioness. But she slid gracefully to the edge of the bed. With great dignity she drew herself erect.

"Never," she said.

CHAPTER
twelve

~⚮~

R*avishment. The word that meant both rape and* rapture. Maggie understood it now.

She looked in the tarnished mirror over her commode and saw the eyes that glowed, as if with a fever, and the lips that were abraided by Wolf's scalding kisses only a few minutes earlier. And she knew, despite the incredibly pleasurable sensations that Wolf had initiated, she desired the rapture even less than she did the rape. For when Wolf's passion began to grow more demanding, she began to feel she was losing herself. Before, she had withdrawn from the degrading action.

But now she had no control over herself, over her passions that rose to the bidding of Wolf's prowess in lovemaking. She had stood on the threshold of some mindrending discovery—and she was, as Wolf accused, a coward. She was afraid of submission, afraid of being nothing but a tool for another's will, the pawn of another's whim.

She recalled the exact moment when she had realized he was in the garage with her, that moment when a sudden current of air had rustled the hem of her skirts. Without even looking, she had known he was there. How?

The servant's buzzer interrupted her uneasy reflections. Damn, her one day off! She sighed, and went to see what Mrs. Van der Rhys wanted. From the gymnasium she could hear the sound of Mr. Van der Rhys's handball slamming against the wall. When she entered the bedroom, Sedalia sat in the pillow-piled window casement that overlooked the rear of the grounds. She turned, and Maggie saw the fury that contorted the woman's face, creasing the wrinkles into a witch's mask.

With clenched hands, Sedalia came slowly to her feet. Her satin robe swirled around her as she advanced across the Bokhara carpet toward Maggie. "How dare you, you little slut!"

Maggie held her ground. "I don't know what you're—"

Sedalia's teeth bared. "Don't lie to me. Look; look at yourself. Your hair looks like a bird's nest, your cheeks are raw from his beard stubble... You've been wallowing in the bed with Wolf, haven't you!"

Maggie recognized the jealousy that literally turned the woman's complexion a sickly shade of green. She knew there was no placating the woman. "It is my day off, madam," she said quietly.

"It's your year off!" Sedalia screamed. "You're fired, do you hear me!"

"What's this all about?" William Van der Rhys stood in the doorway. Behind him Maggie saw Franklin's worried face.

Sedalia pointed a trembling finger at Maggie. "Her, William. The girl's been whoring around with, with the local men. Next thing you know, she'll come sniffing around our son like a bitch in heat. She's a hound hot on the trail of money, I tell you."

Franklin pushed past his father to take Maggie's icy hand. "Mother! You're wrong."

"So, she's spread her legs for our son, too!" Sedalia said.

Maggie jerked her hand from Franklin's and whirled to leave. Where could she go? Back to the factories? With all the emigrants vying for a job, it was hopeless.

"If Maggie goes, I go with her," Franklin said.

"Just a minute here!" William Van der Rhys shouted. He caught hold of his wife and forced her to sit down on the ponderous, tasseled Turkish chair. "Let me handle this."

"I'm going to marry her," Franklin blustered. His handsome face glowed a beet red.

Maggie threw him a startled look. The last thing she wanted was marriage. Whatever independence she had achieved would be shattered.

Van der Rhys turned to face Maggie and his son. A stern, shrewd expression, that Maggie imagined he must have used in his business's boardroom, hardened his countenance. "I do not underrate you, Miss Moran. You are a very intelligent, ambitious young girl. I feel you and I can come to some settlement on this, and do what's best for everyone in the bargain. Some sort of settlement."

He was watching her, gauging her. His face was a palpitating red. She was willing to bet it had nothing to do with the effect from the recent exercise. "Shall we say five hundred dollars?" he asked.

She felt like she had been hit on the head again by a falling meteor. It was unreal to even attempt to imagine such a sum. The idea was so staggering that no words came to her. Van der Rhys frowned. "Miss Moran, you're not dealing with one of your vegetable-stand hawkers down at the Bowery. You and I both know you don't love my son."

Franklin's hand gripped hers. "Father, I won't have this sort of—"

"For once, Franklin, shut up." Van der Rhys rounded on her. "My last offer, Miss Moran, is a thousand dollars. Do you have any idea what that kind of money could do for the likes of you?"

The likes of you. There it was again. The capillaries beneath her skin constricted, draining her face of blood.

"Maggie, don't listen to him," Franklin pleaded.

"Oh, my God!" Sedalia moaned. "She has even turned my son against me!"

Blood roared back through Maggie's body and flushed her complexion to the same shade as her rose-tinted lips. Her skin burned with shame. Tears sprang to her eyes. "Don't cry, Maggie," Franklin pleaded, trying to gather her to him.

She jerked away. "I'm not crying because I'm hurt," she raged. "I'm crying because I'm so damned mad! And there's nothing I can do about it."

Yes, there was. She turned to Franklin. "I'm leaving. If you still want to marry me, I will."

His shoulders hunched against the New Year's biting wind, Wolf walked along the concrete pavement. As he passed through Harlem's slums and neared the outskirts of Manhattan's midtown business district, the wide esplanade of Broadway became more and more congested. It should be easy enough now to catch a cab.

But he didn't want one. Although he knew there would be plenty enough time later for walking, too much time and too much distance, he wanted to walk now, to let his long strides eat up the distance between Riverdale and Manhattan—and eat up his restlessness.

Sedalia had stormed and raged and eventually cried when he had given his notice. And he had felt nothing. Not even pity for the aging woman whose husband and son had deserted her for other women. That was it: he felt simply nothing. And he liked it that way.

He knew that Maggie Moran—no, Maggie Van der Rhys—was no doubt making the most of her new wealthy status. She was something else he was glad he was leaving. He reminded himself that she was a scheming little bitch, that she had played Franklin right into her hands. She was part of that Old World he had thought he was putting behind him when he set foot on Ellis Island.

His footsteps quickened and finally brought him to Penn Station, the vast railroad terminal with labyrinthine arcades of shops and immense public concourses buried far underground. Here trains daily disgorged and sucked in a multitude of travelers. Here he would escape the remnants of the Old World standards. The lure of the western country whispered to him.

He bought a ticket for the farthest destination west he could afford. For five days he sat in the train seat and ignored the curious glances of the other passengers who eyed the young man who was so graceful they hardly realized he was tall. Instead Wolf watched the big industrial cities—Pittsburg, Cleveland, St. Louis—glide by his window. At last the train left behind the tall grasslands of western Kansas, crossed the Colorado Rockies, and traversed the deserts of Utah to reach his final destination, Salt Lake City.

But putting Maggie behind him—was he really? Something in him recognized an affinity for the young Irish girl.

CHAPTER
thirteen

❧ ❧ ❧

*M*aggie *set the high toque trimmed with tulle and*
osprey feathers at a tilt over her left eye. "You shouldn't
have, Frank," she said, looking at his pleased expression
in the mirror.

It was what every female replied when receiving a gift,
but Maggie meant it, though she tried to minimize the disapproval in her voice. Holy Mary, they couldn't continue
to spend money at such a fast pace! She had to make Frank
understand that one day the well would run dry.

But he loved to spend money. At first she was both
delighted and dismayed at the aristocratic world he introduced her to, beginning immediately with their installation
in the honeymoon suite at the prestigious Waldorf-Astoria.
And she knew he enjoyed her wide-eyed, childlike response.

During the day they frequented the art dealers and the
fashionable, exclusive shops that jostled for room on Fifth
Avenue. At night, after a sumptuous dinner in the Waldorf-
Astoria's crystalline Palm Garden or at Delmonico's, Frank
might take her to visit a movie house on Broadway, the
Great White Way, to Carnegie Hall for a concert, or con-

descend to watch the new dance craze, the *danse des Apaches*, taking place in the cabarets springing up in New York City.

Much later, when they returned to their suite, he would make love to her with a response that was in itself almost childlike. He would begin by brushing out her hair. He delighted in the way it fell to the small of her back in a tangled skein of honey-gold silken threads. But too soon his delight in her willow anatomy would be replaced by his impatient desire, and he would roll atop her.

Their wedding night he had been surprised she did not wear a corset. If he was surprised she was not a virgin, she never knew. She believed that such was her initial fear, he was too preoccupied with trying to make her feel at ease to give much thought to any actual physical barrier. She did discover that an intimate sexual relationship with a man did not hold the terror, nor the pain, she had both expected and dreaded. It was easier than she thought to numb her mind during those endless minutes when Frank possessed her body.

But several times that first week, he awoke her during the night with his urgent strokes and caresses, and she responded with glassy-eyed fright. "Maggie," he asked after the third such occurrence, "what is it? You're as cold and stiff as an icicle."

Through chattering teeth she tried to reassure him. "'Tis just that I'm a deep sleeper, and, and I don't always know rightly where I am when I'm awakened like, like that."

After that he was always careful to intimate his desire beforehand by words or gestures. For this she was deeply grateful and would feign some sort of response, howbeit a passive one.

Time and again that first month she castigated herself for her Irish temper. Perhaps she did have some of her father's Black Irish in her. Her rage was responsible for her marriage to Frank. And although she did not love him, she knew she owed him something for his defense of her. She felt she could help him break the strangling web that bound him to his family's wealth and background. But though his father had disinherited Frank upon his marriage to her, Frank still had the resources of wealth available in his private bank accounts, established prior to the marriage. Which brought Frank no closer to achieving his own independence. This was something she had to make him understand.

He bent and pressed a kiss in the hollow of her shoulder. "You're lovelier than a Gibson Girl, Maggie," he murmured, "and much more real. And if it weren't for those damnable wire-rimmed glasses you insist on wearing, no one would know you were such a bluestocking."

"'Tis for reading, Frank." That first week of their marriage she bought the glasses with the money she insisted on using that was leftover from her saved wages. But the glasses were not just for reading; she liked their effect. The lenses erected a barrier between her and the men who might be tempted to flirt with her, men like the Russian. Wolf! What an appropriate name! It was all his fault she had been trapped into the marriage!

She slipped her hand up to caress Frank's smooth cheek. "Let's not go out tonight, Frank. Let's stay home." *Home?* her mind echoed, looking at the elegant impersonality of the room's reflection in the mirror.

"Not this evening. I have a special surprise for you. I've tickets to see Irene and Vernon Castle dance. They're performing the Innovation and the Lame Duck tonight."

She turned to face him, catching his hands in hers. "Frank, what about the future? We can't party forever."

His blue eyes smiled down at her. He patted her hand with a reassuring gesture. "Why not? I don't have to worry about earning our bread for a living."

"But . . ." she paused, groping for the right words. Only now did she begin to realize that the temptations of wealth were greater than the moral dangers of poverty. The temptation to sink back and enjoy one's privileges was well-nigh irresistible. Why should Frank fight when he already possessed what everyone else was fighting for?

"Don't you see, Frank," she tried again, "that the qualitites that come from struggling, that build moral fibre, that these wither like the heather and die in an atmosphere of wealth?"

He laughed then. "All right, I'll struggle. I'll begin with earning the butter and jam for the bread. Okay? I'll start with the Stock Exchange. There's a runaway bull market down on Wall Street."

It wasn't exactly what she had in mind, but he looked so pleased with himself that for the moment she gave up trying to make her point and allowed him to parade her down the Waldorf's amber-marbled corridor that, furnished with luxurious blue and green-brocaded sofas and chairs, was known as Peacock Alley.

The winter days winged by for Maggie, seemingly without any end to the idyllic time. Frank was incessantly gay ("It's being away from the mausoleum," he explained, referring to his parent's mansion) and never seemed to lack for ideas for entertainment. He took delight in introducing something novel to captivate Maggie's inexperienced but curious mind.

Once he took her into Harlem to explore the nocturnal pleasures of the city's Negro community, revues featuring blues singers like Ethel Waters or the tap dancer Bill "Bojangles" Robinson. Another time he rented a private trolley car decorated with banners and electric lights, and a German band to sit on the front seats and furnish music.

Later in the evening there was always dining and dancing at the Sans Souci, Maxim's, or Murray's Roman Gardens with its revolving dance floor and exotic decor. Maggie absorbed the elegance and sophistication like a sponge and never made the same mistake in social conventions twice. At night in bed, she repeated to herself like a litany the rules of society: a woman is seated first, a man orders, a woman always wears gloves and hat . . . and on and on.

Smoking was one of society's taboos she purposely broke, though not as a visible expression of the newly liberated woman as a few other brave females were doing. While she did not enjoy smoking that much, she found it put her more at ease around the men who dropped by the tables to talk to Frank. The cigarette figuratively erected a protective wall of smoke between her and the men.

The plutocratic style of life began to grow wearisome for her. Once, on one of March's first springlike days, she was able to persuade Frank to bicycle with her through Central Park and up Riverside Drive to Grant's Tomb. This he acceded to more easily than he did her next request: to accompany her down to Mulberry Bend to see Peg and Jamie.

In the small, dingy room both Frank and Peg looked so uncomfortable in each other's presence that Maggie knew it was best to leave. She hugged a much thinner Jamie, who kept looking with interest at her glasses. She knelt and whispered, "Take good care of your mom, sweet pea." The boy nodded mutely, his intelligent eyes glowing in the grimy face.

Outside, in the malodorous hallway, she turned to Peg. "Please," she murmured to her friend, and tried to press the last of her own wages in Peg's hand.

Peg, embarrassed before Frank, pushed away Maggie's hand with a gentle, "Nay, me dear."

"Good God," Frank exclaimed after they caught a cab, "you used to live like that, Maggie?"

"Aye," she whispered. And that day not one of Frank's gay attempts to charm her out of her somber, reflective mood succeeded.

Two things happened that spring to change their blue-blood's type of life-style. The first Maggie had been expecting. Frank walked into their suite from one of his occasional trips down to Wall Street. His face wore an ashen look. She put aside the book, another novel by Dickens, and tilted the wire-rims atop her head. "What is it, Frank?"

He passed her the sheets of paper. "My bank says I'm twenty-one hundred dollars overdrawn."

She glanced down the line of numbers and looked back to Frank, who was pacing the floor. "Why didn't they notify you before this?"

He ran his hand through his hair. "The vice-president figured my father would cover the overdrafts. I did, too."

She rose from the bed and went to him. "Frank, Frank, dearest, you knew better than to expect help. 'Tis clear your parents made it, the day you told them we would be marrying."

"That's not all," he said, ignoring her remark. "Downstairs the management presented me with a running bill, requesting—ingratiatingly, of course—that I bring my account up to date."

Before the checkerboard street plan of Manhattan was mapped out in the early nineteenth century, Greenwich Village was already a maze of twisting streets that seemed to cross and recross one another without ever arriving anywhere. It was on Waverly Street that Maggie found quarters for her and Frank in one of the old homes that had sunk to the shabby estate of a rooming house. The quarters were innocent of modern conveniences, but contained large, stately rooms.

Maggie loved it. Life in the Village, fortunately, was simple and cheap. It was a place where people were free to be themselves. *La vie bohème.* In the old, low-dormered red-brick houses Maggie met artists, writers, and social radicals, all introduced to her by Vera Walden.

It was the memory of that first visit to Vera's house that

inspired Maggie to move to the Village. Not only did the former socialite locate vacant quarters for Maggie, but she freely talked about her prior life as she helped Maggie settle in. "You see, darling, I had the nerve to touch up my face at the table at Sherry's. For that I was asked to leave. But for appearing at the Plaza Hotel smoking, for that I was ostracized from the stodgy, socially elite Four Hundred. Such a double standard, my dear! And that was ten years ago. Things haven't progressed that much."

Despite Maggie's efforts to cheer Frank out of his despondency, he continued to mope about the place. There was simply no work available for "a gentlemen," he would tell her in a quiet despair.

She knew that he felt he had failed her, but she was happier in those shabby, respectful quarters than she had ever been in the Waldorf-Astoria. Where before the maid straightened the bed and tidied the hotel room, Maggie now cleaned their "home," as she enjoyed thinking of it. The sybaritic plumbing, as Frank exasperatedly called it, bothered her not at all. There was a time when she had lived with no plumbing.

With extra time on her hands, she gave in to Vera's suggestion to help out on the weekly column the woman wrote for the local suffrage newspaper, *The New Woman*. "It doesn't pay worth a fiddler's damn," Vera said, "but it's something." Before Maggie could respond, she plopped the unwieldy-looking typewriter on Maggie's kitchen table. "I'll collect the news, my dear. I'm good at wheedling information. You do the typing. You do know how to type?"

Maggie laughed. "I'll learn."

She tried to share her happiness with Frank, and she succeeded, at least, in driving away his moroseness when night fell and they came together in the privacy of their bed. "Maggie, Maggie," he would whisper in an erotic litany as he took a handful of hair and buried his lips in it. And she learned to whisper also, soft urgings that stirred him to reach a peak of pleasure that she assumed was denied to the female.

When the end of the month arrived, and there was no money for the rent, she suggested to Frank that they sell some of the things he had bought her. "After all, dearest, where would I be wearing such grand things now?"

He rounded on her. "Don't throw it up to me that I can't afford to take you out in style anymore, Maggie Moran! You didn't even know what style was until I showed you!"

"My name is Maggie Van der Rhys," she said with a quiet dignity that caused him to catch her to him.

"I'm sorry. It's just the damn bills and no prospects for a job. I know that father's put the pressure on the people at the places where I've applied. After all," he said bitterly, "he's on the board of almost every company in the city."

After that, Maggie began to notice that Frank came home with the smell of alcohol on his breath, though he seemed completely sober. She began to worry, but said nothing. Then the second event happened, which dispelled Frank's depression.

The United States entered the world war by declaring war on Germany. "Don't you see, Maggie!" he yelled, elated with the front page headlines on the *New York Herald* that he had been searching through for jobs. "President Wilson Declares War on Imperial Germany," the headlines screamed.

"I can apply for an officer's commission," Frank explained. "A guaranteed job!"

This time it was Maggie who caught Frank to her. "What if something should happen to you? You could be killed."

He hugged her against him and looked down at her with laughing blue eyes. "No chance of that. The Germans wouldn't dare shoot at a Van der Rhys."

He took her to the bed then, though it was still early afternoon, and made love to her with such great tenderness that Maggie almost forgot her fear and repulsion. While she did not actually experience the joy that some of the liberated women around the Village openly talked of, neither was she an outsider, watching the intimate act with a detached curiosity.

The next morning after Frank went down to the local recruiting office, Vera came over to leave several sheets of handwritten notes for the column. "We're having another one of our evenings, darling," the pretty, plump, intense woman told Maggie. "You must come."

"And what cause is it this time?" Maggie asked her as she got out the precious little coffee she had left. "Let's see, last week, t'was the meeting for free speech I typed for *The New Woman*—or was it the new art?"

"Birth control, this time. It's the only way we'll free the female."

Maggie knew that Frank was skeptical of the liberal ideas of the women's movement but could not openly forbid the work she did for them since it did contribute a very small amount to the rapidly dwindling funds. And while she did not think he would come to the evening's meeting, she knew that it was one meeting she would not miss. She did not want to introduce a child into the world like the Bowery—a level to which she and Frank at that point could so easily slip.

She turned back and sat the sugar bowl and spoon before Vera, saying, "Perhaps I can persuade Frank to come tonight."

But Frank did not return that afternoon. She was worried, but Vera reassured her. "He's probably just out celebrating, darling. You know, the last of his freedom before the service gets him and all that."

Maggie suspected that what Vera said was probably all too true. But she was surprised when Vera added, "You know, darling, your husband is a very charming man. A chauvinist in some of his ideas, but very charming."

It was something Maggie had forgotten, Frank's charming appeal.

She let the woman pull her along to the evening's cause. Emma Goldman, with cropped hair and dressed scandalously in sandals and flowing robes, was there preaching anarchism and free love. Margaret Sanger stood up, and everyone fell silent when she began to talk about the necessity of birth control.

Maggie had turned crimson at what Emma Goldman had to say, and she found herself blushing again as the Sanger woman discussed the intimate details of preventing conception. But she felt that what the woman had to say was justified. She was glad she had come, but prepared herself to face Frank's disapproval.

His disapproval she did not have to worry about, since he was not there when she returned to their apartment. She was thinking of going to the landlady's and calling the police, when he entered. He said nothing, but walked unsteadily to the dilapidated sofa and slung his body across it.

Slowly Maggie pulled out her hatpins and laid the leghorn hat on the table. "I was getting worried about you."

"No need." He folded his arms across his face, as if to shut out the room's light. "I can take care of myself."

She sat down beside him. A terrible fear sprang to her mind. "How did everything go?"

"My dear, dear Maggie, they didn't want me. Flat feet. We are now facing destitution." He began to laugh. Maggie listened with an anguished face while she smoothed back the damp curls from his forehead.

CHAPTER
fourteen
⊷⊶⊷⊶

With the dawning of the electrical age, the com-
ing of the telephone and telegraph and the furnishing of
electricity to homes and industry, the mining of copper
became paramount. But Wolf, digging the teeth of the steam
shovel's scoop into the rock and earth, thought it ironical
that Bingham Canyon, Utah, with the greatest open copper
pit in the world, was one of the most primitive of towns.

Due to the steep walls of the gigantic Oquirrh Mountains
and the narrow winding roads, access to Bingham Canyon
was still mainly by horse and wagon and, of course, by the
Rio Grande High Line Railroad that connected the Utah
Copper mine with the company's mill some seventeen miles
farther up Bingham Canyon. Only two telephones existed
in Bingham Canyon, both controlled by the Bingham Canyon Mercantile Company.

The men who worked the open copper pits were too poor
to afford the luxuries of telephone and electricity. These
men did not stay long. For the most part they were drifters.
The work was hard, and exposed them to the blistering
summer sun and frostbiting winter blizzards. Wolf had known

both hard work and the polarlike weather in Russia. The summer sun that baked his already swarthy skin a darker brown was only a little better than the staggering heated conditions he had endured working around the furnaces of the St. Petersburg steel mill.

That searing summer of 1918, the number of employees suddenly increased as the United States called on the Bingham Canyon copper mine to produce more of the much-needed copper for the war effort.

Wolf ground the Vulcan steam shovel to a halt on its rails when one of the track gang crumpled to his feet like a string puppet. Wolf jumped down from his perch in the mammoth machine and crossed to the inert man. The Ute Indian called Bear, for his massive, barrellike build, halted his rhythmic swinging of the sledgehammer and watched silently as Wolf checked the man's pulse and raised his eyelids. "It's the damn heat again," Wolf murmured.

The Indian dropped his sledgehammer. "I will take him up to the fieldhouse." With an effortless motion he swung the unconscious man up over his broad shoulder and trotted off along the bench, the fifty-foot-wide dirt road that grooved the open pit.

When Wolf had first come to work at Bingham, the other laborers had had a field day in comparing the lean Wolf and the large Bear, though the men were always careful to make the jokes with a certain amount of friendly respect. Bear would merely grin good-naturedly, displaying the gap between his two front teeth. Wolf occasionally returned the jokes with a sardonic quip of his own.

At last the mine foreman called it quits, and Wolf trudged along with the others back to the fieldhouse, where the men were loaded on wagons bound for the quarters provided for the mine's employees. Wolf wiped the perspiration from his forehead and dried his sweaty, calloused hand on the chest hair curling riotously in a triangle that apexed at his navel. A thick-set blond who had migrated from Minnesota called out, "I keep telling the boys that with all that hair, Wolf, you probably run with a pack at night."

Wolf's deeply curved lips formed a feral smile. "In that case, Swede, I wouldn't walk out alone in the dark. You've heard of werewolves?"

Chuckles erupted from the other men. Bear called out, "Hey, boy. You don't let anyone make fool of you, eh?"

Wolf halted and ran his gaze up the mountain that was Bear. Wolf was very tall at eighteen, almost six foot four, and Bear was maybe only an inch or so taller. But the twenty-five-year-old Ute carried almost three hundred pounds of sheer muscle on his giant frame. "I would bet you don't either," Wolf said at last.

Bear's stomach, pure muscle also, shook with laughter as he fell into step alongside Wolf. "Every day you go back to that boardinghouse and eat the lousy food. You no drink or gamble like the others. Why not?"

Wolf evaded the personal question. "You don't either."

Bear laughed. "You know no Indians allowed in the beer halls."

They reached the clapboard fieldhouse, and Wolf grabbed the faded plaid flannel shirt from his locker and went back outside to climb aboard the waiting mule-drawn wagon. The big Indian slid in next to him. "Why not come home with me. My mother, she fix fine food. Then there's smoking and good talking afterwards."

"I'll think on it."

He did think about the Ute's invitation that evening as he sat down in the large dining room with the boardinghouse's other occupants, all steam shovel and locomotive operators. He looked at the heaping bowl of mashed potatoes and the tureen of baked beans, food he once would have been happy with. But after seeing the same fare night after nights for months on end, his stomach longed for a change. The cook was an old man who cared more for his whiskey bottle than he did for a cookbook.

Precious few restaurants—and precious few women—populated Bingham Canyon, and the thought of a home-cooked meal by a woman was enough to make him accept Bear's invitation the next day. The big Indian smiled, both surprised and pleased. "My mother will cook her best," he promised, rubbing his stomach expansively. "Old Molly one bitch of a cook."

Wolf rode home with Bear that evening in the Indian's ramshackle buckboard—a far cry, Wolf thought, from the Van der Rhys's smooth-riding Bentley or Pierce-Arrow. The memory brought back Maggie's face and her unforgettable fey beauty, and he quickly shoved the image from his mind.

Home was an hour's ride through half desert, half canyon that was stubbled with aromatic sagebrush, and gnarled cedar trees before they reached the cabin of lodgepole pine. At the wagon's approach, five boys of varying heights ran out of the cabin to greet their brother. Two women, dressed in calico skirts and overblouses, came to stand in the doorway.

Bear rattled off the names of his younger brothers—George, Jefferson, Abraham, Ulysses, and Teddy, all named for United States presidents. The boys, ages six through twelve, dutifully and silently shook Wolf's hand. He waited for Bear to introduce his mother and presumably his sister, who looked to be about the same age as Wolf and Bear. But Bear led him into a cabin that was amazingly immaculate considering the number of children living there. Silver fox furs dotted the cabin's walls, which were incongruously plastered with circus posters. The few pieces of furniture—a table and chairs and a cupboard—were hand hewn and functional at best.

The Ute offered him a seat on a three-legged stool and produced thin, yellowed sheets of paper. He began to roll tobacco from a bag of Bull Durham while his mother and sister retreated to the cooking area to set the table. To smoke a cigar or cheroot was one thing, but to smoke a cigarette was considered unmanly by some. Wolf couldn't have cared less. Accepting the cigarette Bear proffered, he agreed to a game of checkers. The boys gathered around the two men and stoically watched the game.

Wolf, who had been raised on the more intricate game of chess, found the game of little challenge. While Bear spent a great deal of the time deliberating his moves, Wolf watched the two women of the house move quietly about the table. The older woman, Old Molly, was short and stolid, with coils of braids about her round, flat face. The daughter was of short stature also, with the same heavy melon breasts but a more slender frame. Sleek dark brown hair falling down her back framed large expressive brown eyes in a dusky, moon-shaped face.

"Got you!" Bear said, jumping two of Wolf's checkers. Jubilant, he swatted Wolf on the shoulder, and Wolf's body vibrated with the impact.

He dragged his gaze back to the worn board before him and focused his attention on quickly vanquishing his opponent. By then dinner was ready, and the family grouped about the table for one of the best dinners Wolf had eaten in a long time—stewed mutton, Indian bread, and fried squash. The children ate noisily, and no one bothered to talk. Every so often Wolf felt Old Molly's gaze on him, but when he looked at her across the table, her lids would be decorously lowered, as were those of her daughter.

After dinner, while the women cleaned up, Bear led him outside for another "big smoke." The chilly night mountain air carried the clean scent of pine. In comfortable silence, he sat with Bear on orange crates and puffed on the cigarette. After a while Bear said, "It will be late by the time we get you back to Bingham tonight. Why don't you stay with us, eh?"

Bear and his family retired to the one bedroom, and Wolf

was left with the main room to sleep in, and a pile of brightly colored Indian rugs. He found the Indian-rug bed more comfortable than the lumpy mattress at the boardinghouse. Presently, he drifted off to a state of semi sleep, only to come wide awake at motion above him. He did not move, but his eyes searched the darkness—to encounter the dim face of Bear's sister.

Then there came the shock of her nude skin as she slipped between the blankets. She made no further move, but lay quietly beside him. "What are you doing?" he asked the girl, not even certain if she could speak English. He felt for the first time like an inexperienced youth.

She did not reply. But she turned on her side, facing him. A work-roughened hand slid along his chest to entwine in its hair. His breath sucked in. He took the hand and brought the palm to his lips. He was paid off with an intake of breath, from her this time. Still holding her palm, his free hand came up to catch one heavy breast. He liked the weight of it, and his head bent until his lips could take in the brown aureole. He felt the tremor ripple through the girl when his tongue found her nipple. Still, she did not speak.

Her continued silence annoyed him. His hand moved down to slide through the soft nest of curls below her navel. He heard her first word, a softly gasped, "Oh!"

He knew that he was violating his host's hospitality, but he could no longer control himself. He had been too long without a woman; yet he was not desperate enough to bring himself to visit the few heavily rouged, coarse-faced women who drank with the men at Bingham's Topsy Turvy Bar. His fingers plundered the girl's nest, finding there the small, hard bud of her femininity. This time her gasp was more like a sigh. Two of his fingers searched deeper. The exploration was made easier by the smooth fluid that suddenly coated his fingers.

He moved up over her then, slowly but with the sureness of one purpose only, and plunged into the warm but resisting cavern entrance. *"Milais Deevs!* Good God," he whispered at her small outcry. "You were a virgin!"

Still she uttered no words. With the knowledge of the female that older women had taught him, he proceeded to give Bear's sister what little pleasure he could, considering the lingering discomfort he suspected her to be experiencing. The small kisses he planted on her shoulders, neck, and face, the gentle teasing of her breasts, even heavier now with the languor of passion, were rewarded when she at last slipped her arms up around his neck and drew him closer and embedded him deep within her.

Sometime later, still an hour or so before sunrise, he was awakened as she left his side. His hand caught hers. "Where are you going?" he asked lazily, not really expecting an answer.

"To herd the sheep," came her soft voice. The cold air of predawn swept between the blankets to take her suddenly vacant space.

During the breakfast that Molly cooked, Wolf tried but could read nothing in Bear's gap-toothed grin. Wolf knew a moment of shame, and resolved never to accept another dinner invitation from the Indian. But at the end of the work day, when Wolf set off on the walk back to the fieldhouse, Bear fell into step along side of him. "Old Molly's cooking so bad, you don't go back?"

Wolf looked up into the kindly smiling face. He looked back to the other men who trudged wearily along the bench toward the fieldhouse. Hell! "Sure, I'm coming, if the invitation still stands."

Bear's family came out to greet them again. But this time the sister was not with them. Wolf kept his silence and lit up a cigarette with Bear while Old Molly prepared dinner. Bear talked laconically of all the strangers pouring into Bingham, and Wolf desultorily mentioned he was glad to see the tall poles that meant the government was bringing a more modern electrical system to the primitive town.

He jabbed out his cigarette, nervously wondering where the daughter was. Should he expect some savage Indian reprisal for the rape of the sister? But it had not been rape, he tried to remind himself.

Just as Old Molly began to put the dinner on the table, she said something to Bear that Wolf did not understand. The big man turned to him and asked, "My sister's up in the pasture just above the house with the sheep. Would you mind getting her for dinner, eh? Just follow the trail."

Reluctantly Wolf went in search of the girl, keeping to the trail worn smooth by the sheep hooves. It was almost dusk by the time he came upon the girl, in a large clearing fringed with the ever-present stunted junipers and greasewood. She sat on an outcropping boulder while she watched the small band of sheep below. He knew that she had to be aware of his presence as he made his way across the clearing toward her, but she never once looked in his direction. He had the time to study her face in the diminishing sunlight. The face was not a beautiful one, but the features held a serenity that moved him, especially at that moment when the last shafts of sunlight glazed the clearing with a pastoral tranquillity.

He made his way up the rocky incline and came to stand before her. She looked up, her brown eyes as gentle as a doe's. He hunkered down near her on the rock, but not near enough that he touched her.

"I know you can speak English," he said.

She didn't reply, and unperturbed, he continued smoothly, slowly.

"I would like to know your name. I've been thinking on the walk here that it must be something with a very soft sound—like Little Star or Running Stream."

He was gifted with her smile, an amused one with teeth that were reasonably even and white. "Maude," she replied with a voice that threatened to erupt in laughter.

He chuckled. "Well, Maude," he said taking her hand,

"I've achieved at least some headway between us today. Come on, your family is ready to eat."

Nearly the same pattern was followed as the previous night. Before dinner he arm-wrestled with the five boys and let each win once—which paid off in a solemn smile from each. Several times he caught Old Molly's eye on him and thought, *She knows*.

When Bear offered his muscle-bound arm, Wolf threw up his hands and laughed. "I give up." Though the muscles that striated his chest and upper arms were like thick ropes from his years of work at the steel mill, Bear's whole torso was corduroyed with muscles that were more like steel cables.

After dinner Wolf sat and played checkers with Bear while his eyes followed the ample curve of Maude's buttocks beneath the calico skirt as she moved gracefully about the room. Still he retained enough presence of mind to win the checker game.

But all the while his mind was on Maude. Would she come to him that night? After everyone retired the time seemed to take forever to pass, until Teddy's giggle was hushed by Bear's gruff voice and the last cough of Jefferson's died away. Then she was there, her ample body sliding in next to his, accepting his, returning his kisses with shy ardor. And with the dawn she was gone again.

Bear seemed to expect Wolf's presence at his dinner table each evening, and the summer days fell into a delightful, restful repetition, though the nights were anything but restful as Maude learned to take the initiative through Wolf's gentle urgings. Oddly, she was most reticent in other areas, and Wolf had to draw her out about herself. Few times was he alone with her, usually only when he went to the clearing at dusk to call her for dinner.

"Don't you ever get lonely or bored?" he asked her once as he helped her drive the sheep back down to the cabin's corrals.

He had expected a simple no or yes in keeping with her pattern of few words, but Maude said, "Sometimes. I daydream a lot."

"What about?"

She looked at him bashfully before turning her attention back to the sheep. "About things." She waited a minute, then said, "I haven't always herded my mother's sheep."

Wolf had learned that the Indians were basically a matriarchal race, and that the sheep or cattle belonged to the wife to be passed on to the daughter. But it wasn't sheep that interested him. "What else did you do?"

"As a child I went to the Mormon school at Salt Lake City. But it meant living away from home. After I finished the sixth grade I went to work at the Bingham Canyon Mercantile Company."

"Why did you leave?"

The sun had dropped behind the Oquirrh's peaks, and he could barely make out her face. "After my father died, my brother became the head of our family. And he did not like the way the miners looked at me, or tried to... touch me."

Self-disgust stabbed at Wolf. Here he was screwing Bear's sister nightly. A curious thought hit him. His hand at her wrist halted her. "Does Bear know you come to me at night?"

There was only the silence of the cool evening to answer him. Wolf watched while Maude joined her mother inside the cabin, then he went to Bear who sat on the porch smoking. "Why?" he asked, planting himself in front of the big Ute. He had been duped, and he was angry, most of all at himself.

For the first time Bear did not smile. "Because I love my sister," he said quietly. "And I want the best for her. But the best is hard to find, eh? Until you came along."

Wolf grunted. He slumped down against the cabin's rough

timbered wall and closed his eyes. "You've made a big mistake, Bear," he said tiredly. "There is a restlessness in me. A restlessness that won't let me stay long in one place."

Bear grinned into the darkness. "That's fine. Me and Old Molly, we take the chance."

CHAPTER

fifteen

❧ ∼ ❧

"*It's sure I am it will work, darling,*" Maggie said.

Frank kept his gaze on the wintery landscape that sped by outside the Pullman's window. The farther west the New York Central took them, the fewer cities and towns that rose up to remind him that civilization still existed.

Maggie knew he did not want her to see the uncertainty in his eyes. She stretched out her hand to clasp his. "National Firearms wouldn't have hired you if it wasn't a good job they thought you'd be doing."

Frank groaned. "A traveling salesman. Old Sylvester Van der Rhys would rise up in his coffin at the idea."

Maggie smiled. Her spirits could not be dampened. For the first time since coming to America, she felt really freed of the Old World oppression. The ad she had spied in the *Times*, guaranteeing traveling expenses plus commission, had been enough for her to convince Frank that it was the answer to their problem. For more than a year they had lived off her small salary as a typist for *The New Woman* and the money from the valuables they sold. It was not just the financial solution the ad offered that caught her interest, but also the opportunity it supplied to escape from his parents' dominion.

"You'll make an excellent salesman, Frank. You're able to express your ideas clearly and," she squeezed his hand, "you deal well with people."

A self-mocking smile formed beneath the handsome pencil-thin mustache he had begun to grow. "My 'gift of charm' you keep referring to." He sighed. "Well, it landed me you, Maggie Van der Rhys. So some good must come of it."

He had rescued her from a hopeless future and forfeited his heritage in doing so. She owed him so much. She would do her best to repay him.

In the days and weeks that followed, Maggie realized that he did not like the bothersome tasks of accounting for the orders and all the paperwork entailed. Thus, during the day when he was gone and she sat in the hotel room, she began to deal with those "dreadful details" of business, as Frank called them. She totaled the number of sales and the dollar amounts each day, made out the accompanying reports, kept track of the traveling expenses, and saw to it that all this paperwork reached the New York home office.

At first she worked laboriously, her teeth tugging at the tip of her tongue as she struggled to make the numbers balance and to write grammatically correct reports. For all the classical reading she had done over the past year and a half, her arithmetic and penmanship did not come easily. A small dictionary she purchased helped, as eventually did the repetition of her work.

Apparently a good deal came of the charm that Frank mocked. At the end of the first month Maggie sat on the bed in Omaha's Blackstone Hotel and looked over the sheaf of orders he tossed her. "Like taking candy from a baby!" he said, and closed the lid on his sample case of firearms. He caught her hands and pulled her up against him. "We'll eat out tonight to celebrate. Omaha is supposed to have some of the best steaks in the country."

She put aside the orders and took off her glasses. "Frank, we don't have that kind of money yet."

"We will have." He kissed her soundly. "Now don't disagree with the master. Put on that straw picture hat—the one trimmed with the green velvet ribbon. We're going to do the town."

Maggie thought the California Restaurant's steaks heavenly, and afterwards at the Rialto, as they watched Texas Guinan's performance in *The Gay Musical* Frank was exceptionally attentive. In the darkness of the theater he leaned over to apparently whisper something and instead attempted to kiss her sensually on the ear. She repressed a sigh.

She was trying in another way to repay that debt to Frank—giving him in the darkness of their hotel rooms the acquiescence of her body. She wondered if he ever suspected her indifference to sex.

No, she thought irritably, that was not true. Wolf had managed to expose her indifference as a sham, to shatter her indifference as easily as shattering glass. She closed her eyes in the darkened theater and involuntarily recalled how Wolf, with a mere kiss, had made her weak with wanting as Frank never had.

Later, after they returned from the theater, Frank made love to her. Perhaps a bit more roughly than usual, as if he wished to possess more than just her body, as if he knew her thoughts had not been of him.

She tried to tell herself her marriage with Frank was basically a good one, with neither of them demanding what the other could not give. With her help, Frank was becoming moderately successful. His love of drink and cards with the men and his natural charm with the women, who were especially lonely with all the young men off to war, made selling easy for him.

She and Frank began to establish a good working relationship. In every city—St. Louis, Kansas City, Wichita, Denver—it was the same. He made the sales, she handled the details. His sales began to increase. Some evenings he returned to the hotel later than usual, always in a gay mood, always a little tipsy. "Entertaining the clients, Maggie. A game of cards is always worth an extra order, you know."

Then one sunny November day in Ft. Worth, when she had escaped the stifling boredom of her Worth Hotel room for a breath of fresh air, she caught a glimpse of Frank in the lobby with another woman, a pretty young brunette who batted her lashes with obvious coyness. Maggie's heart sank. That night, he did not return until the early hours of the morning. And there was not just the smell of alcohol about him, but also that of a woman's expensive perfume.

He was more than tipsy. "Just out celebratin' the war's end." Silently, Maggie helped him remove his shoes and pants. "Thanks, Maggie," he murmured with a little-boy smile. "You're the, the greatest."

She closed her eyes with a sigh. He had been using the Kaiser's surrender the week before as an excuse to celebrate every night since. She sat beside the bed and watched him drift off into a gentle snore. Pain gnawed inside her like a small rat. His betrayal stung. But then, had she not expected as much? She had married Frank with eyes wide open to his weakness for the opposite sex . . . No, her eyes had not been wide open. They had been clouded with rage. She deserved exactly what she had gotten.

What was she going to do now?

She rose and went to the window to stand looking out at the city with her handkerchief pressed tightly against her lips. Ft. Worth's arc lights twinkled in the night like fireflies, imparting an illuminating beauty to the cowtown that by daylight looked rough and hard. But she did not see the beauty of the night; she could feel only her disillusion and hurt.

While he traveled on, she could stay there in Ft. Worth and find work—though it would be difficult to find anything better than domestic help, with the war over and the soldiers returning home from Europe. But why should she and Frank get a divorce? She should know there was no such thing as happily-ever-after. If he came home drunk sometimes, if in some ways he was still childlike, did it honestly matter? Could she fault him for his occasional sprees of carousing when she obviously could not supply the sexual enjoyment he sought?

She would not cry!

Slowly she wadded the handkerchief into a tight ball. Her pride and anger may have shackled her to marriage; nevertheless, never again would she let herself be dominated by the male sex. The years of suppression under her father had taught her that much. She was slowly escaping the limitations imposed by poverty, and she would establish her independence yet.

The handkerchief fell to the floor and rolled across the frayed carpet. Her head drooped. Dear God, but she felt older than her almost nineteen years.

"Come with me, *malutit*," Wolf said, unconsciously using the old Latvian endearment. "It's been too long since you've been into Bingham."

Maude glanced down at her enlarged belly and back up to where he sat on the wagon seat. "No, it's better I wait here."

He grunted with exasperation. "Carrying a child is nothing to be ashamed of." He abruptly bounded from the seat to land on his feet with a catlike grace. "You are going, Maude, and you are going to enjoy yourself." Against her murmured protest, he slipped his hands around her thickened waist and hefted her up onto the wooden seat.

The bright November sun gently warmed the two young people as the horse team clip-clopped along the undulating dirt road that crawled upward toward Bingham. Wolf, who was learning to handle the reins with the consummate skill of his cossack ancestors, could sense the disquiet of the young Indian girl at his side. For all her stoicism, she sat with tightly folded hands. Was she regretting her refusal of the offer of marriage he had made the night before?

He had not been forced into the offer, though he knew Maude thought differently. For some weeks after he suspected her pregnancy, he had deliberated on what he would do.

He knew that Bear was wise enough not to force him into the marriage. Bear realized he could not hold him, that Wolf was just that, a lone wolf always traveling, always loping to the next rise just beyond the horizon. No, the decision had been his own. He could not keep running the earth forever.

As he drove down Bingham Canyon's main street, still unpaved, with only raised boardwalks for sidewalks, he sensed Maude's agitation grow. But his attention was diverted by the three men standing before the general store. They wore the tunics and slouched caps of the old slavic countries, but the baggy knee breeches had been replaced by western trousers. He parked the wagon outside the store and set the brake, all the while trying to pick up their words.

Russian! Wolf helped Maude down and approached the men. Two of them were older, wearing the long beards of the mother country. *"Labdeen,"* he said, greeting them in the ancient language.

The men turned excited faces toward him, and the younger one stepped forward. In rapid Russian the man pointed to the vanlike wagons on the other side of the street and explained that their families had come from Wyoming's Big Horn Basin, where they had harvested the fall crop of sugar beets. They had been on their way to the sugar beet farms of Gunnison Valley in southern Utah when they lost their way. For a moment, as Wolf gave the man directions toward Salt Lake City and Gunnison Valley, he experienced a sharp pain of nostalgia.

As he led Maude into the store, he put from his mind the memories the itinerant Russian workers had stirred up and did not once glance in the direction of their departing caravan. The old country held nothing for him but the past. Looking at Maude, whose gentle face was bathed in splendor as her hands fingered a bolt of baby-blue flannel, he reminded himself that his present and future were here.

"Can I help you, son?" the old man in a white apron asked.

Wolf pointed to the Barlow penknife in the showcase. "I'll have that one."

From the back of the store a voice called, "Give squaw man one of them fancy pearl-handled knives, Clem."

"Now, Bill," the storekeeper admonished.

Slowly Wolf turned in the direction of the voice. A large, red-bearded man leaned against the whiskey keg. The man was only a couple of inches shorter than Wolf, but much more stoutly built. He held in his hand a tin cup that was tied conveniently to the keg for sampling the free whiskey. The man let the cup drop and ambled down the aisles stocked high with dry goods. "On the other hand," he taunted, grinning, "an Indian lover's gonna need something more like a Bowie knife."

Black anger washed over Wolf. His muscles twitched as if he had been poked with a cattle prod. He perceived the frightened, warning shake of Maude's head, but it was too late. His anger exploded, and his fist arced up to clip the man beneath the granite jaw. The man staggered backwards into the aisle, and zinc washtubs, saddle blankets, irons, and washboards came raining down on his head.

"Ssshit!" escaped between Wolf's clenched teeth. He caught what had to be a shattered hand beneath his armpit.

Old Clem hurried over to inspect the damaged wares burying the decked-out Bill. Wolf's free hand took the hand of a trembling Maude.

"Come on," he said, grinning. "We're getting married."

CHAPTER
sixteen

❦ ∘❦ ∘

The Chicago, Burlington & Quincy Railroad's
locomotive crawled at a slow chug as it hissed its way along
the North Platte River into the outskirts of Casper, Wyoming, passing the cattle cars on various sidetracks by the
shipping pens. When the engine rolled through the fringes
of Casper proper and passed the hastily erected canvas tents
and temporary shacks of scrap lumber and metal, Frank
said, "You are looking at the product of black gold, my
dear."

Maggie raised a skeptical brow. "Apparently we are not
looking at the same thing."

"Look again. Black gold—oil—has changed the old fort
from a cowtown to an oil boom town. Boom towns are
notorious for land-grabbers, claim-jumpers, and shyster
lawyers. And it's here we'll make our fortune selling National Firearms."

She doubted it, but Frank's spirits remained high as they
later shouldered their way down crowded Center Street to
the Midwest Hotel. If possible, it seemed even more crowded.
To her astonishment and Frank's delight, stockbrokers were

operating in small rooms off the lobby. An auctioneer standing on a desk seemed to be shouting himself hoarse. Maggie looked around her to see an aproned housewife supporting a baby on one arm and waving greenback bills at the auctioneer with her free hand. A minister in a black frock coat haggled over leases and margins—terms Maggie had learned from Frank.

The World War, which had ended the year before, had precipitated the pandemonium in the oil market that resulted in the construction of the two pipelines from Casper forty miles north to the newest boom town of Salt Creek. "What did I tell you?" Frank said at her ear to make himself understood above the shouting. "Even the poor here are rich and the rich are richer"—he laughed—"or broke."

Entertained by the uproar, Maggie and Frank patiently waited their turn at the hotel counter, only to be told by the desk clerk that all rooms were full. "Surely you must have something," Frank protested.

The man peered over his glasses. "Fellow, people are sleeping in garages and basements. They're even walking Casper's streets all night."

Frank raised inquiring brows at Maggie. She turned to the desk clerk. "We're strangers here. Do you have any suggestions?"

"You could try another town."

He began to turn away, and, desperate, she asked, "Where?"

"Medicine Bow. Or Buffalo—it's north of the Salt Creek oil fields. There's a stage leaving for there twice daily; you can catch it at Bob's Auto Livery."

"A stage?" Frank echoed. "You must be joking."

To Frank's relief, the Salt Creek stage was a 1914 jitney bus with isinglass side curtains and windshields that were flecked with oil. "I never would have believed it," he muttered, watching out the window as trucks and wagons jostled for room with the bus on the road of shale that ran between Casper and the oil fields.

Maggie loved it. Wyoming had all the excitement of New York without that claustrophobic feeling that occasionally had seized her. She was staggered by the infinite stretch of land that here and there was quilted with zigzagging snow fences, called buck fences. A silver-dollar sun in a brilliantly clear sky showered sunlight over umber-brown hills dotted with sage. Red buttes crested in wondrous rock formations, such as the Teapot Dome pointed out to her by one of the passengers, a gray-haired man who was a geologist for the Midwest Oil Company.

When the bus broke over Forty Mile Hill, as far as sight could reach was a great forest of derricks that seemed to grow over the hillocks like rigid, branchless trees. Closer inspection revealed steam-powered cable tool drill rigs and strange wooden machinery that worked like a duck's bill. "Pump jacks," the geologist told her and snapped his suspenders with pride.

The geologist left the stage at Salt Creek, a desolate-looking little town fringed with tents and tar-papered shacks that contrasted with uniform company houses in neat little rows. Maggie shivered as the dry summer wind blew down the town's one street, whipping dust through the bus's open windows. "You can't be cold!" Frank said, wiping the perspiration from his brow with a monogrammed handkerchief.

"No, just impatient to get to Buffalo." But she knew it was more than that. An eerie feeling possessed her. Some force over which she had no control seemed to be drawing her as a lodestone draws the iron. She tried to tell herself it was the damnable wind. It seemed the wind had increased in velocity from the time they arrived in Wyoming.

Wyoming. A strange coincidence, she thought, as the bus jerked to a start and caterpillared its way north to Buffalo. Wyoming was the name of the steamship that had brought her to America. And if her memory served her correctly, it was the first state to give women the right to vote and hold office.

The uneasy feeling decreased in intensity as Salt Creek fell behind in the windswept dust—and as Frank's depression increased. He shifted about in the bus, uncomfortable and rumpled. He could see the fortune he hoped to make selling firearms in Casper dwindling with each mile the bus took them toward the town nestled in the sheltering belt of Russian olive trees at the foot of the magnificent Big Horn Mountains.

And Maggie—even as the old bus rambled into Buffalo, she sensed her journey was not over. Somewhere near was her final destination.

"Where you bound for, mister?"

Wolf swung up into the Bulldog Mack truck's cab. "Big Horn Basin." It seemed as good a place as any. He recollected the Russians he had chanced upon in Bingham mentioning a Russian colony of sugar beet farmers somewhere up there.

Strange. He really wasn't interested in meeting up with any of his excountrymen. He was no longer a Russian in any sense of the word. He neither dressed, spoke, nor held to any of the old customs as a Russian colony no doubt would. So why was he heading in that direction?

Any direction would have been fine. Any way to put distance between him and the memory of Maude. And the memory of her death. Over the past year he had come to care deeply for the gentle young Indian girl . . . and deeply for the child she was to have borne him.

The hundreds of miles of walking had not diluted his anger at his own helplessness the day Maude went into labor. She should have been in Salt Lake City where a doctor could have attended her. But the labor had come so suddenly,

with her barely seven months with child. Old Molly had
tried to stop the hemorrhaging.

Nor had the hundreds of miles he covered canceled out
Bear's face when he broke the news of Maude's death to
the big Indian. The Ute's expression had gone vacant, like
that of his mammoth animal namesake. And not once in the
next two months that Wolf had stayed on at the bleak little
sheep ranch had the expression altered. One day, Wolf
knew, the antics of Bear's five brothers would no doubt
restore the Ute's placid grin. But he wouldn't be there to
see it.

Intuitively he had known that whatever he felt for Bear's
sister was not enough to ease the restlessness in his soul.
Isolated by the mountain wildness, he had felt his intellect
stagnating. Eventually his survival instinct would have forced
him to leave the Indian family anyway.

Perhaps Maude had sensed that also, for some hours
before her life drained away she opened her eyes and whispered to him, "I'm setting you free, my wild Wolf."

And he had laid his head on the bed and cried, for the
first time since he was five. She had taught him that much:
she had taught him to care again.

His morose thoughts were jerked back to the present
when the rotund truck driver broke out in loud song.

> "The toughest job I ever had
>   in all this western land
> Was freighting with a string team
>   when we linked 'em through the
>   sand."

The truck driver's oblique look satisfied him that he had
the undivided attention of the tall, unshaven passenger he
had picked up in Laramie, and he continued.

"I have hauled feed to the Big Horns
    and loaded back with wool
And logged it in the mountains
    when the woods with snow were full;
But the most heartbreakin' journey
    for the old-time string team load
Was freighting to the oil fields
    way out the Salt Creek road."

At the song's finish, he grinned self-consciously. "Truck-driver's got to do something to keep him from going to sleep."

"Yes," Wolf smiled dryly, "I imagine that would keep me awake."

"Got family in the Big Horns?"

"Nope."

Undaunted by Wolf's taciturnity, the congenial truck-driver said, "Got a job up there?"

"Nope." To ease the backache of riding in the jouncing, battered truck, Wolf slumped farther in a seat whose worn fabric erupted in various places with broken springs. If the Mack truck traveled another hundred miles it would shake itself to pieces.

The button-nosed man held out a bar of Brown's Mule plug tobacco. "Elmo's my name. Wanna chaw?"

Wolf shook his head. "Could use some coffee, though. How far's the next town?"

"Salt Creek? Only a couple more miles or so. You can get more'n coffee there, too. Standard Oil is hurting for roughnecks, what with so many men taken by the war. Say, you seen any time in the service?"

Wolf cocked a brow at the man. "Have you?"

Elmo chortled, and his double chin quivered. "Talk too much, don't I? Uncle Sam tells me I'm too fat." He patted his mounding stomach that barely fit behind the wheel. "A little lard don't bother Standard Oil. All they want is a willing pair of hands. Here it is. Here's Salt Creek. End of the line for me. I'll take a cup of coffee with you, though."

The restaurant was an old Pullman converted into a diner. Wolf and the truckdriver sat down on two of the empty barstools. The chubby man ordered coffee and a large piece of custard pie from the young waitress. She barely noticed him but kept her gaze on the dark-haired man next to him.

Wolf met the thin girl's gaze. "Just coffee." The jangle of the loose change in his pocket warned him maybe he'd better think about taking that job with Standard Oil. "Tell me about roughnecking," he said to the truckdriver.

Elmo was already plowing into the pie, but with a mouthful he launched into the benefits of roughnecking. "... course," the truckdriver continued, now on his second piece of pie, "the derrick man has the best job. Gets to work up high. See for miles 'round. And the best pay. He just stacks the drill pipe as it comes up off the elevator."

At last he finished the pies and said, "If you want me to, I can talk to the foreman 'bout getting you a job with Standard."

Wolf listened now with only half an interest. He had the oddest sensation. He turned from the counter. His gaze swept the diner's oil-sheened windows. But there was no one on the wind-swept streets, only an old prewar bus that rattled off in the whirl of dust.

CHAPTER

seventeen

The cable tool rig monotonously thumped and ground as it pounded and punched deeper and deeper into Wyoming's bosom, searching for pay zones of oil. October's raw wind gusted out of the southwest, swaying the derrick. Wolf snapped his safety belt to the wooden bar of his station fifty feet above the floor of the rig. The wind had to be doing sixty an hour. Most of the men didn't bother with the belt, or any other safety measures around the rig, for that matter. But the first week on the job, Wolf had watched a man fall off a rig after passing out from the gaseous hydrogen sulfide.

Still, there was something about those gas flares at night. Their glow that could be seen from as far away as Casper on the south and Buffalo on the north. If he believed in spirits, he would say that the goddess of fire resided in those perpetual torches, for the yellow, red, white and orange waves of fire were ever changing and so moody. He had seen the torches casting an enveloping yellow glow, murky and uncanny in their mystery on a foggy night. On a clear cold night they gleamed as bright, as silently, coldly blue and white as the snowcapped Big Horn range in the distance.

A brain-piercing scream jerked Wolf's gaze to the rig floor below. A man writhed in agony. "Good God!" Wolf whispered. The man's lower torso was ribboned by a chain that was snagged in the kelly bushing, and the spinning assembly was winding up the chain like a spool. Helplessly Wolf watched as the man's left leg ripped away at the hip.

The old wave of red washed over Wolf. He clung to the safety belt until his vision cleared and below he could see the men swarming like ants about the chain-bound man.

The accident was on everyone's tongue that Friday night at the red brick Liberty Theater. Very few watched Dolly Day's Peacock Review, which was not that unusual, since the six chorines had seen better days and the mind-reading act that followed had played Salt Creek only the month before to less than rave reviews.

Elmo, the friendly truckdriver, sat with Wolf and several of the other roughnecks, who had spruced up for the evening's outing. "Gotta expect accidents like that," Elmo said between the acts. "There ain't nothin' easy 'bout the oil patch. What you're working with tends to blow up, and what you're hunting for tends to burn."

The acne-scarred youth, Bobby, sitting on the other side of Wolf said, "Heard about a man driving one of them nitroglycerin cars—"

"Torpedo trucks," Elmo supplied.

"Yes. Well, anyway, it hit a bump in the road and"— Bobby snapped his fingers—"vanished in a cloud of smoke. All they found was a piece of the well shooter's pants, a finger, and a very large hole in the road."

Wolf paid little attention to the acts that followed. A slow anger simmered inside him. He knew that oil field work was hard physical labor and that the macho syndrome on the rigs made it difficult for the workers to demonstrate any concern for their safety. Worse, the foreman refused to set safety regulations and demonstrated a reckless disregard for human life.

Yet Wolf knew that he could not toss off the careless concern for another life as easily as did the foreman, especially when his childhood nightmare of the winter march through St. Petersburg's bloody streets returned to haunt him.

Thus, when a week later he happened to be in the post office with Bobby and overheard the old man in the black beret inform the postman he needed a manager for his sheep ranch, Wolf knew he was leaving. "Bobby," Wolf said, "drive back to the rig and tell the son-of-a-bitch foreman he has my resignation." The callow youth's eyes rounded like saucers, and Wolf said, "Go on."

Bobby almost stumbled out of the dusty, moldy post office in surprise. Wolf walked over to the old man, who was taking the envelopes the postmaster doled out to him. "I overheard your conversation. I have done some work on a sheep ranch, a small one, and am interested in the job."

The old man pocketed the envelopes and took up his walking stick, a mountain sheep horn cane. In the ruddy face framed by silver hair and handlebar mustache, the old eyes were fierce as he scrutinized Wolf. Then, without a question, "I will tell you about our sheep ranch on the trip back."

Outside, parked next to the boardwalk, was a Stanley Steamer with a canvas top. When Wolf slid inside, he found a young woman wedged between him and the old man. "My grand-daughter, Celina," the old man said.

A pair of café noir eyes in a face of Raphael-like beauty brazenly met Wolf's assessing gaze before the lids dropped like languishing fans. The young woman's hair was hidden by an inky black woolen shawl, but Wolf knew the hair had to be a rich warm brown, like the women in Raphael's paintings. She murmured something to her grandfather in a language that Wolf did not immediately identify, and the old man's lips curled in a contemptuous frown.

"*Barka*, pardon me," he said, "but you must forgive my granddaughter's boldness. Isolated as we are, she has not learned the etiquette of a female. Allow me to introduce myself. I am Jose Bilbao."

Wolf nodded, detecting now the soft fluid speech identified with the Latin languages. More than likely, he judged, French or Spanish Basque.

"*Nire seme*, my son, is in need of a good manager for our ranch. And I have a good eye for men. Benito will be quite pleased with my choice. The pay will be good. The room and board are, of course, included."

Wolf slanted a glance at the woman next to him, who did not once look his way. Still, he sensed her intense interest.

Above the hawklike nose, the old man's eyes studied Wolf for the briefest moment before he wheeled the old car out onto Salt Creek's potholed main street. "La Conquista is not many leagues away, about thirty-five miles northwest on the Powder River's North Fork. If you or *nire seme* do not feel my idea is a wise one..." the old man shrugged, "then I will bring you back to Salt Creek tomorrow, *zergaitik ez*—why not?"

Indeed, why not? In the space of the year Wolf had spent at Bear's place he had come to like the feeling of independence, the self-sufficiency he had derived from working with the elements, not with machinery like steam shovels and drilling rigs. There had been no timeclock to watch but nature's.

Perhaps there was more of the Old World still in him than he knew. Like the old don, he shrugged. But his words held some of the courtesy reserved for the Old World, a way of life he thought he had forgotten. "I will talk with your son, Mr. Bilbao."

Whatever interest Wolf had detected in Celina was not evidenced again on the four-hour-long journey to La Conquista. Celina Bilbao kept her back straight, her gaze cast demurely downwards or away, as if the red hogback hills in the distance were of more interest than the dark stranger at her side. She remained silent.

Her grandfather, though, spoke proudly of being a poor youngest son in the Basque province of Navarra, Spain, and coming in 1868 to the Idaho Territory, of which Wyoming was then a part, to establish one of the largest ranches, La Conquista. "And it was a conquest, Mr. Nicholson. A conquest over the icy winters and strong winds and dry summers. And the Anglo prejudice."

As they left the main road and by a dirt road slowly ascended the wide, rolling country, the landscape became lonelier, wilder. The car began passing through red sheer cliffs that bent in enormous arcs, walls of red that seemed to follow for miles. "Hole in the Wall country, Mr. Nicholson," Jose Bilbao commented. "Cattle rustlers and robbers, like Butch Cassidy's gang, they preferred this country to hide away in."

Wolf thought the country would make an excellent place to hide away from the world and civilization's progress. To have one's own ranch here . . . He could see why Mr. Bilbao chose this place to settle.

"You see," the old man said and waved a hand before him, "all this country was cattle country, cattle brought up by way of the Anglo's Chisholm Trail. A cattle kingdom with cattle barons. *Haundikigo bat*—an aristocracy. In Cheyenne they built castles.

"I had only my allotted hundred and sixty acres. But then come the harsh summer of 1887 that burned the grass and the blizzards of 1887 and 1888 that killed the cattle. *Inoiz ere ez*; never a winter so bad! But my sheep were able to brave the freezing weather.

"The ranges were overgrazed and overstocked. And the

interest rates were at an all time high and cattle prices at
an all time low. Thus I began to buy from the ranchers who
were wiped out. *Azkenez*, at last! I had my conquest, a
rancho thirty miles wide and ninety miles long: La Conquista!"

Wolf considered what the old don told him. He knew
that the year before last the United States Congress had
passed another Homestead Act; that a settler would receive
a tract of land after living on it for three years. Wyoming.
Billed as the last great frontier.

He smiled to himself. He could become the greatest shepherd since Abraham. To the land he could give his love,
for it would always be there. He could not lose it as he had
his mother and sister. It was something to think about, and
the tantalizing idea occupied the rest of the journey until
the low stucco walls of La Conquista's outbuildings came
into view.

Wolf was impressed with the Bilbao operation as they
rode by paddocks, a salt house, wagon shed, feeding yards,
and holding pens. The old man pointed out a machine shop
his son had ordered built only the year before. Here and
there men, mostly hispanics, Mexicans and Basques, ambled, bent on their own business of the moment.

The larger of the buildings, a substantial two-story stone
house, was surprisingly styled like a formal English rural
home, with bull's-eye glass windows. An effusion of ivy
wreathed the spindled-carved porch pillars. On the porch
stood a man of medium height who seemed larger because
of his stocky build. A cigar stump between his teeth, he
waited patiently for the Stanley Steamer to rumble up in
front of the porch before moving forward to assist the old
don out of the car. "*Bila ibili zaren aska ekrrii dizuit*," the
old man told the younger one, who appeared to be about
forty-five or so.

The swarthy, stocky man, chomping on his cigar stump,

watched as Wolf held out his hand to help Celina Bilbao out of the car. When Wolf released her waist, the girl's lids raised, and he knew he had been right about what he had seen in that sloe-eyed gaze. A hunger that had nothing to do with food. Her lids, weighted by thick lashes, lowered again, and without a word she pulled away to glide toward the house.

If the man were aware of his daughter's silent communication with Wolf, he gave no indication. "My father tells me he thinks he has found the ranch manager I have been looking for. Come with me."

Benito Bilbao's office was less an office than a billiard room. "Hauled the table up from Cheyenne," the man said proudly. He took two cues from the rack on the wall and pitched one of the maple rods to Wolf. "You've played before?"

The interview was hardly what Wolf expected. But then neither was Benito Bilbao. Except for the dark coloring and the barest trace of a Spanish Basque accent, the man reminded Wolf of one of the Yankee businessmen. He was tough and shrewd. Wolf lacked experience at pocket billiards, but through sheer concentration he somehow managed to stay even with Benito as the man proficiently knocked the ivory balls into the pockets, all the while keeping a running one-sided dialogue going.

"My father has established a modern-day empire, Wolf, but it won't last if La Conquista can't keep up with modern times." Benito knocked a red ball into the far pocket, took the cigar from his mouth, and raised to face Wolf. "Like my father, you're from the Old World. Think you can handle the job?"

Wolf had never mentioned that he was from Russia, and he thought he had lost most of his accent. But then neither had he mentioned that he wanted the job. So what made Benito so certain on both accounts?

It seemed now that for a long time in some vague, senseless way he really had little choice in the decisions affecting him, that forces outside the realm of the natural were dictating his fate, maneuvering him like a pawn.

CHAPTER
eighteen

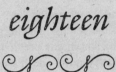

*B*ounded by the cedar-stubbled foothills of the Big Horns on the west, the Salt Creek oil fields to the south, and the open high grasslands in the north and east, the lovely treeshaded town of Buffalo marked where Clear Creek crossed the old Bozeman Trail that snaked through what only a short time before had been Powder River's Indian territory.

Maggie turned the last page and closed the book, *The Virginian*, that she had borrowed from Buffalo's public library. It was difficult to believe that only twenty-seven years earlier, in 1892, the peaceful town was involved in the violent Johnson County Cattle War when the cattle barons and the homesteaders had hired Texas gunfighters to settle their feud for them. But then, looking around the lobby of Buffalo's Occidental Hotel that *The Virginian* had made famous, she still sensed some of that unrest.

Or was it merely the unrest in herself?

Surprisingly, Frank was happy with the small town. Buffalo had a scent to it of grass and fresh mountain air. And she had to admit that in the two months she and Frank had been there its people could not have been nicer. The hotel was a well-known meeting place for the cowboys, the sheepmen, and sometimes oil field roughnecks up from Salt Creek. From Frank's viewpoint they were all potential buyers of firearms.

During the day, using Buffalo as a home base, he traveled in the old Model T, which they had barely been able to afford, to the nearby towns and ranches to sell his wares. But a great deal of each evening was spent in the Occidental Tavern with his suitcase of National's sample firearms propped on the handcarved walnut bar, when he was not gambling. Between the selling and the gambling, he was earning more than he had in any previous town.

He entered the lobby now, and his darkened face told Maggie that this was not one of his more successful evenings. She rose from the circular horsehide sofa to meet him. "It's time we moved on," he told her as he led her upstairs to their second-floor room.

He closed the door and slung himself face down across the bed. His thick voice revealed the extent of his drinking that evening. She went to him and began taking off his fringetongued brogues. "How much did you lose this time, Frank?"

He mumbled something into his coatsleeve about having sold all he could in the area, but she was not really listening. Suddenly it occurred to her that for all those weeks they had been in Buffalo, she had felt a strange disquiet. Yet, oddly, the idea of leaving, it caught at her breath. It was like a nagging thought, as when she knew she was leaving something behind and searched a hotel room one more time.

Quietly, so she would not disturb Frank, she began to pack their camelback trunk. A fine film of perspiration began to glisten on her upper lip. Somewhere at the back of her head a drum started to pound. Each movement became more of an effort. Could she be pregnant? Surely not. Less than two weeks before she had had her menses. Unable to fold another shirt, she sat down in the stuffed chair and rested her sweaty forehead in her hand. She would finish packing in the morning.

She awakened in the chair early the next morning to view a world of white outside the hotel window. A winter blizzard had stormed in during the night, snowbounding the town. She stretched before the window, smiling to herself. Of course, that explained her headache and sickish disposition the evening before. Changes of weather often affected people that way.

Wolf put the treatise on anthrax he had ordered from the Wyoming Stockgrowers Association back on the bookshelf, next to the report on pedigreed Rambouillet sheep. Over the months the shelves he had built in the manager's residence were filling with the books he periodically bought. Any time he had to send a ranchhand into Salt Creek or Buffalo, which were equal distance from La Conquista, he also sent an order for books.

Although Benito operated La Conquista on a patriarchal, almost feudal system, benevolently controlling the lives of the many Mexican and Basque families who lived not only on the ranch but in communities around it, Wolf had no interest in changing the system as he had in Russia. La Conquista, with its high grasslands and the blue-black wall of the distant Big Horns, was a haven for him, despite its reputation for bad winters and barren wastelands. The land was something real, something timeless. He wanted only to make his own way there at La Conquista, left alone.

He returned to the battered roll-top desk and took out a sheet of paper and pen and began to list the supplies the ranch needed, this time from Buffalo. The picturesque town along the winding Clear Creek offered a better variety of stores than the small oil boom town of Salt Creek. And, as the Johnson county seat, Buffalo offered him the chance to file on land of his own, something that had been at the back

of his mind since he had arrived at La Conquista six months
earlier.

Oil cakes, dehorners, picket pins and chains . . . he paused
as he heard the slamming of the screen door. The March
wind again. All winter the wind had whipped down on La
Conquista with all the fury of a cornered Siberian polar
bear. The severe blizzards that raged that winter of 1919–
20 had followed on the heels of one after another, isolating
Wyoming from the rest of the world and straining Wolf's
patience. He felt as restless as a polar bear himself.

With any luck the warm chinook winds with their fur-
nacelike blasts would soon be coming down off the Rockies,
as they did each spring, to dry away the accumulation of
snow that still covered the plains.

A noise behind Wolf caused him to turn around. Celina
stood in the doorway. Her eyes gleamed in the semi-
darkness of the room. A knowing smile transformed the
madonna face into a portrait of sensuality.

It was not the first time she had approached him. Once
he had been alone in the vast barn when she asked him to
saddle her piebald. That time she had been wearing a divided
riding skirt of black velvet that accentuated her lush figure.
She reminded him of a precocious bud whose petals strained
to burst asunder and reveal the exotic flower beneath.

Another time she sought him out in the machine shop
and asked him to repair a broken pair of scissors that one
of the house servants could have fixed just as easily. Always
her eyes were demurely downcast, but he could almost smell
the heat of arousal emanating from her.

"I'm going to Buffalo with you," she said in the Spanish
used by the Mexican laborers, though he knew she had
learned English at a convent school somewhere in New
Mexico.

"Like hell you are." He stuck to English, although with
his natural facility for languages he was speaking Spanish
now almost as well as he did English. Acquiring the Basque

language was a little more difficult for him. "Your father'll have you strung up tighter than barbed wire."

She crossed to him with a fluid grace and, resting her hands on the desk, looked down at him with a sultry, mocking smile. *"Mi padre no esta aqui,"* she purred.

Hell's fires! He had forgotten Benito and his father had ridden out to one of La Conquista's Mexican communities to visit with old friends. He shrugged. "You're still not going."

She leaned over now, and he saw in the open neckline of the boiled high-collar blouse the rise of her full breasts, tantalizing him like juicy, ripe apples waiting to be plucked. "If you don't take me with you," she said softly, smiling, "I shall tell my father you took advantage of me." Her fingers went to her shirt to slip loose the first button, exposing almost the full weight of her breasts. "I shall tell him how you forced my clothes from me."

Wolf's hand snaked out to capture her wrist before any more buttons gave way. "Tell him also that I beat your rear black and blue, because so help me God, Celina, I will if you don't get the hell out of here. Now!"

Unmistakable passion flared in her dark eyes, and her lips parted. "I think I would like that," she said, her voice a husky whisper.

He twisted her wrist sharply, and she gasped. "I don't think you would," he gritted. "Now get out!"

She rubbed her wrist. "You have no feelings!" she spat and whirled, running from the room.

The problem was he did have feelings. Celina stirred them too much. But she was a child. A spoiled child. Yet Maude had not been much more than a child. And he had slept with her. So wherein lay the difference?

The difference, he told himself later that morning as he drove the Stanley Steamer northeast toward Buffalo, was that he meant to settle in Wyoming. And he did not need Benito as an enemy. He would need him as a neighbor and a good friend. Something that Benito would never be if the man suspected an anglo was courting his daughter. Benito, though he might deny it, was as Old World in his way as was the older Bilbao. And Benito meant Celina to be reserved for a match with one of the more prominent Basque or Mexican families of the Powder River area.

Wolf pressed the automobile's pedal. With a little luck and good timing, he might reach Buffalo by sunset. Celina's attempted seduction had aroused him more than he realized. Surely a town of Buffalo's size would offer ample amusement.

CHAPTER
nineteen

᎒ᏛᎧ

Old man Weidemeyer looked over the pyramid of his gnarled fingers at the *Buffalo Daily Leader*'s reporter for the "Political Patter" column. Hhrumph! A woman!

Wire-rimmed glasses, high-collared shirtwaist, and trimly tailored, though somewhat frayed, tobacco-colored corduroy jacket and skirt that appeared almost masculine in their severity. Yet the young woman possessed a classical beauty. Delicate sculptured features set off by that willful jaw. And tawny hair—damned, if it were loosed from that tight knot, she would look like some proud lioness.

Jeez-o-pete! He *was* getting decrepit, to sit there and moon like a calf.

"Well! What the hell information is it the *Leader* wants? And don't bother to flinch, gal. If you're gonna dress and act like a man, you can sure as hell take the rest like a man."

An amused smile dimpled beneath the young woman's arrogant sweep of cheekbones. "Jeez-o-pete," the County Commissioner muttered aloud this time, almost, but not quite, struck dumb by the sheer beauty.

Maggie drew a cigarette from the package. "May I?" she asked and without waiting for permission struck a match to the cigarette's tip. The County Commissioner looked like he was going into apoplexy. She smoothed the twitching curve from her lips.

The glasses, the clothes, the smoking, they produced the effect of understatement she sought. After more than two months of working as a stringer on the *Buffalo Daily Leader*, she had come to realize that men were more apt to relax around her and talk about serious, pertinent subjects if she affected a more businesslike, and certainly masculine, mien. She gained the reporter's job only because she had been able to convince the editor that she had experience in newspaper work, neglecting to inform the reluctant man that it was merely typing Vera's suffragette newsletter.

But, Holy Mary, she had been forced to do something. Buffalo's old timers claimed the 1919–20 winter had been the worst winter since the 1887 disaster. And for her and Frank it had been. One arctic blizzard after another had slammed through Wyoming to snowbound them in Buffalo. Traveling was virtually impossible in Wyoming's wintery wilderness where distance between neighbors was often measured in scores of miles. She would just get their bags packed when another icy storm would come roaring in. It almost seemed as if nature's elements were conspiring to keep them there.

Starvation actually stared them in the face, for both hers and Frank's pride were too strong to ask for handouts. And Frank's pride was too strong to sink to accepting the menial job offered at the Zindal Bar as a bartender. He managed to sell a few firearms as gifts to eke them out through Christmas, and she had snapped up the reporter's job New Year's Eve day.

She softly exhaled the cigarette smoke and took up the pencil. It hovered over the pad in her lap. "Commissioner

Weidemeyer, with Mr. Karcher's resignation from the Zoning Board, the *Daily Leader* wants to know whom you have in mind for his place."

The old man chuckled at the young woman's spunk. From beneath the thatch of shaggy iron-gray hair, his shrewd eyes scrutinized her. "Why, gal? You interested in the position?"

Maggie looked up from the pad. Under the wing-tipped brows, the shamrock-colored eyes narrowed. "And if I were?"

Weidemeyer emitted a scoffing snort. "Whoever heard of a woman in politics?"

With deliberation, she drew on the cigarette until the crack in her composure was resealed. "I might remind you that Wyoming granted suffrage to women way back in 1869. By the state consititution, I could hold any political office." She smiled coolly, watching for the effect of her next words. "Even run for the governor's office."

He laughed out loud and slapped the desk with his hand. "Listen, gal," he wheezed, the laughter still rumbling inside him, "the only reason we granted suffrage to the women was because the territory needed enough votes to qualify it for statehood."

Disgust battled with rage inside her. The pomposity of men! She rose and with deliberation ground out her cigarette in the commissioner's ashtray. She knew what he said was true. A woman had about as much chance being elected governor as an Indian. But there was more than one way to skin a cat.

"Commissioner Weidemeyer, my husband would like to put his name up for the position on the Zoning Board."

The old eyes squinched, trying to read the young woman's inscrutable expression. "By all that's sacred, I do believe you are daring me, Mrs. Van der Rhys!"

Her cheeks dimpled into a leprechaun's smile. "That I am, Commissioner."

* * *

Slowly, Maggie descended the bell-towered courthouse steps. Like a chess master, her mind plotted out the future, and the best course of approaching Frank with her idea. She walked along Main Street, which had once been a winding cow trail but was now bordered on both sides by false-front frame and brick buildings. It really was absurd. She was bent on a fool's errand. Still . . .

Her steps quickened across the Clear Creek bridge, her lids lowered and her shoulders hunched against the March wind's biting cold. That damnable wind again. She really was going to have to learn how to drive the Model T. Then, disastrously, her boots slipped on the ice that coated the bridge. Her hands flailed for the low railing. Wooden splinters scraped her ribs. The railing clipped her temple. Suddenly frigid water washed over her and revived her stunned senses. She struggled to stand against the current of the knee-deep icy stream.

She was dimly aware of the screech of car brakes, and a few seconds later hands gripped her firmly and hauled her up the withered-grass bank. Her lashes, weighted by water droplets, raised with an effort. "Holy Mary, no!" she murmured at the sight of the dark face, the mocking face, that hovered over hers.

Of all the people in the world, why him? Why Wolf? How, over a distance of two thousand miles and three years, could he be there to pull her from the water?

Predestination?

She choked on the water, or the thought, or maybe both, and began to cough. She felt herself tossed like a sack of onions across his back. He scrambled up the bank, and her breath whoomphed from her lungs. Ignominiously she was shouldered through the crowd that had gathered. The sudden warmth of the car's interior was heavenly. If only she could stop shaking. Wolf slid in next to her and gunned the motor.

"My notes," she wailed. "I need them for the *Leader*'s next edition!"

"So you're a reporter now? Why can't you just stay home like an ordinary housewife, Maggie?"

"Because I'm not ordinary!" she snapped back and wrapped her arms about her trembling body.

He whipped the car to a halt before the Clearmont Hotel, a slightly shabbier version of the Occidental Hotel. Before she could protest, he hauled her out and scooped her up into his arms. Her soggy skirts had to weigh three times her weight, but he effortlessly climbed the stairs, ignoring the blustering, "But—but—" of the old man behind the counter.

He kicked open the door to his room with a booted foot and tossed her on his bed, not as gently as he had that first time in his room above the Van der Rhys garage. Shrugging out of his sheepskin jacket, he jerked off her hat, and Maggie cried out as the hatpins pulled at her hair. He ignored her and proceded to efficiently disrobe her, first yanking off the high top boots, then tearing away her jacket and blouse. Her buttons scattered across the wooden floor and she was exposed to his startled gaze.

"Your corset?" he muttered, his swarthy hands contrasting sharply with the pale ivory skin of her breasts.

"I...I..." She tried to control her quivering jaws and at the same time shield herself. "I discarded it ye-years ago."

"You're right; you damned sure aren't ordinary." He tore his gaze from the rose-brown haloes that wrinkled with the cold, thrusting the nipples into a wanton stiffness. His hands worked rapidly at the buttons of the skirt's waistband. "Oh, hell!" he said and ripped the skirt and petticoat away also.

"No!" she pleaded.

He rolled his eyes upward with a grimace. "We've got to get you out of these wet clothes." He proceeded to wrap a rough woolen blanket about her more thoroughly than the

Egyptian slaves bundled Cleopatra in the rug.

"It scratches," she said in a hoarse whisper.

"Damn it, Maggie! Can't you shut up just for once?" The slow drawl was different than the terse formality she remembered, but there was still that exciting edge to his voice. And the youthful recklessness of the lips was tempered somewhat by the faint grooves of patience that had been carved at either side of the long mouth.

He crossed to the cigarette-burned and knife-notched chest and grabbed a half-empty brown bottle and a glass that was filmed with old alcohol. "Here," he said, and passed her the glass that now sloshed with stilled rotgut whiskey.

She shook her head slightly. The mere movement cost tremendous effort. "Drink it," he ordered. "You look like a drowned alley cat."

He held the glass to her lips. Obediently she swallowed. She felt her face flood with the heat of the alcohol and heard the rasp of her indrawn breath. He smiled thinly and refilled her glass. "Aggh!" she said, when her breath wheezed back. "'Tis awful!"

"It gets better. Drink up."

She took another tentative sip and winced. "But it has such a bloody bad taste."

He chuckled and took the empty glass. "That's enough, then. I don't want a drunk female on my hands."

"I'm not dru-drunk."

"Sometimes I wonder if you're female," he muttered, and reached for her bare arm.

She tried to draw it away, but he held it and began to rub his warm hands up and down its length in a massaging motion. The winter's mellow sunlight streamed through the rain and dust-splotched window to play on the strong features of his face: the jutting cheekbones, the straight high-bridged nose and winged nostrils that flared sensuously, the broad jaw that was grooved like God's finger had dented it—or maybe Satan's. And the mouth that seemed to mock both its owner and the world.

The trembling eased from her body beneath the administration of Wolf's firm, warm hands. First one arm, and then the other. The pleasant heat of the whiskey radiated slowly through her bloodstream. Every breath she breathed was as pure as water and as strong as wine.

When the numbness left her lips, she asked suspiciously, "What are you doing in Buffalo, Wyoming?"

"I was at the courthouse, filing on my land," he said simply. "Give me your foot."

Languidly, she did as he instructed, careful to hug the blanket about her body. Her foot arched with contentment like a purring cat arches beneath a stroking hand. "I *am* a female," she said, hazily recalling his previous statement. "I just don't like being treated like a female."

He propped his back against the four-poster and picked up the other foot. "You don't know what it's like to be a female, Maggie. You're afraid of being a woman."

She tried to focus her eyes on the dark face at the end of the bed. "I'm afraid of nothing. Nothing can frighten me anymore! The worst has happened, and I have survived!"

He raked a black brow. "Oh, really." He dropped her foot and leaned forward. "Let me tell you what is worse." Slowly he began to crawl on all fours toward her like some stalking tomcat. Or wolf, she thought vaguely, and shivered.

"It's worse to want something so badly that your guts twist and knot inside you. To live on the same planet with that person and know she is forbidden to you." He straddled her, his fists and knees implanted in the mattress on her left and right. Above her his visage was dark and grim. "Shall I teach you what it's like to want a person, to ache for their mere touch?"

Her instinct perceived some imminent danger. But her fascination with the power-stamped features of the virile face above hers overrode her instinct. She watched, transfixed, as his hands came out to remove the wire-rimmed glasses that now had one cracked lens and lay them on the nightstand. Then his hands came back to caress her shoulders in a gesture that was surprisingly gentle.

Something inside her stirred, a pleasant sensation but yet a tightening, a knotting down low, just as he had warned her. The slowly budding desire warred with her instinctive urge to withdraw. She must not ever forget just what he was: a wolf on the prowl. But some remote area of her brain remembered the exquisite sensations of his last kiss. Almost against her own will, her fingers slipped up to push back the cinnamon-brown locks that feathered across the square brow. Her lids languorously closed, and her lips parted.

His head lowered over hers. She thought his lips touched hers. Then her eyes opened, and he had raised his head. *"Milais Deevs,* Maggie," he whispered, his voice husky with wanting, "I had no idea a simple kiss could be so devastating."

She had no doubt when his mouth claimed hers the next time. His lips were hard, firm, yet, strangely enough, tender. Of her own will she opened her mouth to invasion. There was no savagery in that kiss, rather an impassioned searching of her mouth in an intimate caress that gave life to her own tongue, that gave life to her sexually starved body.

His lips deserted hers to nibble at her earlobe. She shivered rapturously. She clung helplessly to him, the only steady object in a room that began to spin wildly. The tighter she clung, the more Wolf consolidated his attack, taking advantage of every tiny retreat, seeming to revel in each new surrender, until the surrender was complete and her tongue mated with his. Her hips shifted restlessly, wantonly. She could not help herself.

Then he lowered his full length atop her. My God, she thought irrationally, he weighs a ton!

His weight, his length, dominated her. A fear never really

realized beneath Frank's thinner, smaller body—and the belated memory that she had a husband—galvanized her into action. With a desperation born of both guilt and fear, she shoved him from her.

He rolled to his side and looked down at her. "Still a coward, Maggie?" The tone was light, but she heard the scathing contempt in his voice.

She raised on one elbow, holding the blanket close against her breasts. "No. But I'm still against being treated like a woman. A man can decide to end the seduction when he wants. But the woman must—"

"Hell's fires! You don't know the first thing about being a woman." His thumb and forefinger curled about her square jaw. "But, Maggie, you had better pray that you never run into me again. Because I swear by every damp hair on your head that I shall teach you what it's like to be a woman!"

CHAPTER
twenty

❦ ✿ ❦

*"Yippee-yi, ti-yea....And I'll drive my cattle to the
top of the hill.
And I'll kiss my girl, by God, I will. Yippee-yi, ti-
yea...."*

"*Diego!*" *Wolf strode into the circle of ranch-*
hands grouped about the hayracks and came to stand before
the one who had been singing. The man was six years older
than Wolf, but he jumped to his feet respectfully at the soft
drawl with the dangerous ring to it.

"I thought I told you to run those ewes into a holding
pen after breakfast."

The Mexican raked nervous fingers through the dark
brown wiry curls. "*Si, jefe.* I leave pronto!"

Wolf shot a glance at old Manuel, who sat buffing a hide
for boots he was cobbling. "Feel like marking the backs of
the lambs and ewes?"

The old Basque grinned his assent, and Wolf swung and
went to find Benito. The man was in his office with his
father and daughter. Wolf hesitated at the open door, but

Benito motioned for him to come in. *"Nire alaba* is trying to persuade her grandfather and me she should be allowed to ride into Casper to have her hair shingled," he said with a grimace.

Celina turned laughing eyes on him. *"Que pensas,* Wolf?" she said, asking his opinion in Spanish rather than Basque. She stood and pirouetted before him, her hair pushed atop her head with her forearm. It was a seductive pose, and he knew she meant for him to notice, just as she wanted him to be aware she was wearing a new dress with a hemline that was a full eight inches off the ground. The waistline was nonexistent, but the shapely turn of her ankles, encased in beige silk stockings, was very visible. So that's what had been in the package Benito had had him pick up from the J.C. Penney store.

"I think one of the hands could take a pair of sheep-shearers to her and shingle her hair just as well," Wolf said, settling one hip across Benito's desk.

Celina stamped her foot. "Ohh!"

She whirled from the room, and Benito and Jose laughed. But then old Jose, who sat on the horsehide couch rolling his cane between his gnarled hands, sobered and said, "Wyoming is hell on horses and women, Wolf."

Benito passed Wolf a long Havana, and said, "It was hard on my wife, the isolation. She left me when Celina was but a tyke. And I worry about Celina. Being the only young available woman for miles around, she gets to thinking she's the queen of La Conquista. And the hands aren't any help in disillusioning her."

"She needs someone to take her down every so often," Jose said.

Wolf jammed the cigar in his pocket for later. He wanted to change the subject. "Benito, I figure we'll need to let about fifty rams loose to mate with the ewes for a month or so. And while we're at it, with the dry summer and the mountains badly overgrazed, your sheep are in poor shape.

I recommend we buy more hay and oil cake now before the prices go up."

The man grimaced. "You think they're going to? Well, do what you think best. You wanna take on a game of billiards?"

"Don't think so today. Soon as I get the winter shelter sheds going, I'm taking off for a day or so."

Benito grunted agreeably, knowing the young man had earned the time off. "Going to start on your place?"

He nodded. "Brought the mortar back from Buffalo when I filed on the land."

That was not the only thing he had brought back from Buffalo. As the buckboard followed the Powder River's North Fork up towards Pass Creek some hours later, the memory of Maggie rode the trail with him, dogging him, haunting him. Her haughty beauty was still just as tantalizing despite the indication of genteel shabbiness his observant eye had noticed in her carefully mended clothes. He supposed he should feel some sort of elation to find her living with less than the wealth she had plotted for. But all he felt was that damned aching want.

He had thought he had forgotten her; that he had made more out of their meetings than was there. He was wrong. Three years was a long time. But the attraction was still just as strong. The vivid memory of that March day four months before only intensified his want of her. It was the same as all the times before—except that this time she was married.

And this time he was through with drifting. He looked down on the snug little valley sheltered by the Hazelton and Beartrap peaks and knew that he belonged here with the land. Its wildness was a part of his own wildness. Against the western sky towered the massive and heavily wooded Big Horns, whose eastern slopes were cut by innumerable creeks. His land, bordering on the La Conquista, which had first water rights to Pass Creek, had a good stand of sacaton and buffalo grass and plenty of timber for fences, fuel, and buildings. An excellent site.

The rattle of loose pebbles swerved his head toward the butte above him. He grimaced as he watched Celina, dressed in a suede riding outfit, ride down out of a belt of lodgepole pines. He seemed to have lost some of the sharpness in the tricks of the trail that Bear had taught him.

Celina reined in abreast of the wagon. "I followed the noise of the wagon wheels," she said when he offered no greeting.

"You know your father's going to blister you for this one."

She dismounted and walked to the wagon to look up into his face. For once her teasing smile was gone. "I know it. And I do not care." She took his hand from the reins and pulled it down to her suede-jacketed breast. "See. I have no shame. My heartbeat betrays my want of you."

Feeling the weight of the soft breast, he groaned inwardly. "Celina, your father has marriage plans for you, and I'm not in them."

"Bahh!" She dropped his hand and planted her fists on her hips. "Do you think I will marry a common sheepherder?"

"Some of the Basque in the area are not common sheepherders," he reminded her in an effort to restore some practicality to the moment. He wanted no trouble with Benito, who would be his future neighbor. "Some of them are well-to-do ranchers."

"But none of them are like you," she said, and he saw the fire smoldering in her eyes. "I am not ugly. And I will make you happy in bed. I know I will."

"No, you won't make me happy in bed, 'cause we're not going to bed together."

She laughed then. "We will, my Wolf. I always get what I want. But for now, for this lovely afternoon, I will watch you begin work on your house."

"And your father?"

"I will take care of my father."

Why was he hesitating? Celina would make a good lover. Yet he realized there was something in him that would never let him give the kind of possessive loving she demanded.

Maggie typed the last words of the week's column, ending with the reporter's standard "thirty." She removed her glasses and rubbed her eyes with her fingertips. The glasses she had bought to replace the cracked ones in Clear Creek gave her headaches when she worked long hours.

Slowly she shook her head, as if trying to shake what had happened at Clear Creek five months before from her mind. But the memory was always there. She pushed back the chair from the battered desk and crossed to the window, drawing back the yellow chintz curtains to view the shadowy row of lovely old homes, homes with character, whose windows were lit against the darkness of the July night.

With the raise she had received, and Frank's job on the Zoning Board—the Holy Virgin bless old man Weidemeyer!—they had been able to purchase the time-worn but solidly built two-story brick boarding house at the corner of Lobban and Fetterman streets. She had been delighted with the house—her first house—with its green carpet of grass, the many shady cottonwood trees, the large, spacious rooms. Unfortunately, the house overlooked Clear Creek— a beautiful view, but it held one unwanted memory.

Too vividly she recalled redressing herself under Wolf's hard stare, of holding the buttonless blouse and jacket together during the tense, silent ride in the Stanley Steamer back to the Occidental Hotel. Later that evening she had paced the hotel's small room, trying to repress the overwhelming urge to flee, to leave the town. But where to? She had had the eerie sensation that anywhere she went, she would turn around to find him.

But she was finished with running. Convincing Frank to

stay was another thing. When the chinook winds swept down off the Rockies the following week to warm the countryside, Frank was ready to move on. "I don't know, Maggie," he had said at her suggestion to settle down in Buffalo. He dabbed the brush in the shaving mug and lathered his face. "Why this God-forsaken place?" he mumbled through the foam of soap.

She thought about all the God-forsaken towns they had stayed in, towns strung out like glass beads on a railroad track. "Because we would be able to buy a home of our own."

Frank pulled his mouth to one side to shave the stubble just under his mustache. "The rooms at the hotels have always been big enough for us."

"They wouldn't be if—if we were to have a baby."

His eyes left his reflection in the spotted mirror to slide to that of Maggie's. "Are you trying to tell me something, Maggie?"

She saw the apprehension in his eyes. In his childhood there had been no siblings to compete with, and she knew he wanted no rivals now. She turned away and lit a cigarette. "No. I'm trying to tell you that Wyoming is wide open for enterprising men like yourself and that Orville Weidemeyer is considering you for Buffalo's Zoning Board. It's a good place to start, Frank."

Either her suggestion or Weidemeyer's offer persuaded Frank to remain in Buffalo. He accepted the job on the Zoning Board and even opened a small firearms store on Fort Street, though he hired a man to run the gunsmith for him.

Maggie's fears of running into Wolf again had been for nothing. Apparently he was not a resident of Buffalo. But he was still somewhere near. Her instincts told her he was.

She turned from the window as Frank entered the front door. The dapper silk handkerchief (the frayed hems she had meticulously mended), the dove-gray spats, the matching Albert watch chains passing across his old embroidered waistcoat—these accessories combined with the affable smile to lend him an undeniable charm. And she knew he capitalized on that charm. But this time she hoped they both could capitalize on this asset.

He crossed to kiss her cheek. The faint smell of liquor lingered about him. "You shouldn't have waited up for me, darling."

"I was working on a column."

He removed the Baden-Powell bowler and tossed it on the hat tree. "Let's go on up to bed," he said. "I'm bushed."

She allowed his arm to encircle her waist as she climbed the stairs with him to their bedroom. "I want to talk to you about something."

He shrugged out of the double-breasted dinner jacket and draped it over the back of the worn stuffed chair. "I hope it's not about the Hodges' dinner party tomorrow night. God, but they're boring."

"No, the banker and his wife can wait." She picked up his jacket and sat down in the chair. She began to remove the pins from the knot of hair at the nape of her neck. "The primary elections are coming up the first week in September," she said slowly, carefully. "I think you could run for an elected office, like County Tax Assessor or something, and win it, Frank."

His hands paused in the midst of removing his watch chains. "Why would I want to do that? Between the money the county pays me during the day and the money the County Commissioner loses to me in poker at night, I'm earning enough so you don't have to work at the newspaper. You could stay home like a normal wife."

There it was again: the normal woman. She turned her head to look at him over her raised arm and flashed a cynical smile. "But you should know by now I'm not a normal wife."

Frank's breath sucked in at her unknowingly provocative

pose. She was the most goddamned beautiful woman he had ever seen. Each time he saw her he was struck anew by her beauty. And by her coolness. He had thought that when he made her his, he would break down that reserve. But he never seemed able to reach through her. There were other beautiful women who were much better in bed. So what was it that kept him to her like some plodding, faithful husband? Well, almost faithful.

It had taken more than those great green eyes to compel him to rebel against his parents and tie himself down to a nobody. Some dim area of his mind recognized what it was that kept him bound to Maggie, though the idea of her strength of will never occurred in so many words.

"Do you realize the power and position a politician can command?" she asked, returning to the original conversation. "And even the money? Wyoming needs responsible men to lead it, Frank."

He crossed to her and combed his fingers through the hair that now tumbled riotously over one shoulder. "A lion's mane," he murmured.

She looked up at him. "Will you consider it, consider running for Tax Assessor?"

He chuckled. "Maggie, you're incorrigible."

Apparently her suggestion of running for Tax Assessor took root, for he informed her the next week that he had filed for candidacy. "I hope you know what you're getting me into, Maggie." He groaned and sank into the stuffed chair. "We've got to travel again, this time by car instead of train. I've got to cover the county kissing babies and shaking hands."

She crossed to him and kissed him on the forehead. "'Tis a magnificent baby-kisser you'll be."

The spontaneous but rare display of affection caught him unaware. He pulled her down across his lap. "As long as you're there with me, I can probably even manage to kiss little old women."

But not young, impressionable girls, she thought. Which was just as well. A scandal would not help his chances of winning the election.

She started to plan the campaign, beginning with her resignation from the *Daily Leader* so she could devote her full time and energies to the project. She obtained a map of the state from old Weidemeyer. Across the huge breadth of Johnson County she stuck tacks on the various little communities Frank would need to visit. Kaycee, Linch, Mayoworth—those were the county's only other towns; of course there was the nearby Mormon settlement that amounted to nearly four hundred people. And the colony of Russian beet farmers farther north. The tack dropped from her hand. *He* could be there. That she would bypass.

She stuck a tack at Fort McKinney, which was now the Wyoming Soldiers' and Sailors' Home. Frank could gain a lot of votes there. And she mustn't forget the ranching communities like the Double B and the Rocking M, and especially the large Basque one, La Conquista.

CHAPTER
twenty-one

❧❧❧

That same eerie feeling crept over Maggie as it had the day she and Frank had first journeyed to Buffalo. That uncomfortable feeling, an anticipation really...but of what?

She shifted uneasily in the car seat, and Frank asked, "Tired?"

She should be. Traveling over the dusty, pitted road jarred every bone in her back. And the monotony of the vast, rolling expanse of land, whose prevailing tones were fragmented shades of browns and ochres, did not help her restlessness. The somber colors of the treeless hills, traversed by numerous deep ravines, caused one to fade into the next. The effect of relief on the land was lost in the distance, and the barren and desolate landscape seemed almost one-dimensional. Above the unlimited expanse rose bold escarpments and buttes. She decided that rather than making her feel tired, the infinite stretch of land had the power to make her feel insignificant.

No, it wasn't the arduous campaign trail that was wearing on her, nor was it August heat, which was unusual for

Wyoming. It was an uncomfortable feeling, perhaps a premonition of the election to come. After all, Bilbao's support was so important, wielding influence as he did over the Hispanic voting population. Frank would need every vote if he hoped to close the margin between himself and the incumbent.

She decided against telling Frank of her apprehensive feeling, saying instead, "I suppose I *am* tired. Mrs. McIlheney at the Walking R—it's really nice she was, but it's been so long since she's seen another woman that—"

"That she talked your ear off," Frank supplied, laughing. "I think her curiosity about a woman in trousers was what got her going."

The surprise at her trousers at every ranch they visited seemed ridiculous to Maggie. "I warned you in the beginning that, regardless of what other women might have worn crossing the prairies in covered wagons, a dress and heels are impractical for traveling hundreds of miles in isolated areas—and over these unimproved roads, where the Model T could be stranded."

"Well, Mrs. McIlheney's husband was just as curious," Frank said. "And he managed to match her word for word—on other subjects though."

"You listened very patiently, now didn't you?" she teased. "And you were able to talk with Mr. McIlheney about reclamation projects. You surprised me, Frank. I had no idea you knew anything about irrigation and conservation."

His blue eyes danced. "I don't. But old Dykeman at the Bar H served on the Wyoming Board of Control when the Pathfinder Reservoir was built. I merely stored away everything he had to say on reclamation."

"'Tis a born politician you are, Frank Van der Rhys." She hoped so, for he would need all his wits about him if he hoped to gain Mr. Bilbao's support. And according to Commissioner Weidemeyer, the Basque did not embroil himself in politics. He ran his hispanic community the way he felt best and kept politics outside the Mexican and Basque community.

She knew the first time she saw the brawny Basque, when he stepped down from La Conquista's veranda to welcome them, that he was a shrewd man. She saw it in the way his eyes assessed first Frank, quickly but thoroughly, then herself, taking in the tailored khaki shirt and men's trousers she wore. The other ranching families had overlooked her masculine attire, attributing it to eccentricity. Perhaps it was. But would her eccentricity bother him, influence him against Frank?

Looking into those tired, deep brown eyes, she thought not.

"*Ongi etorri*, welcome," Benito Bilbao said. A much older man and a lovely young woman sat on lawn chairs in the shadowy veranda of the ranchhouse—the nicest ranchhouse she had visited during their weeks of campaigning. "Mr. and Mrs. Van der Rhys, is it not?" Benito asked. "Your letter came several days ago, and my daughter has been excitedly preparing for your visit."

Maggie saw the daughter's sloe-eyed gaze flicker incredulously over the masculine attire before moving on to meet Frank's appreciative gaze. *Sweet Mary*, Maggie prayed, *don't let Frank take more than a passing interest in this one, don't let him jeopardize everything now*.

"Celina will show you to your room," the Basque continued, "and later, after you have rested, we will have a fiesta tonight in your honor. I have taken the liberty of inviting some of the neighboring ranchers."

Bilbao's daughter led Maggie and Frank through the spacious twenty-room home. But Maggie noted that Celina Bilbao's languorous smile and sultry, softly accented words of welcome seemed directed more to Frank than to herself. Maggie sighed. The three-day visit was going to seem much longer than she had anticipated.

The hour's nap in the cool green and white upstairs bedroom was a respite for Maggie, though Frank was anxious to be about. Too soon, it seemed, Benito Bilbao came to escort them outside to picnic tables lit by lanterns suspended from the leafy cottonwoods and silvery-gray Russian olive trees. Already, empty buckboards and old Model T's filled the areas about the outbuildings, and through the maze of sheltering trees more wagons could be seen coming down the dusty road.

Everywhere there were people: a few women in dresses and bonnets ten years out of fashion, and a crowd of men in their best overalls and shirts, some sporting the native Basque berets and shepherd's crooks, others sombreros and chaps. Above the fiddle music she heard both the Spanish tongue and, what seemed to be an anomaly of languages, the Basque.

She and Frank moved about the people as Bilbao introduced them to the various ranching families and their ranch-hands who had journeyed to La Conquista for the fiesta. Everyone was eager to take advantage of any excuse to get together and escape the tedium of work. Frank circulated among the men, spending a few minutes with each talking about their ranches, the price of wool, the dry summer. Maggie visited with the women, attempting to make herself understood to the few who spoke little English. She sensed their innate loneliness and curiosity and told them things about the eastern cities, the movie houses, the underground trains, the towering buildings—things that must have seemed to the women like another planet.

Then, Maggie found herself propelled into a group of people lined up for the barbeque. Across the table of potato salad, candied carrots, and baked beans, she looked into the yellow-brown depths of eyes that were fierce and flashing: Wolf's eyes. Taken by surprise, she steadily met that blatant stare of instantly aroused sexual intent, while a voice inside her screamed, *Impossible!*

The young woman at his side said something, and his

gaze released Maggie to fix on the female's slumberous eyes. Only then did she realize the girl was Celina. What was the girl to him? Was she his wife?

With her head held regally, Maggie moved away to join some of the other women who were already at the tables eating. It was difficult enough to follow the mixture of English, Basque, and Spanish conversations without the confusion contributed by the conflict of emotions that warred within her. The instinctive and unreasonable fear that swept over her whenever Wolf confronted her vied with an almost tidal pull toward the man.

Even now, as Basque dancers moved into the circular opening created by the tables, she unaccountably wanted to search among the revelers for that one face. Instead, she fastened her attention on the dancers, who were dressed as sheep. They wore sheepskins on their backs and sported huge bells that thumped and chimed as they bounded about the circle lit by women holding candles in their hands.

Limping to her side, old Jose Bilbao gestured with his cane toward the women, saying, "They are supposed to be all the women who have waited for their men to come home from the sea. They wait—as you wait."

She glanced at the old man, puzzled by his statement, and he went on blandly, "You know, Mrs. Van der Rhys, we lived in Europe before the Romans, and were the first whalers."

Fascinated now, she watched while two Basque men pounded with huge staves on a large oak drum that Jose called a *txalaparta*. Other men, masquerading as sheep, twisted in intricate moves around their counterparts, the herders, who stepped to the music in brilliantly colored costumes of gold and white with red, green, and white streamers, the Basque colors.

But always it was the music that held her. The primordial beat that was supposed to remind one how far back in history Basque culture went, only served to churn up some primitive emotional well of feelings inside her. She closed her eyes, unconsciously swaying with the beat. Abruptly her lids snapped open. She had felt the heat of his gaze again. Her eyes searched about the candlelit circle. Beyond its far side she found what she sought, the gaze that glowed like phosphorous in the dark—like a pair of animal eyes.

The gaze riveted her where she stood. With an enormous effort, she tore her gaze from his and turned away. She found Benito and Frank and, thanking their host for the evening's entertainment, excused herself, claiming fatigue. A headache, which seemed to pound with the *txalaparta*'s incessant beat that seeped through her open bedroom window, made sleep impossible, and she was still awake when Frank came in much later.

CHAPTER
twenty-two

*"**I**'d really rather not stay any longer than nec-*
essary, Frank."

Surprise widened his eyes as he slid into his riding jacket. "It was your idea to visit La Conquista. And a damned good one, Maggie. We can't leave now. I talked Benito into showing us something of La Conquista's countryside. We ought to take advantage of his hospitality. Remember, he has yet to promise us his support."

Yes, the man was shrewd, Maggie thought when they joined him, his father, and daughter for breakfast. Over the hearty breakfast of pancakes, maple syrup, bacon, and strong coffee, Benito casually informed them he would have his manager show them around, thereby, Maggie guessed, excluding himself from being put into a position of having to make a commitment. "A thousand pardons, but there is so much I must attend to, you understand," Benito finished.

Frank turned his warm smile on Celina, who sat with a disinterested expression across from him and Maggie. "You will, of course, join us?"

A breeze rustled through the room at the opening of a

door, and Celina's hot brown eyes moved beyond Frank to
the tall figure that suddenly appeared in the dining room's
doorway. Maggie did not need to turn around to identify
the person behind her. "*Si*, I would very much like to,"
Celina replied.

"My manager, Wolf Nicholson," Benito said, introducing the man who had just come in. "Ready?"

Maggie sat rigid. Damn! So Wolf was the ranch manager!
He was to be their escort. Damn, damn! She could back
out, pleading a headache. But she had already claimed that
excuse the night before. Still, she could feel the throbbing
of an approaching migraine, especially when Frank leveled
an inquisitive eye on Wolf. "Say, haven't I seen you somewhere before? Yes, by golly, didn't you use to chauffeur
for my parents?"

"Done a bit of everything," Wolf replied laconically. He
directed his next statement to Benito. "Clouds are building
over Hazleton's Peak. I'd suggest the sightseeing be post-
poned for another time."

"What's a little rain?" Frank said. "What about you two?
Maggie? Celina?"

Celina's gaze slid back to Wolf before she turned a dimpled smile on Frank. "I will bring my umbrella."

The umbrella turned out to be more like a parasol, a
dainty affair of black silk with a jeweled knob. Celina twirled
it over her shoulder as she demonstrated her expert horse-
manship, riding sidesaddle easily beside Frank, who handled his horse quite well — well enough to keep Celina
amused with small talk about New York.

In front, leading, Wolf rode silently. Maggie had noticed
that all horsemen were narrow hipped, as he was, even when
they were fat from constant riding. But he would never be
fat. He possessed that lithe, catlike leanness. A wolfishness,
she thought ruefully, would be a more appropriate descrip-
tion, especially dressed as he was in the brown leather vest
and hickory nut shirt. Aye, brown and lean and dangerous.

The shotgun in the scabbard reinforced the aura of danger about him that seemed to crackle like lethal lightning.

Behind the three, Maggie wrestled with her fear of her horse. She should have admitted that she had been astride only two or three times in her life, and then on the family's old plow horse. But pride had buttoned her lips. She rode stiffly, sitting like a tailor's mannequin on the roman-nosed chestnut, who decided to crow-hop its way through the outing. Her lids closed in utter misery as the recalcitrant chestnut bounded up a rocky ravine like some mule deer. Sweet Mary, it wasn't even midmorning and her duff was already raw.

Celina had had the idea of having the cook pack a lunch to eat at a place known as the seep, for the oil that slowly bubbled, forming a black pool about the site. And a sigh of relief that was more like a grunt went up from Maggie when Wolf called out, "The seep is just ahead." He seemed as bored by the outing as she was.

There was not a tree in sight to offer shade, but about three-quarters of the inky pool was an outcropping of limestone that threw some shadows for relief. It was here that Wolf led them, instructing his "tenderfeet," as she knew he must think of her and Frank, to toss their reins over the horses' heads so their mounts would not wander. Gingerly, she dismounted, both wary of the enormous horse and miserably sore.

Celina, however, seemed to be enjoying the outing immensely. She spread a saddle blanket on a smooth portion of rock that bordered the seep and with Frank's help began laying out the crusty bread, cheese, and cold slices of barbecued lamb left over from the night before. There was even a *bota* bag of red wine that had escaped the long arm of the government's prohibition agents. Several times something Frank said brought Celina's laughter that sounded like the musical sheep's bells.

Wolf chose a rock to settle back against and lit up a

cigarette. Maggie envied his lithe relaxation. But since sitting was now an impossibility for her sensitive buttocks, she remained standing where the horses grazed on the clumps of sacaton that broke through the rocky crevices—far enough away from Wolf's disturbing presence that she felt she could draw an unfettered breath.

She lit a cigarette and, smiling grimly to herself, watched the interplay between Frank and Celina. Frank was feeding his masculine ego on Celina's attentions, and in turn Celina was playing Frank off against Wolf. Were Celina and Wolf having an affair? The image of his naked body stretched out in a bed both fascinated and repelled her.

She cast a glance at him to see how he was taking the scene, but he seemed more intent on studying the darkening horizon where the clouds boiled. Good; if it rained, they could return to the ranch. Regrettably, rain didn't look at all imminent, and when all the food was laid out, she moved to join the others.

It was then the chestnut chose to show its affection, coming forward to nudge her. Without thinking, Maggie backed away—right off the rock and into the oil sludge. The sticky black substance was less than two feet deep, but enough to coat her from head to foot. She struggled to rise, her clothes weighted by the thick, miry oil, and only floundered about like a fish out of water.

The ignominy was too much, especially when she heard Wolf's outrageous laughter. "Do something!" she gritted at Frank, who stood with his mouth open in shock. Beside him Celina's surprised expression faded as a small grin of satisfaction curled her lips. "You look like *una negra,* señora."

Frank looked down at his dapper riding clothes and held out his hands, palms up, in a helpless gesture. Maggie rolled her eyes heavenwards. Agony of agonies. From the corner of her eyes she saw Wolf mount his horse and ride toward her. Then she was abruptly hauled up and tossed in front of him like she were a stray lamb he was rescuing. She thrashed about in an attempt to right herself. "What—just what—"

His chuckle, followed by a light whack of the palm across her squirming bottom, left her speechless. "I'm taking her over to the Sunk Hole, Celina. We should be back within half an hour."

Each lope of the great gray whooshed the breath from her chest and jostled the eyeglasses on her nose. When the horse scrambled up a rocky hillside, the glasses slid off. With a sickening cringe, Maggie heard next the crunch of glass. "Oh—dear—God—my—glasses!" she yelled out at each rib-bruising jounce.

"You never needed those damned glasses anyway, Maggie," Wolf laughed.

The horse's flanks, coated now with the oil that had dripped from her, steamed with the rank smell. Maggie felt absolutely as loathsome as a leper. Humiliation shriveled her insides. Oh, God! What could be worse?

Then she knew. Wolf reined in and dismounted. She lifted her head, which had bobbled like a broken doll's during the fifteen-minute ride, to see where they were, and then felt herself dragged from the back of the horse and unceremoniously dropped. Before she could cry out, hot water flooded over her. It filled her mouth, and she sputtered and coughed. Hands beneath her armpits roughly pulled her to the surface.

"Oh, please," she strangled out as Wolf knelt over her. There was a twitching of his lips. She wanted to throttle the amusement out of him but, gasping, submitted to lying weakly against his arm, half in, half out of the water, while he scoured her face and hair with grit and water.

"It seems like it's my destiny to haul you in and out of pools and creeks." He grunted and added, "It seems like my destiny is involved with you, period."

"I'll never let"—she choked as water sloshed in her

mouth—"let myself believe that I'm a victim of destiny, or a pawn of—"

She gagged again, and he said, "Good God, Maggie, do you ever shut up? *You* should be campaigning, not Frank. But in essence, you are," he said bitterly, "aren't you?" He did not wait for her answer but scrubbed her scalp more vigorously, as if he wished to punish her.

"Oowww!"

He ignored her yelps, but after a while his hands relented and eased up somewhat on their abrasive administrations. Gradually the hot, mineral-laden water diluted a little of the tension from Maggie. From under languishing lids she perceived she was in some sort of thermal springs whose perimeter was terraced with pastel-hued limestone. The slopes beyond were dotted with quaking aspen that were already gold with autumn's approach.

Her eyes raised to study Wolf's face while he worked. From that close range she could see that his skin had been baked browner by the sun since their last meeting and that tiny weather wrinkles now fanned out from his eyes. It was a hard, virile face that spoke of independence and self-sufficiency; yet he was no less handsome than Frank with his boyish good looks.

His gaze dropped to the sodden pants. "Must you always flout convention, Maggie?"

"Men aren't the only two-legged creatures!" she snapped.

His finger grasped the top button of her shirt. Her gaze flew upwards to meet his, and the now familiar electrical current lightninged through her. Her body jerked with the volatile impact, and he growled. "Do you want to rinse out these oily clothes or not?"

Her hands shot up to lock over his deftly moving fingers. "No!"

His hand halted, and he cocked a brow. She mistook the look on his face for one of puzzlement and hastened to explain. "I—I can do it, wash my clothes. But, go away. Somewhere."

His eyes studied her expression, searching for what she did not know. She only knew the heat of his hand in the valley of her breasts burned through her shirt, surely leaving its searing imprint on her skin. "Please," she breathed.

He rose then and moved away. She waited until he disappeared beyond the limestone terraces before she felt safe enough to begin removing her shirt. She turned her back to the rock-crusted banks while she knelt to wash out her shirt. Her breeches were more stained than actually soaked with the oil, and there seemed little to be done without the benefit of soap.

Imperceptibly she became aware of a shadow moving over her and across the water's surface. Fearing Wolf had returned, she twisted her head upward, merely to find that the sky was rapidly blackening with clouds. She rose, and buffeted by the surging wind, tried to slip into the shirt. But as her fingers began to work at the flapping buttonholes, she was suddenly caught from behind. "Come on," Wolf said, dragging her up the embankment with him. "The storm's coming."

"I'm wet anyway!" she protested.

He ignored her, and she was pulled along behind him, her feet sloshing in the wet boots. Then, as the first icy lumps began to pelt her, she realized the reason for Wolf's concern. A hailstorm in the middle of August! The crazy thought struck her that she'd like to see Celina's fancy umbrella now.

A large hailstone slammed into the middle of her back, and she staggered. Instantly Wolf's arms swooped her legs from the ground. His head and shoulders hunched protectively over her, he carried her toward the stand of aspen. Beneath the sheltering branches he collapsed against a trunk with her still cradled in his arms. She could hear him panting and knew that, weighted by the water-soaked clothing, she was no light load. But then he should be used to that by now, she thought spitefully.

All about them the wind whistled and the hail thudded. It echoed the thudding of Wolf's heart against her cheek. Isolated by the wrath of nature's elements, they were united. For those eternal moments the natural fear of the raging storm overrode her fear of the man who held her. Unwittingly she snuggled closer against the broad chest. She felt his arms tighten about her. His head lowered nearer to hers, and his lips brushed at her forehead.

She stirred, but he lodged her close against him so that her legs lay imprisoned across his lap. When his left hand slid up her bare rib cage to cup one unfettered breast, she gasped. She tried to pull her shirt together, and his hand caught hers. This time it was he who whispered, "No."

Compelled by the intensity in his gaze, her hands halted, and she allowed his fingers to continue their exploration. Her breath exhaled in jagged rasps when his fingers found the taut nipple and began his mastery of her. Her gaze clung to his, as if clinging to a life preserver in the midst of a storm-tossed sea. The fingers that caressed and stroked her breast, cruising over the skin with gentle patience, were irreconcilable to Wolf's previously rough behavior toward her, but it was a difference she was unable to fathom in the languor that slowly took control of her.

A splendid heat radiated from the lower portion of her stomach throughout her quivering body, warming it, sensitizing it to an exquisite pitch. Unable to assert any semblance of self-control, she felt her lids close and her arms and legs relax in complete abandon. Wolf's lips brushed the pulse beating at her temple, his breath fanning her hair. "Love," he whispered against her parted lips, "I have been waiting for you for a long, long time."

"Wolf," she murmured. "It's been so lonely, the waiting."

The hand that slipped down to the buttons of her pants wakened her from the sensual lethargy Wolf had cast over her like an entrapping net. With an effort her lids opened, to focus on the eyes that burned with a fierce domination.

In that terrible moment she knew that when two powerful wills such as theirs collided, one had to subjugate or destroy the other.

CHAPTER
twenty-three

*Like two lovers coming together after a long-awaited tryst: God help him, that's the only way he could think of that afternoon. Yet when Maggie pulled away, she had been as cool, as cold as the ice that fell around them.

Wolf closed his eyes against the fire's blazing light and remembered once more the proud tilt of her chin, the gray-green eyes, narrowed to hard slits, looking like wintery seas. The wet strands of hair had escaped the sedate coil to cling to her cheekbones and graceful neck. He heard again her harsh words untempered by the Irish brogue. "Find another prey, Wolf. It's no man who will be having me."

He had grabbed her arms then, his fingers brutally digging into their slender softness. "Frank has you! His money bought you!"

She shook her head slowly. "No, not even Frank has me."

For one brief second he thought he saw a vulnerability darken those haunting eyes, but whatever he did see quickly vanished when she rose from him. Her wet shirt clung like a second skin to her heaving breasts, revealing the straining nipples. "The storm is over. Take me back."

The storm was not over; it still raged inside him. The thought of Maggie, who should have been his since . . . since that first spark of time, though some quirk of fate had missed uniting them. The thought of her with another man, spread naked below a lust-filled face, was enough to drive him crazy.

He tried to tell himself that it wasn't Maggie who had the power to make him crazy-wild those long November nights. It was the constant and pervasive danger that faced any sheepherder in a remote camp, a loneliness so extreme and oppressive in that great Western expanse, along with a thousand sheep and a couple of dogs for months on end. Not a few sheepherders had gone mad.

Yet it was the opportunity to be alone that had made him decide to spell old Manuel for a few weeks while the shepherd recuperated from a broken ankle. Wolf wanted to sort out his thoughts.

The frigid mountain wind chilled his bones, and he cursed himself for not wrapping burlap bags about his legs against the cold. He pulled the sheepskin coat tighter about him. At his sudden movement the sheep dog at his feet lifted her head. Somewhere out in the wild darkness beyond the fire's yellow light a coyote yipped. The dog's ears pricked, and he scratched her head reassuringly.

He wished he could as easily reassure himself. He knew he had been avoiding making a commitment in life. Even his marriage to Maude had been less a commitment than a whim of the moment. Someday he would have to settle down. The house he was building in the Wyoming wilderness that he loved so much was well under way. But it needed a woman to make it a home. "A home." He had never really had one.

He thought of Celina, and knew she would make as good a wife as any. Below the provocative, exotic surface, he sensed no great depths, which curiously attracted him. No involvement would be demanded of him. He knew he could come to care for her. But to care deeply, to love with a total commitment . . .

"A stroke of genius on your part!" Frank praised. "Without your charming conversation with Benito Bilbao that last evening at La Conquista, we couldn't have swung the vote in our favor."

He rose from his chair and held aloft his cup in toast to his wife. The friends who had gathered in the Big Horn Restaurant's banquet room to cheer Frank's election followed suit.

Maggie could not recall that evening last August with as much enthusiasm as Frank. She remembered returning from the ride that afternoon with a determination to win Benito's support and leave as soon as possible.

Over the glasses of burgundy that Benito served the four drowned picnickers, she watched and listened to Frank and their host. She avoided glancing at Wolf, who stood by the fireplace with a seemingly detached look in those amber eyes. Sometimes Jose contributed to the light talk; Celina seemed bored by it all.

But Maggie waited. "You are, of course, a very educated man, Mr. Van der Rhys," Benito said bluntly when Frank turned the conversation to politics. "Far more than me. But I have no reason to suspect you will be any more effective in the senate than other Anglo politicians have been."

"My opponent is a cattleman, Mr. Bilbao," Frank said, stressing "cattle," and bestowing a diplomatic smile on both Benito and his father, "while I would strive to be impartial."

It was not enough to sway the man. Maggie knew it. She refused to appeal to him with the female's outmoded weapons: subterfuge, chicanery, hypocrisy, flattery, sexual charm. Her strategy was more direct. For the first time she spoke, quietly but firmly. "On the other hand, Mr. Bilbao,

I am of Irish Catholic heritage and would be very partial, since the majority of the people in the county are Catholic."

Certain aspects of her Catholic heritage, especially the doctrine that proclaimed the man the undisputed head of the family, she resented. Yet she nostalgically recalled that it was the Catholic Church and Father Patrick, more specifically, that had instilled in her the desire for knowledge. She owed the Church some allegiance.

She felt the weight of Wolf's eyes, but kept her steady gaze trained on Benito. His father said something rapidly to him in Basque, and the son nodded. Celina's eyes widened. Maggie did not know what was said in the exchange, but Benito did give his benediction to Frank's campaign a few moments later.

And she was able to leave with Frank early the next morning without having to encounter Wolf again.

"Here's to our new Tax Assessor," Orville Weidemeyer said, raising his glass in another toast. He looked at Maggie and winked conspiratorially.

Tin horns tooted, and the people pushed back their chairs to form a victory snake dance about the room, which was decorated in a western motif with wagon wheels and branding irons. Frank, dressed casually in floppy white trousers called oxford bags, latched onto a dishwater blonde's waist. A young redheaded man in saddle shoes approached Maggie. "Would you like to join in?"

"No, thank you," she smiled. Slowly she drank the punch. She wished it were champagne or, better yet, vodka. It would take something strong to dilute the thoughts that plagued both her daydreams and her nightmares.

CHAPTER
twenty-four
❧ ❦ ❧

Spring was the busiest time of the year, for sheep and herder alike. April was lambing time, and when lambing began, Wolf's work swallowed the whole twenty-four-hour day. Celina was petulant. "You never have the time for me!" became the nightly cry.

Wolf tossed his Stetson on the halltree and headed down the hall toward the bedroom. Benito stepped out of the office. "Wolf, have a drink?"

Wolf glanced toward the closed door. He was too tired to face his wife. The offer of the drink sounded pretty good, especially considering that he had had no dinner. He nodded and followed Benito into the office. The man crossed to the desk and took out a bottle from his secret cache of liquor and glasses. "I'd say whiskey is more in order than wine this time of night," his father-in-law said, pouring a generous amount in each glass.

Wolf took the glass, saying, "A watering hole on the desert couldn't be more welcome right now." He slouched down on the horsehide couch and tossed off half the glass. His eyes closed as the fiery stuff burned its way down.

Benito watched the young man. He had been tremendously upset when Celina had told him she was going to marry Wolf. Wolf was not of the Catholic faith, much less of hispanic heritage. But ultimately he had welcomed Wolf as a son-in-law because he recognized the young man's strength of drive and felt he would make a contribution to La Conquista's ranch operations.

He had been right, of course. Wolf put in far more hours than he himself did. The Basque's eyes narrowed, wondering if there were another reason for the way his son-in-law drove himself. The couple had been married almost a year and a half now, and though his daughter was carrying Wolf's child, she showed no signs of delight over her impending motherhood. She no longer laughed and teased as she used to.

"The last of the sheep sheared?" he asked the young man.

Wolf nodded. "And the pregnant ewes have all been herded into the corral." He thought of the ewes, their bodies, naked of wool, looking awkward and swollen, until the time came to drop their lambs. And he thought of Celina's own swollen body. The fact that she had put on so much weight so rapidly concerned him for her health.

He finished the drink and came to his feet with a graceful movement unexpected in a man with such height. "Tomorrow I'm moving the ewes with lambs into the mixing pens."

"Why don't you take off for a few days. Diego can handle things while you and Celina get away. Maybe take her out to your house and work on it. Celina can help you finish out some of the inside, doing little things."

Wolf knew what Benito was thinking, that perhaps living with an in-law accounted for the strained relationship between the husband and wife, that things would get better if they moved away from La Conquista. How could he tell Benito that the house he was building with his own hands was a special place that he didn't want to . . . oh, hell, he couldn't even explain it to himself.

"Too much going on right now," he told Benito.

Benito had sensed something of Wolf's uncompromising character, so evident in the thrust of the jaw, and he didn't force the issue, saying only, "You're as stubborn as a Basque, Wolf Nicholson."

Celina was a dark lump on the brass bed. Wolf didn't bother to light the kerosene lamp. He would be glad when Benito applied for the Rural Electrification System. In the darkness he stripped to the nude and slid into the bed, too tired to bathe.

Celina shifted on the lumpy wool mattress and turned to him. "Why have you not come to bed sooner?" she whispered. "I have been freezing without you to warm me." She slipped one cold foot up between his calves.

He knew what she wanted. Her need for sex was insatiable, as he had discovered shortly after their marriage . . . just as he had discovered she was not a virgin. But her lovemaking since she conceived was aggressive to the point that after a while he found himself losing interest.

When he made no movement toward her, her hand glazed the hard ridge of his thigh beneath the quilt and after a second brushed upward to lightly cup one testicle. "You are heavy with the need for release," she breathed into his ear.

He slid his arm under her shoulder and pulled her to him, kissing her on the temple. "And my lids are heavy with the need for sleep, *amado*."

She pushed at him, her nails raking a path through the hair on his chest. "You do not find me beautiful anymore!" she hissed. "That's it, is it not? I let you plant your seed in me like some rutting ram, but when I grow large with your child, you do not want me!"

He closed his eyes. Her ponderous body was not as enticing as it had once been, but he knew that if he really loved her, it would make no difference. And he knew that for the same reason her desire for sex had increased, that she sought his reassurance of her former beauty through their lovemaking.

He lowered his lips to her eager mouth, while his hand embraced the heavy breast that sagged unflatteringly with milk. Celina rolled from him to spread her legs wide. "Now, Wolf!" she urged. "Do not wait!"

He moved up over her then, burying himself between her undulating, ample thighs. But his thoughts were of a small, slender child-woman whose cool green eyes burned him as Celina's touch never could. As if sensing his errant thoughts, Celina sunk her teeth savagely into his shoulder. "You smell like a sheep!" she snapped, but her fingers ground into the muscular hips to draw him deeper into her.

Maggie folded the May 23, 1922, edition of the *Wyoming State Tribune*'s front page and passed it across the breakfast table to her husband. He glanced up impatiently from the sports column, "Billy Evans Says," that announced Dempsey had triumphed in the twelfth round. "What is it?"

She knew he had lost fifty on Harry Greb and wasn't in the best of tempers that morning. "Look at the second column, Frank," she said gently. "Demming has decided not to run for another term in the senate next year."

"So?"

"Why don't you announce your candidacy on the Republican ticket."

"For state senator?" he asked incredulously.

She leaned forward. "Frank, you could win. I just know it. You're good at mixing with people, from the grass roots level to high society. With your charm, you could convince the people of Wyoming's Red Desert to buy the Brooklyn Bridge. And with your education to back you, you'd be a natural politician."

"Why would I want to be a senator?"

More than once in the last few days she had asked herself

another question: why *was* she nudging Frank into the political arena? And she knew the answer went further back than old man Weidemeyer's blatant insinuation that women had no place in politics.

"You don't want to be hidden is some backwater town like Buffalo for the rest of your life, do you, darling?" she asked persuasively. She certainly did not. As much as she loved Buffalo, she wanted to run as far as possible from this small town—and from Wolf Nicholson. Just knowing he was so near made her constantly uneasy. Every time she stepped out onto Buffalo's Main Street, she expected to see that diabolical face.

She laid her hand over his. "If you run for senator, you could spend more time in Cheyenne. And you know how much more cosmopolitan the capital is than Buffalo," she added, calculating that the lure of a big city like Cheyenne would appeal to her husband.

Still he resisted. "It'd mean just twice as much work. And you know how I would hate being bothered with writing speeches and keeping up on the issues."

"I could write your speeches. And I enjoy reading the capitol's daily reports anyway." It was true, she liked knowing about the decisions—all made by men—that affected her life and the others in the state.

"Aww, Maggie, are you sure this is such a good—"

She used her last ploy.

"Besides, this time we *will* be able to use the additional money. 'Tis a baby we'll be having, darling."

The joyous expression she had hoped for did not appear. She should have known better than to expect excitement from him. But then she had refused to analyze her own sense of doom, as if her pregnancy were a capitulation of all achievement for her equality.

"When?" he demanded after a long moment of silence.

"The last of November."

He ran his hand through his hair. "Maggie, right now

we don't need a child. It'll only hold us back, especially if you plan for us to campaign for the senate office."

She withdrew her hand. "'Tis—'tis glad I'd have thought you would be," she whispered, wounded.

He caught her arm as she made to move away. "Can't you find some way to get rid of it? We can always have another one. But not now, Maggie. We don't need a child to hang on to us now."

Fury boiled in her like an erupting volcano. Her hands balled into fists. "You should be pleased. Now you can travel and campaign without me—and have all those affairs that you couldn't when I was with you."

"I never—"

"Don't be lying to me, Frank. No longer am I the naive immigrant you married."

He wadded up the newspaper and hurled it at the faded papered wall. "Asked? I was forced!"

Slowly Maggie rose. Her chin came up, and her eyes narrowed to slits. To Frank she looked like some Celtic warrioress. Something inside him thrilled to her fierceness and her implicit strength. His arm encircled her waist and pulled her to him. His voice was low, cajoling. "Maggie, Maggie, those women meant nothing. I swear there won't be any more flings. And we'll even have the child, if you really want to."

She knew he was using her as a mother substitute. Yet, could she condemn him? Had she not used him both as a vent for her rage and as a means of escape from poverty? She had even been less than honest, telling herself that she married him because she felt she could help him.

Perhaps she could still help him, help their marriage. With a child of his own, perhaps Frank would be more ready to settle down to responsibility. Perhaps she would be more fulfilled, so that she would—should—need nothing else, so that the restlessness that drove her would at last be ended.

She held his head against her breasts and ran her fingers through his wavy hair. "I'll campaign with you, Frank. I'll always be at your side."

As a final appeasement, she held back her shudder of distaste as his hand sought the softness of her breast through the opening of her robe. "Maggie," he murmured, "I need you so."

CHAPTER
twenty-five

*W*olf *stood at the side of the crib. Like the ewe* that commonly has twin lambs, Celina had just given birth to twin boys, a month early. They lay there, two tiny mites wrapped in blue receiving blankets. Their faces held a blue tinge, and the effort to breathe expanded their little ribcages spasmodically.

"There must be something we can do," he muttered, his hands gripping the crib's spooled railing. Celina turned her head to the wall. Never once since Wolf had drawn the babies forth from her womb had she glanced at them, as if she knew they would not survive the ordeal of birth.

The image of Maude, pale on the Indian blanket as her life ebbed away with the blood flowing from her thighs, darkened Wolf's vision. He spun from the crib. "I'm going to Buffalo for the doctor."

Celina looked at him then. Tears shimmered in the coffee-brown eyes. Beneath them, dark circles shadowed the sallow skin. "You waste your effort."

For the first time, he felt really close to her. He perceived the depth he had overlooked, a depth formerly centered on herself and now filled with her private suffering. He crossed to the bed to take the plump hand. It did not respond to the warm pressure of his fingers. "They won't live," she said hollowly. "They weren't conceived in love."

He heard the break in her voice and turned away. How could he refute what she said? Despite the intellectual he had always supposed himself to be, he knew there was another side of him, a darker side that believed in fate, destiny, whatever one chose to call it. And he knew Celina was right. The children were fated to die.

But something in him raged against being a victim of the hand of fate, as Maggie had raged against it. He tore through the house, not even stopping to tell Benito and Jose, who waited in the office, where he was going. Of course, by the time he returned with the doctor, the faint light of life had flickered out of each infant.

"Within minutes of each other the babies died," Jose informed him in a voice heavy with grief. He laid a gnarled, consoling hand on the young man's heaving shoulders.

During the 1880s to 1890s when the Lords—the foreign-born nobility—and the Lordlings—the capitalists from the eastern United States—created a cattle empire in Wyoming, the city of Cheyenne was the richest city of its size in the world.

The houses for the most part were elegant mansions, with stables of fine horses, and the people lived as though Cheyenne were Paris or Boston. The cattle barons and wealthy stockmen, many who commuted between Cheyenne and Europe, even organized the most exclusive club in the West, the Cheyenne Club. Furnished like an English smoking club, it sported fireplaces with carved marble mantles in each room, a dining room that was known throughout the world for its cuisine, billiard room, several card rooms, reading room, wine cellars, lounges on the main floor, and apartments for members and their friends on the second floor.

The cattle empire collapsed after the blizzard of 1886–87, but during the annual Frontier Days, when Cheyenne staged the "Daddy of 'em All," the largest and richest rodeo extravaganza in the world, the essence of the Old West captured the city. The Cheyenne Club was called the Industrial Club now, but during Frontier Days, the last week in July, the cowboys' spurs still jingled as they walked across the club's wooden veranda that ran on the building's south and east sides, and the women still guided their children to the far side of seventeenth street to avoid the fisticuffs that occasionally broke out.

That particular July afternoon of 1923, Wolf threaded his way through the dining tables that dotted the veranda. Men in three-piece business suits enjoyed dinner alongside cowboys in chaps and Stetsons. Wolf conceded to meeting the variety of fashion halfway, and wore a smoke-gray suit of broadcloth and hand-cobbled boots of old Manuel's best leather.

Unlike most of the men there, who were a part of that human tide that flooded Cheyenne that week, he had not come for the rodeo. He had hauled La Conquista's fatter lambs, packed into the World War surplus truck that he had convinced Benito to purchase, to the market to be auctioned.

He had hoped to convince Celina to accompany him. The festivities that went on during Frontier Week would have cheered them both. More than a year had passed since she had given birth to the twins, but their deaths seemed to have erected a wall between him and Celina. She had lost a great deal of the weight that pregnancy had added, though she was now larger in the hips and breasts. Yet the generous curves were voluptuous in a sensual way. He entertained hopes that he could yet salvage something of their marriage.

For a brief moment he had glimpsed the excitement in

her eyes when he asked her to come with him. Then her lids dropped, and she murmured, "No, I think I would rather stay here."

He had left for Cheyenne with a bewildered mind. Before, Celina would have been delighted to even ride into the raw boomtown of Salt Creek; now this reluctance on her part, which was so unlike her. He puzzled over it as he took a seat near the veranda's railing.

The waiter came, and he ordered coffee. The rodeo would begin in another hour, and already firecrackers were exploding down at the Frontier Park grounds where twenty thousand people were gathered to watch the parade of clowns, covered wagons, mounted soldiers from nearby Fort D.A. Russell, beauty queens, and the Sioux who came in from the Dakota Indian Reservation to dance.

Wolf listened to the clang of the streetcar bells that overrode the raucous conversations going on about him while he finished the remainder of his coffee. He thought he'd take in the rodeo that afternoon before returning to La Conquista. A man wearing a smart straw hat rose from the table nearest the window and said something to the other four men at the table. Preoccupied, Wolf watched the man with only a passing interest. When the man paused before him, he realized the man was Frank Van der Rhys, who was now no less than a state senator. Wolf recalled that word was out the man was being considered by his party for Secretary of State in the next election year.

"Wolf Nicholson!" Frank said, extending his hand. "What a surprise."

Wolf knew better than to be surprised at anything anymore.

"How about joining the rest of us for a cup of coffee," Frank continued with a congeniality that curiously—or maybe not so curiously—had been missing upon Wolf's return with Maggie after that hailstorm almost three years before.

Apparently, Wolf deduced with an inner grimace, Frank knew about his marriage to Celina. No doubt with the elections coming up, the man hoped to capitalize on the power he, as Bilbao's son-in-law, now carried. "Thanks, Van der Rhys, but I'm on my way over to the rodeo."

Frank was not to be deterred. "Great! You can join Maggie and me and some of the others in our box."

Wolf drew a deep breath. He knew the terrible chance he was taking, just when he was getting her out of his mind again after going all those years without seeing her. But the urge was too great. "All right."

Shouting, cheering adults and children already packed the grandstand by the time he and Frank arrived in Frank's Niagra blue Lincoln convertible. A fine dust churned up by bucking broncs and charging bulls filtered over the lower rows of bleachers. Higher up sat the boxes reserved for dignitaries; it was there that Frank led him. But even with the press of people Wolf felt like a homing pigeon making its way toward a destination on instinct alone. The nearer he drew to those boxes, the sharper were his senses. The hair prickled on the back of his neck like the hackles on a wolf who has sensed danger.

Maggie's head turned at his approach, and behind the lenses her liquid green eyes widened in stark surprise. The damned glasses didn't hide her fey beauty, but she wore a new aura of sophistication—like a cloak of protection, he thought. Though he had yet to know her in the intimate way a husband knows a wife, he felt he knew her as no other man would. And yet he didn't know her at all, did he?

Apparently Frank was doing well as a state representative, for with the straw broadbrim hat she wore an expensive-looking white linen suit. Or maybe the way she carried herself just made the clothes she wore look expensive. That day he had noted so many of the Cheyenne women had bobbed their hair or frizzed it with the Marcel, yet she nevertheless had kept her hair sleekly swept back into a sedate coil at the nape of her neck. What would it be like to bury his face in that long, wildly curling hair?

"Maggie, you remember Wolf Nicholson?" Frank said.

Wolf watched her face assume a controlled politeness. "Of course," she said. He took her outstretched gloved hand, and felt the sudden tremor at his touch. Or was it his own hand that had jumped with something akin to static electricity?

She quickly withdrew her hand, and Frank went on to introduce him to the other couples in the nearby boxes, some whose names he recognized as holders of state offices—the state auditor, a director for the Health and Social Services, the Land Commissioner. He found himself wedged between Maggie and a pert-looking brunette who was introduced as Barbara, the wife of Jim Whatley, a local attorney.

Everyone's attention turned to the arena, where a cowboy sat astride a gargantuan cream-colored bull penned in a chute. "Powder River, let 'er buck!" the cowboy yelled, using the battle cry adopted by American soldiers in the World War. The bull raged out of the chute. After mere seconds, the unlucky cowboy astride the bull was catapulted off like a stone out of a slingshot. The cowboy began to scramble out of the way of the flashing hooves, and the spectators surged to their feet with drawn breaths—all but Maggie and Wolf.

He ran a deliberate eye over her and felt some perverse pleasure at the crimson that slowly blotched her throat and cheeks. "What happened to your men's pants? Or is that style out of keeping with your position now that Frank may be up for the Secretary of State nomination?

"I heard you married Celina Bilbao," she countered. The cowboy safely over the fence, the spectators settled back onto the wooden benches, and there was no time for further exchange of words between the two of them.

Barbara turned to him then with friendly eyes that ran

up and down the length of him. "You look tough enough to be out there riding one of those beasts," she said with just the mildest hint of laughter.

He smiled blandly. "I'm afraid, ma'am," he said with a purposely inflected southern drawl, "that I'm no cowboy, just an ol' sheepherder."

Barbara grinned. But her eyes glanced curiously at Maggie's flushed face, as if she sensed something between her Irish friend and the tall, good-looking man.

Maggie studiously ignored him for the rest of the rodeo, but he knew she was as intensely aware of him as he was of her. He had been foolish to accept Frank's invitation. The sight of Maggie had only stirred up the old longings. He was determined to return to the Plains Hotel as soon as the rodeo ended. But he changed his mind at the sight of Maggie's sudden stiffening when Frank pressed him to attend a private party being given at the home they kept when in Cheyenne. Something of the old recklessness caught fire in Wolf. His gaze met Maggie's with a challenging flash as he assented to Frank's invitation.

Their home, a three-storied red-brick mansion, elbowed for room among the other palatial buildings that lined Seventeenth Street, which was known as Cattle Barons' Row. The hardwood floors inlaid in intricate patterns, the elaborate ceilings, the stained-glass windows—Wolf had seen such pretentious estates in St. Petersburg, and was not impressed. He recognized Frank's hand in the acquisition.

But the other touches, the warm ones—the lone wood carving of a shepherd boy on the fireplace's marbled mantle, the muted deep blue drapery that set off the soft brown of the Empire furniture, the lack of the Victorian bric-a-brac that usually cluttered such rooms: Maggie's hand was evident in the interior's decor.

"We hired the orchestra up from Denver," Frank said, gesturing to the musicians who softly played from the stairwell behind large palm plants.

A maid served citrus punch and coffee from the buffet, but Wolf noted that a few of the men casually spiked their beverages with liquor poured from hip flasks. A simpering blonde cornered Frank. "There you are, Mr. Van der Rhys! You must meet my sister, who's in from Dallas."

Frank raised his eyes heavenward and flashed Wolf a roguish grin as he allowed himself to be dragged off in another direction. Wolf's gaze flickered to Maggie, who was giving instructions to the maid. Was she oblivious to Frank's philandering charm? Or was she just immune by now? Wolf remembered the stories of the number of maids Frank had seduced. But not Maggie. She had been too smart for Frank.

An older woman with powder-creased wrinkles, whom Wolf recalled being introduced as the Land Commissioner's wife, approached him now with a flirtatious smile. Where the hell was the woman's husband? Wolf tried to politely answer her questions, but he was only aware of Maggie. No, he had not seen Clara Bow's latest film. Who in the devil was Clara Bow? Oh, the "It" girl.

Even as the woman continued chattering, he watched Maggie finish speaking with the maid and turn to survey the room with a hostess's critical eye. "Excuse me," he told the Land Commissioner's wife and strode off toward Maggie.

Her shoulders straightened imperceptibly, her chin lifted. He knew then she was aware of him shouldering through the milling guests to her. Their gazes collided, and their energy charged the room. "Lo! Behold, the shepherd cometh!" she said to him in a quiet, sarcastic voice.

He matched her mockery. "Not this time, but one day you'll know when I do come." His crudity was rewarded by the sudden blaze behind her veiled eyes.

"Has Frank introduced you to everyone?" she asked coolly, disdaining his remark. "The distinguished old gentleman over there is Senator Kitteridge. He's back from

Washington to look after his fences, political and otherwise. "John," she called, and Wolf knew she was summoning a defense.

She made the introductions, and Wolf shook the man's hand, saying, "I read that President Harding has appointed you to a Senate investigation committee."

Kitteridge seemed to flinch. "The Naval Reserve thing at the Teapot Dome? Wyoming has nothing to fear from any scandal."

"But John," Maggie said, "the committee did find that the Department of the Interior leased out the Teapot Dome area to Sinclair Oil without competitive bids."

Her soft County Kildare voice acted as a benediction on Wolf's weary mind. She withdrew a cigarette package from her skirt pocket, and he lit the cigarette for her, watching her lips part as she exhaled. He found himself barely listening to Kitteridge's long-winded explanation. He studied Maggie. Behind her intelligence, behind her political rhetoric, was hidden the real woman, the woman he wanted to know.

He realized he was treading on dangerous ground. And his thoughts were not conducive to reestablishing an intimate relationship with his wife. He thanked Maggie for the evening, noting with an irrepressible grin of amusement her relief.

Instead of returning to the hotel, he drove all night back to La Conquista and Celina's surprisingly welcoming arms. The trip had at least accomplished something.

CHAPTER
twenty-six

T*he drapery of glass beads, glittering like gems* under the artfully tinted light of the Making Whoopee stage, was a prophetic symbol of the new era—the era of peace, prosperity, and prohibition.

The great World War was over, prosperity was registered by the unprecedented bull market at the Stock Exchange, and Prohibition was signaled in the defiant revolt of the younger generation, or at least so said the myriad newspapers that Maggie weekly scanned. It was a decade that would be remembered for its unrestrained hedonism, and to Maggie, 1925 seemed the epitome.

On the stage a young woman in unfastened galoshes, her flesh-colored stockings rolled below her knees, and her skirt barely covering them, leaned against the baby grand piano and belted out "I'll Say She Does," then launched right into "Running Wild."

When the singer began to dance the Black Bottom shimmy, the audience clapped in time to the syncopated music. Later that evening marathon dancing, a new craze that was sweeping the country, was scheduled. Maggie sat back in the booth, her gaze running over the people in the speakeasy, which was a rowdy roadhouse on the outskirts of Cheyenne.

The women she studied wore their shingled hair peroxided or hennaed, their eyebrows plucked and penciled, and their cheeks and lips piquantly rouged. Except for the raccoon coats draped over the backs of their chairs, the sum of what they wore could almost have been packed into their handbags.

In contrast, Maggie's starched white shirtwaist and severely tailored black wool knit suit and jacket appeared quite businesslike and was tempered only by the sensuous line of her lips and the obvious curve of high, ripe breasts. She had made one compromise in her dress code over the years, giving up trousers for the sake of Frank's career. She had come to realize that not all people accepted her eccentricity about trousers so lightly.

She thought of her friend Vera in Greenwich Village. Now that the women had finally been given the right to vote, which was more a result of their entrance into male-dominated labor markets due to the World War rather than as a result of their protests and demonstrations, Vera and her suffragettes had achieved the liberation of the female. But for this inanity? Maggie wondered, watching the women about her, some reeling in their chairs with sloshing glasses of gin or scotch and others half-sprawled across tables in drunken stupor.

It was Maggie's first time in a speakeasy. Only Barbara Whatley and her husband Jim, whose gregarious smile was pinched, looked as uneasy as Maggie felt. In the roadhouse's dim interior she finally located Frank, who had excused himself from their party a few minutes before to talk to some friends he had spotted. For a change the "friends" were not female, but their identity made her just that much more uneasy.

In that giddy, glittering era of night clubs and speakeasies, which pedants insisted should be called "speak easilys," no one had foreseen the rise of a new plutocracy dominated by bootleggers, gangsters, and racketeers. And Maggie was certain the men Frank was talking to were in that unsavory category.

She stubbed out her cigarette with an impatient gesture. She had sworn off the cigarettes more than three years ago when she knew she was going to have a child. She remembered the sense of panic when her stomach started to get larger, a sense of doom. Analyzing the feeling, she realized the pregnancy had stamped her irrevocably as a woman, the very thing of which she had always been afraid. Women were victims. Women were destroyed.

Then everything changed. As the baby started to move, she became fascinated by her pregnancy. She felt a tremendous bond with the subterranean forces of womanhood. But shortly thereafter, she lost the child. A doctor in Cheyenne told her the miscarriage had been brought on by the rigorous campaigning she had participated in with Frank. Whatever the reason, she had resumed the vile habit of smoking.

She really did not like smoking that much; yet she found that when Frank's constituents and co-workers called upon her for her opinion, the pause to inhale gave her more time to formulate a sensible, intelligent answer. It was a small ploy, part of a style that was rapidly bringing more and more intellectuals, artists, writers, politicians to both her home in Buffalo and the Cheyenne one on Seventeenth Street. She thought with a wry smile that she was being cast into the role of a courtesan, a Madame Pompadour who influenced the affairs of the state. A madame: Wolf would love that!

She shook off the unwelcome thought. There were other things that needed her attention more than raking up unwanted memories, things like Frank's cohorts at the far table.

She waited until after they left the Making Whoopee roadhouse and were driving home to broach the subject of the three men he had talked with earlier.

"'Tis bad enough that we attended such a place," she said quietly.

"Everyone goes to the speakeasies these days, Maggie. Look, with an attorney and his wife accompanying us, how wrong can it be?"

"That doesn't make it right, Frank. 'Tis still illegal."

"Get off my back, Maggie," he growled. "You have nothing to complain about. I'm making you a better living than you ever knew as a chambermaid."

She laid her head back on the seat and closed her eyes. "All right," she said in a firm voice. "But I'm finished doing your groundwork for you—writing your speeches, reading up on all the bills, keeping up with your social appointments."

She slanted a glance at him to see if her tactic had worked, and was gratified by the worried look he shot her. "Look, Maggie, I need your support for my career." Then he tempered his entreaty. "You're good at entertaining, and talking with both the men and the women."

She realized he was attempting to increase his own importance by demeaning her value in his career. But she also knew that what he said held some truth. She was able to talk with seeming ease to women or men, especially, in the case of the male sex, if the subject were politics. In fact, she had to bite back her answers more often than she liked. A female's visual and vocal involvement in politics too easily incurred male disapproval.

On her advice, Frank had turned down the nomination for Secretary of State. "The office is a nominal one, a lieutenant governor of sorts," she had told him. "I've studied

Wyoming's past Secretary of States, Frank, and none of them went on to become governor."

Frank's blue eyes had widened. "That's what you have in mind for me, the governor's office?"

"Aye." It was what she had had in mind since that first conversation with old man Weidemeyer.

That fall of 1925 the *Wyoming State Tribune*'s society column deemed her the Patroness of Politics. She wanted to become even more involved in politics and less in entertaining. Already she had relinquished control of both her and Frank's personal books and those of his gunsmith store to a public accountant, so she would have more time to assist Frank. He even suggested she hire a woman to actually manage the household affairs.

Immediately she thought of her friend Peg. Perhaps now she could return the favor Peg had done for her and give her the opportunity for a fresh start outside of New York's slums.

It took two weeks for her letter to find Peg, three days for the train fare for Peg and Jamie to reach her, and another two weeks before the two arrived at Cheyenne's Union Station depot. With mounting excitement Maggie waited in the red and gray sandstone Romanesque edifice, pacing the tiled floors, occasionally speaking to acquaintances who passed. She had missed the close friendship of another woman over the years since she and Peg came to America. Barbara was a good friend, but she had not been through the deprivations that sometimes sealed a friendship such as the one between her and Peg.

The woman had changed little—still plump, with outlandishly red hair and engaging freckles. But Jamie at fourteen was as tall as his mother and had the same vivid coloring. Maggie hugged him, and he blushed, lowering his head shyly. "'Tis a man you've grown to be, Jamie O'Connor."

She turned to Peg then, and hugged the woman while

she blinked back the tears of happiness.

"Well, glory be, just look at 'oorself now!" Peg said, standing back to run an admiring gaze over Maggie's elegant attire. "You've done well by 'oorself, Maggie Moran. Maggie Van der Rhys it is, isn't it? Has it really been almost nine years? Just listen to me. I run on like a blithering idiot. Jamie, fetch the bags now, won't 'oo, son."

Maggie laughed, glad to hear Peg's Irish brogue. She linked her arm with the woman's and led her toward the exit. Peg paused under the depot's archway and looked down the long ten-block stretch that terminated in Wyoming's state capitol. The gold-leafed dome on the stately gray sandstone building glistened beneath the October sun. "So that is where 'oor husband be working, Maggie gal?" She looked critically at her friend, noting the thinness. But of course the boyish slimness was the fashion now. And despite her friend's paleness, there was an etheral beauty in the wan complexion. "Does he work so hard that there be no time to make children?"

Maggie blanched at the bluntness. "There was one, almost. But I just . . . don't seem to be able to carry his child."

"You'll be happy here, Peg," she said, not wanting to linger on the question. "Wyoming is so clean and beautiful and spacious. Remember that feeling we had when we first arrived in New York, that all those cement buildings were closing in on us? And the climate is marvelous. Warm, sunny days and cool nights in the summer, and in the winter when it snows, 'tis confectioner-sugar powdery, not slushy like New York's. Even when it's five above zero you won't be noticing the cold, it's so dry in this high altitude—except when the damned wind blows."

She took Peg on a tour of the city, a cow town where still lingered some of the vivid frontier color, the lavish extravagance, the adventure and gaiety of the Old West. Turning off the main thoroughfare, Lincoln Highway, she pointed out Minnehaha Lake to Jamie. "By January it'll be frozen over so you can skate, and in the summer there's boating."

She took them by old Fort D.A. Russell. "Tom Horn, who was a range detective," she told Jamie, "was hanged here some twenty-odd years ago."

"What for?" Jamie asked, his face alight with interest.

She smiled. "For the murder of a sheepman's son." Jamie's black eyes widened when she added that the sheepman's son was about his age.

Peg seemed more interested in the fact that Maggie could actually drive a car. "I had to learn," she laughed. "There were too many trips back and forth to the capitol to be made." When Peg raised a questioning brow, she explained, "I research the issues and bills proposed for Frank."

Peg accepted the statement without comment. But later, after the weeks fell into a routine, when the woman noticed that Frank was absent more than he was present, she asked, "Maggie, are 'oo happy?"

"Aye, Peg," she said slipping into the Irish brogue that she had always worked so hard to lose. Not wanting Peg to see the sudden emptiness she sometimes felt, she turned her attention to her knees, which she was powdering before donning her short skirt. "I enjoy the challenge that Frank's job brings," she added. "And with you to help here at the house, I have more time to devote to helping him."

She told herself that she *was* content, much more so than other women bound to the home by only the drudgery of housework. Her hours were filled so that she rarely had private time to think, to feel. In addition to the political issues she assisted Frank with, she remembered the birthdays of the politicians' families, visited ailing neighbors, and read up on the issues of the day.

So it was with shock that, as her eye glanced over the weekly "Political Patter" column, she saw Wolf's name.

He had announced his candidacy on the Democratic ticket for the state senate. Shaking, she let the newspaper drop to her lap. Dear God, what if he won? He would be invading the citadel she thought she had found in Cheyenne.

Peg, dressed in the plain black dress that slimmed her buxom figure, glanced up from the menu she was preparing. "What is it?" she asked at the sight of Maggie's stricken face.

Maggie blinked and looked over at her friend. Peg rose from the table and came to kneel at Maggie's side. She picked up the newspaper. Her gaze labored over the print. Reading had never come easily for her. She looked back to Maggie, who sat wordlessly. "Is something wrong, Maggie gal?"

"Peg," Maggie began hesitantly. She had never told anyone about the strange hold Wolf had over her. "Do you remember the young Russian on the ship?"

Peg nodded, and Maggie continued. "Our paths have crossed several times over the last ten years. Too many times. Each time I think—I hope—it's the last."

The memory of their last meeting flashed through her mind. It had been the year before at the County Examiner's office. She had come to apply for her citizenship papers. And he was already there. His back was to her, his hand raised as he took the oath of citizenship. But when his deep voice had spoken the last word, he slowly pivoted, his penetrating gaze searching the room for her, as if he knew beyond a doubt she was there. Their gazes locked. Then she turned away and began filling out the necessary papers. Her temples pounded and her mouth turned dry at the fear that he would cross to her, corner her, say something that would force her to acknowledge his presence. But a clerk had signaled that she was next, and she had escaped him— that time.

"There is something about Wolf Nicholson that makes

me uncomfortable," she finished. How could she explain what the man's sheer masculine virility did to her?

"I know it sounds foolish, Peg, but I have the uncanny feeling that, like his namesake, he is tracking me down, running me to the ground."

CHAPTER
twenty-seven

ϾℛℳϾ

He switched off the truck's ignition. Laying his arms atop the steering wheel, he rubbed his forehead against the sleeve of his sheepcoat jacket. He was tired. He had stayed up the entire night in Buffalo's Occidental Hotel, which was the official polling place, waiting for the election results to be tallied.

"Hey, Wolf," Benito hailed from the veranda. "Well? Are you a legislator?"

Wolf swung down from the cab. "Afraid so," he grinned, suddenly feeling much better at the recognition that he had succeeded after months of campaigning.

Benito gave him the traditional *abrazo*, kissing him on each cheek. "Congratulations! How about a drink?"

"How about five?" he countered, following the Basque into the office. He missed Jose's presence. The old man had died the same day Wolf had become a United States citizen, the same day he had last seen Maggie.

Now he knew what was meant by Snow Queen. That day at the County Examiner's office he had wanted to cross to her and pull her to him, to set her on fire as she did him.

But he owed something to Celina, who at least wanted him with a passion of which Maggie was incapable. And he owed something to himself. He had been a lot of things in the short span of his life, but there were certain abstractions he knew he owed to himself to live by. Words like loyalty and integrity. Damned difficult words.

"Take it easy on the wine," Benito joked, passing him a half-filled crystal-lead glass. "Prohibition is slowly consuming our wine cellar." He raised his glass to Wolf. "Here's to Wyoming's best: best politician and best son-in-law."

Wolf acknowledged the toast with a deprecatory smile and took a sip of the wine. He crossed to the leather sofa and sprawled his long body out with a sigh. "Why'd you do it, Wolf?" Benito asked, looping one husky leg across the corner of his desk. "What made you decide to run for an office?"

Wolf slit one lid and eyed his father-in-law. He caught that worried look that he had glimpsed several times before over the seven years he had lived at La Conquista. With a sigh he sat up, leaning forward with his forearms resting on his thighs, his large hands cupping the fragile glass. He looked down into its ruby-red contents.

"Before I came to America, Benito, I was involved in Russia in a political movement. A revolutionary movement, really. It was all that occupied my life, even as a child. My family more than once took part in protest marches." His voice had assumed a harsh, clipped accent; his words halted as the unwanted vision of his mother and sister's sprawled, blood-splattered bodies ringed his memories.

In precise, emotionless words he forced himself to tell Benito of their deaths, of the difficulty he had in giving his love. "Since then," he continued "since their deaths, whatever I have wanted I have fought for. Taken but not given."

"You've given me a son's affection I never had," Benito said gruffly.

Wolf swallowed the lump the man's warm words brought. He kept his gaze fixed on the wine. Why was it so difficult for men to vent their feelings? "And you gave me the father's affection I never knew," he said at last.

"But why politics?" Benito asked briskly, changing the emotionally colored subject.

"I suppose my love of politics has been dormant over the years since my arrival in America," Wolf said in the soft drawl he had acquired. "When I came here, when I saw some of the terrible wrongs, the oppression that existed even in a great city like New York, I told myself that I wanted no part of changing such a system. That politics was behind me. I wanted only to make my own way, left alone. I've reaped democracy's benefits, and now I guess it's my turn to sow something."

He didn't add that he had grown bored with Celina, nor that it had been Frank and Maggie who had reintroduced politics into his life, though he was certain that Benito was astute enough to draw that conclusion on his own.

"Where's Celina?" he asked Benito, only at that moment realizing her absence. "Still asleep?"

"She rode out early. Said she wanted some exercise. Why don't you catch up on your sleep? I'll tell her you're here when she gets back."

Wolf rose from the sofa in one smooth movement. "I need to get the kinks out of my muscles. I'll saddle up and ride a while. Maybe I'll find her." He looked at Benito and added, "I think she'll be happy living in Cheyenne during the month the legislature is in session. It'll give her something to do."

The older man turned away. "I hope so."

Wolf headed for the stables, his hands buried in his jacket's pockets. His thoughts were riveted on Celina. She had put on a few more pounds over the last few years, but she was still an enticing young woman. His preoccupation first with the ranch and more lately with campaigning had not helped their marriage, and he knew she deserved more than he was giving of himself.

The morning sunlight sifted through slits in the rafters to warm the stables with the scent of musty hay and manure. He found the saddle he wanted and hoisted it over one shoulder. The pleasant odor of old leather reached him, as well as soft, husky laughter from one of the far stalls. Celina was back. Meaning to surprise her, he trod with the fluidity of a puma. The layered hay hushed the clank of his spurs.

He surprised all three of them—himself, Celina, and Diego. At the squeak of the stall door the Mexican's slender brown body rolled from Celina like a precipitous rock slide. Wolf was left staring at the black shadow between his wife's spread legs. Quicker than a feline, she came hissing to her feet. For the briefest second he thought she had never looked more magnificent. Her auburn hair burned beneath the shaft of sunlight, and the rosy glow of lingering passion suffused her skin.

But her detonating anger abruptly diffused, to be replaced by a look of fear in the coffee-colored sloe eyes. Diego glanced warily from her to the tall man who loomed in the stall's doorway like some diabolical fiend. The explosion he expected from the ranch manager never erupted.

Wolf slung the saddle at Diego's feet. "Try the saddle," he said quietly. "It rides a hell of a lot better."

He swung away. "Wait," Celina cried out and scrambled to don her clothes. Wolf kept going. She caught up with him in their bedroom. "What are you going to do?" she demanded.

"What does it look like?" He flung denims and shirt into the canvas bag.

Her hand grabbed his arm, clutching like a vulture's talons. "What you just saw—it means nothing. Nothing!" she repeated desperately. "I wanted *you*."

He shook off her hand and looked down at her. "Don't say anything else."

"It's all your fault!" she shrilled, but tears stood in her eyes. "You never were here. Even when you were."

He returned to the packing. "Just chalk it up to preoccupation."

"Preoccupation? *Merde!* Try disinterest!"

"Tell Benito I'll get in touch with him later." He closed the bag and walked out of the room.

The Magic City of the Plains. A name given to what was once the worst of the tough western towns. Some said the sobriquet was bestowed when the Union Pacific building operations wintered in the area. All the flotsam and a good deal of the jetsam of humanity, who had been following the railroad as it built west, moved from Julesburg, Colorado, their last place of revelry, to the newest scene of building, Cheyenne: the Hell on Wheels.

When spring came and the railroad men, ladies of the night, soldiers, bull-whackers, and ragtag and bobtail moved on with the railroad, enough of them stayed to realize that cattle could be raised profitably in that grassy wilderness. With the continual pouring of settlers into the West after the Civil War, Cheyenne perpetually overflowed with adventurous souls.

Lots sold for outrageous prices; stores, banks, schools, and churches sprang up. So quickly did the town erect itself that it earned the name of "The Magic City of the Plains." Or perhaps Cheyenne derived the name from the fact it was the first town in the country to have electric lights, even before gas mains were laid.

Wolf did not know the truth behind the nickname. He only knew that Cheyenne had a magic about it that rivaled even that of Czarist St. Petersburg.

And there was the magic of Maggie.

He told himself it was the lonely two months he had
spent holed up in his cabin, only braving the subarctic wind
and snow to take feed to his sheep, that made him hungry
for the sight of her. He had spent the long days and nights
profitably, reading before the fire the English classics by
Milton, Defoe, Coleridge.

He had neither radio nor newspaper to keep him abreast
of public affairs, but he knew that before the first general
budget session began in January he wanted to spend some
time in Legislative Services poring over past legislations,
familiarizing himself with the bills and proposals. And it
was on that first day back in Cheyenne, in the Legislative
Services' dim, musty archives, that he came upon Maggie.

She sat at the long wooden table, her head bent, as she
scribbled notes from a text. Did it seem that her golden hair
cast a glow in the small radius of her person? He stood
watching her graceful movements, drinking in her beauty.
After a few moments, her hand paused. Her head raised.
He saw her nostrils flare, her eyes dilate.

He moved forward out of the darkness. The subtle, sweet,
musky scent of her perfume reached him. Swiftly his mind
calculated the number of words they had exchanged over
the years. So few. Nevertheless, he knew her thoughts as
well as if they had corresponded like old friends. But he
knew they were more than that. And he knew she knew it
also.

"Hello, Maggie."

"Wolf." Her voice held an almost breathless quality. He
noted the way her fingers tightened on the pen.

He hitched a long leg over the corner of the table and
leaned forward. "I read that you have been elected President
of the Women's Club of Wyoming."

The eyes she raised to him were cool, calm. Nevertheless, he sensed the struggle for composure that went on
behind the shuttered gaze. "Aye. It was quite an honor."

"Does the world of politics occupy all your time?" he asked quietly. "Is there any personal time left over for Frank?"

Picking up the manilla folder, she slid from the chair and stepped to the file cabinet behind them. "Congratulations on your election," she said, her voice prim, contained, proper.

He rose and came to stand over her, his hand on the open file drawer and the other on the cabinet, entrapping her. "I want you, Maggie."

She turned around and opened her mouth, and he laid a blunt fingertip across her lips. "You can only run so long a time from yourself."

Her eyes frosted over. "Leave me alone."

"I'm telling you now," he said softly, dangerously, "that I won't let you run roughshod over me as you do the other men. I won't let you dominate me. If we can't meet on equal terms, then one of us will have to surrender to the other. And it sure as hell won't be me."

Against his better judgement, his hands caught her shoulders and pulled her to him. He kissed those startled, parted lips. Shock, resistance, uncertainty—he felt all the emotions, one succeeding the other, course through Maggie's pliant body that contrasted so with her unyielding nature. Abruptly he released her, half afraid he would make love to her on that table like some damn tomcat.

He saw the indignation and the fury that burned in her eyes hotter than any furnace blast. It was only the second time in all the years he had known her that he had seen a chink in her ice-block facade. He grinned.

Her hand arched out, and his jaw jerked with the impact. He laughed aloud and caught her hand.

"Let me go," she hissed and tried to yank free.

He brought the resisting hand to his lips. When his tongue tickled the palm's sensitive skin, his eyes watched hers cloud and saw her visibly tremble.

Suddenly her other palm came up. This time he was quicker. He caught the hand in mid flight. Tears of anger flashed in her eyes. "I hate you. I hate you. You've done nothing but upset my life."

He smiled and drew the other hand up to his mouth. "You hate your helplessness," he said, his lips brushing her palm. "And you hate your weakness for wanting me." This time his teeth sank with a soft nip into the palm's tender cushion. Her breath sucked in.

"Maggie, if this is what it takes to get through that barricade you've erected, then I'll break you open like a shotgun if I have to. I'll break down every barricade quicker then you can erect it until the moment comes when you surrender."

He released her then. If looks could burn, he would have been a pile of cinders at that moment. His unrelenting gaze held hers until, by a great effort of will, she turned away.

He watched her gather her papers in cold, precise movements and listened bleakly as her heels tapped staccato clicks down the hall's black-and-white checkered tiles.

CHAPTER
twenty-eight

*M*aggie *sat in the gallery with Barbara Whatley* and watched the proceedings of the State Senate's legislative session being enacted below. "Maggie," the attorney's wife whispered, "I can't imagine what brings you to this stuffy place. Wouldn't a game of bridge be more tempting?"

Maggie smiled at the pregnant woman, who shifted uncomfortably in the wooden seat. "Now as a member of the elite Cheyenne Women's Club, would you deny such an opportunity to improve your mind?" she teased.

"But every day?"

"Sssh," Maggie whispered. "The President of the Senate has recognized Frank." Her husband rose from behind his desk, handsome and distinguished in the gray pinstripe suit. His fingers seemed to absently rub at his neatly trimmed mustache. Maggie knew it was a delaying tactic. He was surreptitiously scanning the expectant faces of his fellow legislators, numbering those he felt he could count on to back him.

A born orator with the gift of charm, he had become a much better politician than she had anticipated. Watching

225

Frank, she could understand his success on the floor. As majority floor leader, he held the legislators spellbound, his words drawing their attention in soft-spoken tones at one moment, then the next compelling, urging, motivating.

She leaned forward as he began his introduction of the bill he was sponsoring, a proposal to establish several state-controlled hunting and wildlife areas with privately operated dude ranches located on the grounds.

"It's not an original idea," he said smoothly, summing up the proposal. "Our illustrious president, Teddy Roosevelt, who often hunted in Wyoming's Big Horns, spoke of the need for just such ranches. They provide access to an enjoyable sport for the public, while controlling unlimited decimation of our wildlife." His knuckles rapped the desktop. "We owe it to our constituents, gentlemen, to see that this bill passes!"

It had been her suggestion to mention Teddy Roosevelt. Reading through some old newspapers at the state archives, she had come upon Roosevelt's hunting expeditions into the state some twenty years earlier, and had suggested that Frank use the fact to reinforce his proposal. Apparently a good suggestion, for applause broke out on the floor when her husband finished and took his seat. The President of the Senate banged his gavel to quiet the chambers. "I recognize the Minority Floor Leader, Wolf Nicholson."

Maggie's breath hissed in. It wasn't the first time the two had clashed on bills before the legislature. The year before Wolf had opposed Frank's proposal for a 25 percent tax on oil revenue to private industry by declaring it should be twice as much, that they were practically giving away the state's minerals. But Frank had insisted that such a low tax would draw more speculators and in the end achieve as much or more revenue than a 50 percent tax.

Wolf had spoken firmly but in spare, terse words against the proposal, saying no more nor less than was needed to make the point. But Frank had won the legislators to his

side that day, his reverberating oration leading them as if
they were a flock of sheep.

Wolf rose now, tall, roughly masculine in a black three-
piece suit and flowing string tie. "Now I know why I came,"
Barbara whispered, her gaze fixed on Wolf's lean figure.
"What do you think it'd be like to kiss that pit in his chin?"

Maggie flashed her a withering look, and she said, "I
may be pregnant, but I can still fantasize, can't I? Besides,
Maggie, there *are* other things in life besides politics."

"What you hope to achieve for our constituents, if I
understand you correctly," Wolf began, "is a greater inflow
of the tourist dollar through the appeal of the dude ranches?"

"While the state, of course, monitors the wildlife numbers available to the hunters," Frank interjected.

"What the state cannot monitor is the destruction of the
historical sites and trails by such ranches. Gas lines, telephone wires, car tracks would destroy the primitive beauty
of places like the Big Horns. You can't put a price on
historical sights like Independence Rock, the Fetterman
Massacre Site, or the Oregon Trail."

Frank smiled thinly. "Could it be you're worried about
your one-hundred-and-sixty-acre homestead that sits on the
edge of the proposed area rather than concerned about some
archaeological anachronism?"

Wolf cocked a black brow. "Could it be, Senator Van
der Rhys, your concern is more for the investment you have
with parties interested in building such a dude ranch?"

Maggie's mouth fell open. She knew nothing of any such
negotiations by Frank. She saw her husband quickly suppress his surprise. "Naturally, there are people interested in
backing such a worthy cause. But my concern is foremost
for the investment of the people, Senator Nicholson."

During this exchange, a muted hum of words over the
debated subject began to build between the other legislators.
"Gentlemen!" the President called, rapping his gavel again.
"Some compromise can be reached. I propose that the bill

be tabled until the next session. In the meantime, I request Senators Van der Rhys and Nicholson research the aspects of the bill more thoroughly and come prepared to present their findings then. Mr. Nicholson?"

"Mr. President," Wolf said clearly, "I propose Senator Van der Rhys and his investors—and, of course, his family, if they so choose—spend one week in the Big Horns this summer, using my cabin as a base. I feel certain we can come to some kind of terms over the Ranch Bill then."

"With you as our guide," Frank replied pleasantly, "there can be no question that we did not give the matter our closest regard."

Wolf's feral smile chilled Maggie to the bone.

"The bill is duly tabled," the President of the Senate announced.

"Breathe deeply," Maggie told Barbara.

The young woman winced at the stab of pain and squeezed Maggie's hand. When the contraction passed, she exhaled. "Was it so bad?" Maggie asked, smiling.

"Damn bad," she whispered with a weak grin. "Hey, Maggie, thanks for coming over to sit with me in the middle of the night. Jim can't stand pain. Mine nor his."

"I wasn't really very sleepy anyway." Which was an understatement. When Jim's call came at two-thirty, she had been sitting in the kitchen over a cup of coffee and a cigarette.

She had quarrelled earlier with Frank over his neglecting to inform her about his involvement with the dude ranch investors. It wasn't that he had kept his involvement from her that bothered her, it was the investors themselves.

He had hedged on revealing their identity. "Just three or four wheeler-dealers I met at the Club. They're reaping it big at the stock market right now and are looking for a good deal to invest some of their earnings in, that's all, Maggie."

She suspected those "wheeler-dealers" were some of the

nsavory characters who had sprung up after prohibition ike mushrooms after a rain. She openly accused him of onsorting with such underworld figures.

The bitter exchange of words that followed had been all he excuse Frank needed to leave the house. Maggie knew e wouldn't return the rest of the night, that he was no doubt eeking solace in the arms of any one of a number of women who would readily make themselves available for a man of his importance.

Not that she cared. It was in fact a relief when he took his desires elsewhere. His parting words had hit their mark: 'You're not a natural woman, Maggie!"

It was not something she did not already know. Rape at twelve quite adequately covered that. But how could she explain the compelling feelings she had for Wolf, the fear and the attraction for him that controlled her mind and her body?

Barbara moaned with the next onslaught of contractions, and Maggie smoothed the young woman's damp hair back from her forehead. "Why don't you let me call the doctor now, Barbara? The pains are close enough that he would want to be awakened."

Barbara closed her eyes and nodded. Maggie slipped from the room and met Jim in the hall. "She's all right," she reassured the husband. "But it's time to call the doctor. Why don't you sit with Barbara while I make the call."

Jim grimaced. "All right, but I don't like watching her suffer, Maggie."

"It won't be long now." Why was she reassuring him? What did she know about having babies—she, the unnatural woman? Yet she had lovingly cared for Hugh. Where were her brothers, and what were they doing now? And her father? She rarely thought or cared about him. She shrugged off the guilty feeling that assaulted her and made the telephone call.

After she roused the doctor, she sat down in the darkened

parlor and lit up a much-needed cigarette. Like the drifting cigarette smoke, her thoughts wafted back to the scene at the capitol chambers earlier that day and Wolf's open challenge.

Foolish Frank. Wolf was not challenging him over the Ranch Bill. Wolf was challenging him for his wife.

CHAPTER
twenty-nine

The four ball ricochetted off the cushioned edge, spun diagonally across the green baize, and dropped into the far pocket. Benito grunted. "You're getting better, Wolf."

Wolf moved around the end of the billiards table and positioned his cue stick before the five ball. "If I spent as much time playing as you, I'd beat you one day."

"You could try spending more time here," the man said softly. Beneath the grizzled brows his rock brown eyes watched the younger man, waiting.

Wolf hated to dash the hope he saw there. He knew Benito thought of him as a son more than a son-in-law. He drove the cue tip against the orange-striped ball. "It won't work, Benito. I'm sorry."

He picked up the square of chalk and rotated it over the cue's tip. The action kept his attention on what he was doing so he would not have to meet the Basque's eyes. "I want Celina to divorce me."

"I was hoping for a grandson."

The jocularity in the man's voice did not fool Wolf. "Not from me, Benito. The best thing for everyone would be for

Celina to divorce me and find someone who will love her."

"She's waiting for you in the bedroom."

"I'll talk with her, Benito. But I'm leaving as soon as the Van der Rhyses and their party arrive."

"You really think you can sway Van der Rhys from going through with that damned Ranch Bill?"

He laid the cue stick down. "It's worth a try."

Celina had redecorated their bedroom in bright yellows and oranges. She sat with her legs folded beneath her in the old Sheridan that was recovered in an orange-flowered print. An open magazine, *Vogue*, lay in her lap. He saw the wariness that shadowed her eyes before she lowered her lids. "I've missed you, Wolf," she whispered.

He jammed his hands in his pockets of his denim pants and went to stand before the window. New curtains of lemon yellow chiffon draped either side. "You shouldn't. I'm sure Diego fills my place quite adequately."

He heard her skirts swish as she rose and came to stand behind him. "He fills your place only as ranch manager." Her hand tentatively touched his shoulder. "I want only you to fill my bed."

He caught her hand and pulled her around in front of him. Purposely he made his voice rough. "Look, Celina, it's no use. We don't love each other."

She jerked her hand away. "You don't know how to love anyone!" she cried, her voice high and shrilly pitched.

"I know," he said softly. "That's what I'm afraid of."

The two cars, the Pontiac following the Niagra blue Lincoln convertible, bounced over the potholed road that wound steadily upward through La Conquista's juniper- and cedar-peppered hills. From the Lincoln's back seat Jamie called out, "Wow! Look at those deer, mom! Up there, on that cliff. Look!"

Beside him Peg laughed. "I see, I see, me lad."

Maggie smiled. "If it's camping out for three days you

be planning, sweetpea, you had best learn your wildlife. Those animals are antelopes, not deer."

"Pronghorn antelope," Frank qualified, keeping his eye on the bumpy road that swerved and dipped over the ravines and hogbacks that ribboned the desolate moonscape.

Peg reached forward and touched Maggie's shoulder. "I can't be thanking ye enough for inviting us, mum."

The formal address was for Frank's benefit. Though he was openly friendly toward Peg and Jamie, as he was toward everyone, Maggie had realized long ago that he liked proprieties to be observed. "I thought Jamie would enjoy the week's outing, Peg."

"Now that he would. The only wildlife he saw in New York was an alley cat or the policeman's nag."

Maggie felt a slight pang of guilt. Her invitation had not been wholly one of thoughtfulness for Jamie and Peg. True, she knew that Jamie would be ecstatic at the prospect of roughing it. But she also knew that she did not want to face Wolf alone.

Of course, Frank would be there. But there was the possibility—no, the probability—that he would wind up the evenings drinking with Crawford or Wright, who followed in the Pontiac. Crawford, a dark, pear-shaped little man in his thirties, and the older, balding Wright comported themselves with an array of good manners that would have bested Sir Galahad. Nevertheless, Maggie sensed something sinister lurked beneath their unctuous manners. She trusted the investors no more than she did her control of her emotional response to Wolf Nicholson.

Through the web of cottonwoods and poplars, La Conquista's ranchhouse came into sight. Maggie pushed the wet strands of stray hair off her neck. It was the July heat. Where were the winds that seemed to forever plague Wyoming? She put the wide-brimmed Spanish hat back on and pulled the leather strings tightly beneath her chin against any sudden gust, though she doubted she would be so blessed.

Already her khaki shirt and trousers were damp with perspiration. The one blessing of the trip, besides the opportunity afforded Jamie for an outing, was that she was back in trousers. If more women only knew how comfortable they were!

She spotted Wolf first, before her husband did. He was in the larger corral, the holding pen, with several other men. She recognized him by his height—but something more, too. The powerful, fluid movements of his body, the feline grace that had nothing of femininity about it. He wielded the long shepherd's crook deftly, hooking one of the bleating ewes by the left leg. The shuffling sheep kicked up dust, obscuring the men for a moment.

As their Lincoln drew near, she saw him pass the crook to one of the other men and shove the Stetson back on his head, his gaze following the cars. When he vaulted the corral's wooden slats and strode toward them, she drew a deep breath. "Afternoon, Frank, Maggie," he said, his gaze sweeping over Frank to rest first on her lips before moving upwards to meet her eyes.

"Didn't think we'd take you up on your offer, did you?" Frank asked, grinning.

"I felt certain you would," Wolf replied with an enigmatic expression. His gaze released her and moved beyond to Peg and Jamie.

"I hope you don't mind us bringing two extra," Maggie said, wishing she did not sound so breathless. "Peg and Jamie came over on the *Wyoming* with me."

"I remember," Wolf said. A warm smile creased the lines on either side of his mouth. It was one of the few such smiles Maggie could recall.

"I remember, too!" Peg said, matching the smile. "And methinks half the female population on board remembered also."

Traitoress, Maggie thought. One smile and her friend quickly went over to the other side.

Crawford and Wright joined them now, and Benito, who wore his black beret at a rakish angle, came out on the veranda to greet them, shaking the hands of the three men. He removed the cigar stub from his mouth and gave Maggie a gruff peck on the cheek. "For the most part, you've done better in the legislature than I expected, Frank," he said. But his eye was on Maggie, as if he were acknowledging her part in Frank's success.

She watched with surprise that was replaced by pleasure as Benito's boulevardier gaze moved past her to linger on Peg. Beneath the Basque's open appraisal, the woman seemed to almost visibly grow prettier. Her already ruddy cheeks flushed even pinker, and the sky blue eyes brightened. Could freckles dance across one's cheeks? Maggie wondered. Peg's right hand came up to shove the wild parrot-red hair into place as she pulled Jamie forward and introduced him.

Maggie wondered where Celina was and was about to ask when Wolf said, "I suggest we have lunch before striking out for the wilderness."

"Wilderness?" Peg echoed. "Does it get more wild than this?"

Benito laughed. "That it does," he said, and put an arm over Jamie's shoulder, leading him and the other adults inside to the dining room.

Celina was there, with an old Mexican man, setting the table. The woman's full rose-tinted lips, seeming almost swollen, the dark eyes veiled by thick lashes, the voluptuously plump body—she reminded Maggie of some overripe fruit. Celina acknowledged her father's introductions with a nod, but Maggie caught the secret look that peered from the ambush of hungry eyes, a look the woman directed toward Wolf. Only then did Celina glance at her, fixing her with a brief puzzled look that Maggie did not want to interpret.

Over the vegetable soup and lamb chops, Wolf explained the itinerary for the four-day weekend outing. "Using my cabin at the foot of the Big Horns as base, we'll tour by horseback Tensleep Canyon, Powder River Pass, and, if we've the time, Cloud Peak. I hope by the end of the outing I've convinced you, gentlemen, how unsuitable dude ranches would be for the people you hope to entice to the area, besides how damaging to the land."

"And we hope to convince you to the contrary," Crawford said smoothly in that gravel-mixer voice peculiar to the East. "In fact, we thought we might be able to make some sort of proposal that would interest you."

"I doubt it," Wolf said and finished off the coffee in his cup.

"Jamie," Benito said in the awkward silence that followed, "if you'll stay here at La Conquista, we'll go hunting. A big cat's been bothering our sheep, and we need to take care of it." He turned a warm gaze on Peg. "Could I persuade you and your son—and Maggie—to keep an old man company?"

Peg's look took in the barrel chest and dark hair that coiled above the cotton shirt's V-neck and seemed to say, *You're definitely not old*. She glanced at Maggie with questioning brows.

Maggie bit her lip, feeling herself on the horns of a dilemma. To stay with Peg and Jamie meant she would be freed from Wolf's disturbing presence. On the other hand, Benito had issued the invitation to her out of politeness. Her own presence would only inhibit the interest that seemed to be blossoming between Benito and Peg. She cast a glance at the petulant Celina, who sat next to her husband. With Celina along on the outing, Maggie reasoned, there should be no problems arising.

Meeting Wolf's challenging gaze, she told Benito, "Thank you, but I believe I'll accompany my husband and the others."

CHAPTER
thirty

@~~@~~@

The first few hours on horseback were not so bad for Maggie. In fact, she thought she rode as well or better than Crawford, whose round beetlelike body rolled precariously from one side of the saddle to the other. Wright seemed to manage his mount a little better, but he had neglected to wear a hat, and his shiny pate was pinkening rapidly beneath the blistering sun, which seemed much nearer in that high, dry altitude.

The wind seemed to have risen, bouncing the Russian thistle and other tumbleweeds before it over the sun-baked plateaus and semi-arid foothills. The route Wolf was following took its time climbing the Big Horns' foothills, winding up through a series of sweeping, comfortable switchbacks that ultimately presented views of canyons splashed with the red and yellow of wild currant. Slowly the hills, their sides already splotched with frost-touched golden aspens, began to bulk up about the riders.

The higher they rode, the cooler the air grew, and gradually lodgepole pines rose in clusters to offer some scanty shade. Occasionally Maggie glimpsed a miniature jewellike lake or tumbling mountain cascade. She was enjoying herself much more than she had anticipated, though she would have felt more comfortable had Celina come along. She glanced at the broad shoulders of Wolf, who rode immediately in front of her. Were the rumors that drifted into Buffalo true, that Wolf and Celina did not live together as man and wife?

She shivered, feeling as if some unseen trap were slowly closing on her.

Behind her, Frank must have noted her sudden trembling, for he asked, "Tired, honey?" and called out to Wolf, "When's that rest period you promised?"

Wolf hitched halfway round in the saddle. "There's a clearing a couple miles ahead. We'll rest there."

"It can't come too soon," Crawford grunted from the rear of the line.

Wolf called a halt in a boulder-strewn area sliced out of a portion of the mountainside by wind, water, and time. Dotted with chokecherry bushes and ribboned by an indolent, pine-bordered stream, the sun-warmed pocket gave an unobstructed view of eastern Wyoming, the lush grasslands that stretched out to the "mile wide and inch deep" Powder River and, beyond, the broken badlands with their tawny buttes rising like vast prehistoric monsters of the plain.

Maggie, who was sure her bottom must resemble raw meat by now, dismounted without any urging and eased down into the grass that tufted the stream's bank. She closed her eyes and heard the water lapping against the mossy rocks. "Here," Wolf said.

She opened her lids to find him haunched on one knee. He passed Maggie his canteen. She wanted to refuse the drink, but she was too thirsty and too tired to get her own canteen. For a moment her eyes met his as she placed her lips over the tin rim, and she was jolted by the intimacy that bridged the intervening space between her and Wolf. What forged this extraordinary bond between them?

Frank dropped down between them. "This is the life, isn't it?" he asked, apparently unaffected by the afternoon's exertion. "Smell the pines! Easterners would pay a pretty penny to trade their dirty, smoke-filled cities for a week up here."

"That is the point that I hope to make, Van der Rhys," Wolf said, taking the canteen Maggie returned to him. "Wyoming's wilderness won't remain a wilderness if your dude ranch bill passes."

Wright, whose head was now a bright plum pink, put down the canteen he drank from. The man's hooded eyes did not conceal the irritation that flamed there. "But we'd put restrictions on them, Nicholson. No littering, smoking in designated areas only, no hunting—rules like that."

"That doesn't begin to protect the wildlife," Wolf said harshly. "For the ranches you are planning, you would need some sort of mass transportation. Careless use of your motorcars could result in the destruction of wildlife food and cover and even in soil erosion. Your improvements will drive the bighorn sheep and wapiti and bear from places like Crater Lake and Tensleep Canyon." He nodded toward the beaver damn some yards downstream. "How long do you think things like that will last once your ranches blight the land?"

The tension among the men shattered the peace of the pastoral surroundings. Maggie said, "Arguing won't settle anything. That was the purpose of the trip, to see the primitive areas for ourselves and then decide." She looked at Wolf. "When do we ride up to Tensleep Canyon?"

His gaze met hers, and she warmed under the piercing regard. His head nodded almost inperceptibly, as if acknowledging her attempt at a truce among the five of them. "We spend the night at my cabin and leave early tomorrow for Tensleep."

Keeping with the established harmony of the moment, he went on to explain that the canyon was named by Indians

because it was exactly "ten sleeps" between two big camps
From there the conversation turned to safer subjects, and to
Maggie's relief the journey once more was resumed under
pleasant conditions, though her bottom protested by di-
recting flashes of pain upward at every jolt her chestnut
gelding made.

Wolf led them in a westerly direction now, but the trail
seemed to gradually drop back down out of the pine forests,
revealing more and more of the mustard-color boiling hills.
The five riders passed fields terracing the hills where the
grass was corrugated by grazing black-faced sheep—Wolf's
sheep, Maggie learned.

Watching the four mounted men, an impish smile curved
Maggie's lips. She was reminded of the fairy tale about the
big bad wolf and the three greedy pigs.

The sun rocked in the cleft of Bighorn's gray granite
humps when they rode into a sunlight-shafted valley patched
with great gnarled gray cottonwoods and Chinese elm. Wolf
led the way down a narrow pebble-layered trail to a cabin
of native rock and timber. The land was not as beautiful as
the meadow higher up where they had rested, nor was the
house as imposing as the one Maggie kept in Cheyenne.
But both the land and the house had a rugged permanence
about them.

She had expected to find Celina's touch inside, yet neither the main room and kitchen nor the bedroom were softened by any feminine frills. Old mine timbers supported the
roof. Two chairs—constructed of horns, no less—an old
camelback couch, and a low leather-bound coffee table
hugged the stone fireplace that was ridged by a pine mantle
filled with various books. Next to the couch stood an Edison
Player, the only concession to modern times.

While the men unsaddled the horses, she wandered into
the kitchen, noting its rustic sparseness: an old cast-iron
cooking stove, a cigarette-burned table of walnut, and a

white-enameled cupboard filled with a few utensils and can-
sters of staples. At least everything was clean.

Her curiosity led her to the bedroom. The single bed
covered with a brown and orange Indian blanket answered
her question: Celina had had nothing to do with furnishing
the house, had never lived there even. Maggie spun at the
clink of the spurs on the uneven oak-planked floor, feeling
like she had been caught trespassing. Wolf filled the doorway. "This is where you'll sleep tonight."

"And the others?" she asked nervously. "Frank?"

He set her duffel bag down on the low chest of drawers
and nodded back toward the main room. "In there." She
did not miss the taunting grin that tugged at the corners of
his lips. He purposely wanted her separated from Frank!

"While I get the fire going," he said, "why don't you
start the coffee?"

"All right," she replied tersely.

But he made no move to return to the other room. With
one hand propped against the doorjamb, he stood watching
her, his eyes almost daring her, it seemed. In his eye, in
his face, in his stance, in the whole man, there dominated
something potent to be felt.

Behind him Frank and the two cronies spilled into the
room, carrying their bags and laughing. Wright said something she could not hear, and tipped a flask of bathtub gin
to his mouth. Her gaze went back to the mocking slash of
Wolf's lips. It was going to be a long three days.

Her breath held, she slid past him. Surely he wouldn't
dare do anything before the others. While she measured the
coffee, Frank, Crawford, and Wright spread the map of the
Big Horns before them and began marking sites they wanted
to visit over the next three days. Wolf, working on the fire,
occasionally answered their questions. Maggie's hand shook
as she put the lid on the battered tin coffeepot, wondering
what it was about his deep, soft drawl that stirred her so.

When he strode into the kitchen, she almost jumped. He took out a charcoal-flaked black iron skillet and began cutting up sausage he had packed. "Can you slice some potatoes?" he asked.

She nodded, not trusting herself to speak. The two of them worked side by side, and for a while she lost some of her wariness as she pumped water and washed the potatoes he had mounded for her. The resinous scent of the piñon burning in the fireplace and the pungent aroma of the perking coffee filled the cabin. She began to relax slightly in Wolf's silent company. But when raucous laughter erupted from the three men who were all drinking, she jerked abruptly. The razor-edged knife she was using sliced cleanly through the pad of her thumb.

At her sharp gasp, Wolf came immediately to her side. His gaze took in the crimson blood that puddled and spilled over her rigidly knotted hands. With no waste of words and an economy of motion, he grabbed her hand and at the same time reached for a bottle of rotgut whiskey one of the men had left on the table. Standing behind her, he positioned her before the sink and poured the alcohol over the gaping wound. She swayed at the burning that fired her hand. Even when he finished, she could not stir from the alcove of his arms. But he put her from him and swiftly tore a strip from a dish towel to bandage the cut thumb. They stood as one for what seemed a very long time. Then he bent his head so that his lips were next to her ear. But he only said, "Go lie down. I'll finish up here."

Frank, Crawford, and Wright sat before the fireplace, too busy exchanging jokes bordering on the obscene to notice as she made her way past them on wobbly legs. The shock of the badly cut thumb, the loss of blood, had little to do with her shaking limbs. Not bothering to light the kerosene lamp, she removed her boots. She lay in the dark on the narrow mattress and listened to the laughter which grew louder the more the three men in the outer room drank.

After a few minutes, the subtle odor of Wolf enveloped her emanating from the pillow and the blanket—a combination of sweet-scented tobacco and a faint, lingering masculine odor that stirred some primitive response in her.

Could she never escape him?

Half an hour later, an arc of light fanned across the room, and Wolf stood in the doorway. "Do you feel like coming to eat?"

With her husband and the other two men linked by the companionship of alcohol, it would almost be as if she were eating alone with Wolf. "No," she murmured.

"I'll bring you something, then."

He turned to leave, and she said, "No!" He looked over his shoulder at her, his brow raised, and she was afraid that he detected her fear of him. "I don't feel much like eating," she rationalized.

After a moment he shrugged and turned away, leaving the door open. She could hear from the safety of her room first the drunken jokes and laughter that amplified as the summer night crept toward its apex, then, in the long hours that followed, the dwindling of the conversation, and finally the loud silence, broken only by the occasional cricket's chirp or the dismal hoot of a night owl. From the outer room, the fire's warming light stretched across the plank floor to dance on the timbered and mortared walls just beyond her bedroom door. She burrowed her body deeper beneath the woolen blanket, seeking warmth against the night's cold.

Then he was there, filling the doorway, blocking the fire's light that offered reasoning and clear thinking. He moved toward her, silent as cat paws, formidable as his namesake. When he stood over her, she whispered, "You planned this, didn't you?"

"I hoped for it." His voice drifted down to her, husky with desire. On one knee he knelt over her, sinking his hands into the fluffy wool mattress at either side of her head. His dark head was so close that his warm breath fanned her face. "I've waited for a long time, Maggie."

She tried to inject some logic into her wildly tumbling thoughts. "You don't seriously think you could take me, with Frank just in the other room?"

"I think that Frank would offer you to me if he thought it would help the Ranch Bill."

"That's not true!"

"Isn't it?"

Frantically she cast about for some defense, but found no adequate reply. In her heart she was not so staunchly sure that Frank wouldn't do just that. "Regardless of what Frank wants, I don't want you. Can't you understand that?"

Anyone who knew her well would have recognized the uncompromising tone of her voice. Many a man had backed down when she spoke in that cold, clear, and utterly final tone. Why then, she wondered wildly, didn't Wolf seem to recognize it?

"No, I don't understand it," he said in a level voice. "And I don't accept it. Because I see it in your eyes, Maggie." He laid his hand atop her blouse-covered breast. "I hear it in the pounding of your heart." He buried his head in the hollow of her neck and murmured against the pulse throbbing in her throat, "I smell it in your skin."

Her eyes fluttered closed, and a soft moan escaped her lips. His land loosened the blouse's buttons and freed one breast. When his fingers embraced the cocoa-tinted nipple, it sprang up with a life of its own. "Deny me, Maggie," he said. "You can't. You can't deny what was meant to be."

She wanted to. She tried. Her lips parted. His lips moved over hers, breathing tobacco-scented air into her mouth, air that flowed down into her lungs and was distributed throughout her blood system so that he was as much a part of her as if he had entered her. Dear God, but she wanted him! But she wanted even more to keep herself. She twisted her

ead back and forth to escape the kiss that would drain her
f her will.

He pinioned the hands that pushed against his chest above
er head and anchored her legs with one knee. He raised
lightly so he could look at her face. "What is it?" he grated.
What is the wall between us?"

She tried to wrench her hands free, but he held her firm.
It can't be your rape by the soldiers," he continued. "Be-
ause then you wouldn't want me at all. You'd be as frigid
s a Wyoming glacier. And you're not."

His mouth claimed hers then, crushing her lips in a re-
entless kiss. His tongue lashed at hers and his breath stole
he air from her. With one wild gasp, her teeth sank into
is lower lip. His head jerked upwards, leaving the salty
aste of his blood on her tongue. The yellow-gold eyes
lazed with anger that did not override their desire. "When
feel strongly enough about an issue, Maggie, I always
win. Before this is over," he promised, "I'll make you come
o me. I'll make you understand what it is to really surrender.
am done with waiting."

CHAPTER
thirty-one

The four horses picked their way among the many lakes scattered along the eastern slope of Cloud Peak's glaciersided mountain. Every so often they would stop at one of the alpine lakes bounded by thickets of white-flowered hawthorn and towering pines, and Wolf would point out the markings on the maps for Frank and his two partners.

Wolf had to wonder what he was doing there. There wasn't a chance on God's green earth that he would persuade Frank of the danger the Ranch Bill presented to Wyoming's dwindling wilderness. He had castigated Frank as a weak man, but he himself was just as weak—weak for wanting a woman he could not have, for wanting a woman no man could ever have. And yet he meant to have her. He should not have been surprised when she had decided to forego the trip that morning, claiming that she did not feel well.

He haunched over the map now and marked off their present location. He pushed the Stetson back on his head and looked up at Crawford, who was tilting a flask of hooch to his mouth. "I'd go easy on the stuff," Wolf said. Noting the man's frown of resentment, he tried to be patient in his explanation. "The higher we go, the colder it gets, and alcohol reduces the body's heat production."

Crawford tossed the empty flask into bushes of wild gooseberry. "I'm getting tired of your nagging, Nicholson. Don't smoke, don't shoot at the wildlife, don't drink. Do you think you own the land or somethin'? It's free, Nicholson—for everyone!"

Wolf shrugged. "Those were the rules if you wanted a guide."

"Well, we don't need a guide!" Crawford snapped.

Frank came over, his eyes moving nervously from Wolf to Crawford. "Why don't we break for camp and have some lunch?" he said, his politician's voice smooth, placating. "We'll all feel better after we get something in our stomachs."

Crawford pulled out the revolver that was hidden in his waistband beneath the roll of fat. Wolf shot to his feet, too late to stop the man from firing at the meadowlark. The bird's song ceased in the middle of its trill, and feathers wafted down through the sudden stillness of the air. "How about blackbird pie?" Crawford asked with a belligerent glare at Wolf.

"Crawford," Wright cautioned, and cast an anxious glance at the tall man whose long legs quickly ate up the distance between him and Crawford.

Wolf jerked the .45 from Crawford's hand. "Hey, what—" Crawford began. His words broke off abruptly as Wolf's hand smashed against his jaw.

Wolf shoved the pistol beneath his belt. "We're going back," he told the three men.

"You're going back," Wright said. "Not us. We came here to scout the land, and that's just what we're going to do."

"Now, Wright—" Frank began.

Wolf looked at Frank and Crawford, who rubbed his rapidly reddening jaw. "Are you coming with me?"

"You go, Van der Rhys, and you lose our backing," Wright warned.

Frank darted a glance at an impatient Wright and said, "Maybe we'd better meet you back at your cabin tomorrow, all right, Nicholson?"

Wolf's gaze swept over the three men, trying to gauge how competent they would be on their own. Wright looked the most levelheaded. Crawford could survive if he didn't load up on the alcohol. And Frank? The man would survive anything. He always hung on to the coattails of the winning side.

Wolf swung away and headed for the pinto. He had not really expected to convert the men. But there was still one battle he wanted to win.

The fire cracked like a gunshot as Maggie added the last log stacked on the stone hearth. She dusted the shreds of bark from her hands and held her fingers up to the heat that sizzled off the leaping tongues of tangerine flame. The evenings were usually cool enough to warrant a fire, even in the summer in the Big Horn's back canyons. But had she been perspiring, she still would have built the fire. There was something about the warm glow that was reassuring.

And she needed reassurance, there in that small cabin where every item was stamped with Wolf's virile personality, from the swift-bladed ax propped against the rough stones of the fireplace to the pewter humidor that served as one book end on the mantle. She lifted the humidor's lid, and the masculine fragrance of tobacco swirled about her, then wafted upward to join the aromatic scent of the burning piñon. Her fingers played along the beveled edges of the lid before they drifted over to trace the backs of the haphazardly arranged books, some of them surprisingly recent:

F. Scott Fitzgerald's *This Side of Paradise*, and *Main Street* by Sinclair Lewis.

She went to the door and looked out. What was she expecting? The night was immensely quiet. Somewhere in the distance, the bugle of a bull elk broke the silence. Across the summer sky the northern lights spread long pale-green streams. The Campfires of the Dead, the Indians called the phenomena. A golden haze seemed to cling to the valley. Was it stardust? She sighed and went back inside. The Edison Player caught her eye, and she cranked it up. The tinned-cylinder revolved, and Mahler's *Song of the Earth* filled the room.

A draft of cold air fanned the fire, and she spun to find Wolf framing the doorway, a load of logs in his arms. Her breath drew in. "I didn't expect you back tonight," she said when her breath rushed back jn. Her gaze went beyond him, searching for Frank and the others.

Wolf strode across the room toward her, and the light she saw in his eyes made her shiver. He moved past her and, kneeling on one knee, began to stack the logs on the hearth. "Where are the others?" she asked warily when he made no reply.

"There are no others."

She tried to rein in her growing nervousness. Automatically her hands went to her package of cigarettes on the low table. Before she could find a match, Wolf was standing before her, a mocking look on his lips as he snapped a match into flame and held it up for her. Refusing to show fear, she inclined her head to the match and inhaled, feeling some steadiness seep with the smoke through her lungs. Slowly, eyes closed, she exhaled. When her lids lifted, his amber eyes were studying her.

She shied away, turning to one of the two horn-framed chairs. "Why didn't they come back with you?" she asked, trying to sound nonchalant.

Wolf tossed his hat on the antler rack pegged on one

wall, hitting it accurately, and shrugged out of the sheepskin coat. "They elected to continue without me."

The smoke eddied from her lips while she struggled for composure. After a safe interval, she asked, "Why, why did you turn back?"

He crossed to her in that graceful, powerful roll possessed by the predators of the animal world—except that he was a predator of her world. He hunkered before her, his weather-browned hands clasped between his knees. The fire's glow played over the harsh sweep of the cheekbones and his square forehead that was rifted by the dark, unruly hair, casting the penetrating eyes into shadows. But she saw the slight predatory curve of the well-defined lips. The wolf was on the prowl.

"I could tell you I came back because your husband and the others were violating the rules laid down when the trip was agreed upon. And it would be partially the truth."

Agitated, she ran a hand through the hair that tumbled below her shoulders. She should have put it up, as she always did, but that day she had used the respite from her many social obligations to relax. "I see."

"No, you don't see." His hard gaze held her. "I came back for you, Maggie."

She ground out the cigarette in the tray. "That's impossible. It's absurd."

"Absurd, maybe. Impossible, no. I mean to have you— but on your terms."

She rose, shaken by the conviction that carried in his voice. Her breath hammered against her lungs. "Hell will ice over first."

He stood, towering over her. His laugh was low. "I'll wait." Then, as if losing interest in her, he turned away, heading for the kitchen. "How about bacon sandwiches for dinner?"

"I'm not hungry," she said perversely.

"Fine. I'll fix us a drink."

"I don't want a drink." She fumbled for the cigarette package and shook out another cigarette, and it dropped on the floor. Damn! What had happened to the savoir faire Jim and Barbara always commended her for?

She knelt to pick up the cigarette and when she rose, Wolf was coming toward her with two glasses in his hand. She couldn't help but notice the way the blue plaid flannel shirt was stretched taut across the expanse of his chest. Nor the way the devilish grin played around his lips. He passed her one of the glasses. "You look like you could use one anyway."

He settled his long frame on the couch and propped his feet on the low, rustic table before it. The Edison Player jarred with the couch's movement, and the music skipped a note. With a free hand he reached into his shirt pocket and pulled out a pack of Camels. While he lit a cigarette, she took a sip of the whiskey. He was right, she needed a drink. "But you're not always right," she unintentionally said aloud.

Wolf blew a ring of smoke and it drifted slowly upward, seeming to encircle the two of them as its circumference spread. "I'm right about us," he said. "It seems like I've waited forever for you, Maggie. It seems like you were meant for me, as unrealistic as that might be. I can't explain it, but nevertheless I'm right. You were meant to be mine."

Her hand was shaking. She set the distasteful drink down. "You're right again," she said unsteadily, "it's unrealistic. You're married."

"I've left Celina. I'm getting a divorce."

She closed her eyes so she would not have to see the wickedly handsome face before her, and tried again. "But *I'm* married."

She heard the grunt. "I know," he said roughly. "Don't you think I've told myself that a thousand times over, Maggie?" He stubbed out the half-smoked cigarette and came to stand before her. He put his hands on either side of the chair's slatted arms, imprisoning her. "But it doesn't change what was meant to be," he said softly. "Somehow, some crazy way, when our lives were cast by God or the fates or what have you, ours went awry."

"I can't accept that," she said desperately, feeling herself fall under the spell of those mesmeric eyes. "I've got to believe that I have a choice of actions."

"I know. At least, that's what I keep telling myself, Maggie, that I have free choice." He sighed and straightened. "But somewhere the choices went wrong. And it might be the next lifetime before this mess straightens out. But I'll wait, Maggie. I'll wait, no matter how many lifetimes it takes to have you."

The fire's flame sputtered low, leaving the room in a semi-darkness before it flickered to life again, blazing the room with its warmth. The cylinder on the Player clicked tonelessly, but he made no move. The machine ran down slowly until it came to a grating halt. At last he turned away and picked up his drink, finishing it off. "Go to bed, Maggie," he said harshly, looking down into the empty glass. "You're safe enough from me. I want what your damned body can't give."

"You'd have my soul and everything!" she cried, springing to her feet, her hands clenched at her sides.

He pivoted and caught her arms, jerking her up against him. "Yes!" he gritted against her mouth. "I want everything—your soul, your damned lawyer's mind, your body."

Maggie stiffened against the arrogant, overbearing sexual onslaught she had learned to expect, first from the soldiers, then Frank. But Wolf only brushed her lips with his in a warm, lingering kiss before he set her away from him. "Go to bed," he said, his voice empty.

Stunned, she watched him leave her and go into the kitchen. The absence of his hard body's warmth enveloping her was like a cold wave dashing over her. She heard him pour himself another drink. She spun and fled to the bedroom. It was colder in there, but she was safe there—safe from herself.

Quickly she undressed and slid into her gown. She lay beneath the bedcovers, listening to the sudden wind that had arisen outside, seeming to beat at the shuttered window, demanding entrance. In the outer room the fire crackled, and she watched as its tongues of light licked at her doorway. Had her subconscious bade her leave the door open? Why then could she not open the door to herself?

She closed her eyes, willing herself to sleep, but her legs stirred restlessly. The image of Wolf's legs shimmered into shape on the canvas of her mind. They would be long, as hard and muscular as his bare chest had been the one time she had seen him shirtless. She remembered that one time, at his garage apartment, and the effect his near nudity had had on her. Her fingers had desperately wanted to reach out and stroke the satiny toast-colored skin, to entwine in the dark thicket of hair that splotched across his chest and veed downward toward his navel—and the weapon that threatened her security and ultimately stayed her hands that time.

Yet her mind whispered treacherously, *Will you never know what it is to have been fully loved as a woman?*

Her thighs burned, the pit of her stomach ached for the completion of her womanhood. She knew she would never be wholly independent until she experienced that completion and triumphed over it, until she ultimately destroyed her fatal fascination for Wolf. She had been running rather than meet that nebulous fear of sexual surrender. And Wolf Nicholson epitomized for her all that was superior in the male sex. Could she find anywhere a more worthy foe?

How ironic! Wolf meant to win her body by appealing to her intellect!

Initially the oak floor was cold beneath her bare feet, but it grew warmer as she padded steadily closer to the beckoning flames. Stretched out on the couch, Wolf lay awake, as she had known he would be. A blanket concealed the essence of his masculinity. His sun-browned torso gleamed in the firelight. His animal's luminous eyes held her, consuming her with their hunger. He raised his arms, and she glided into his embrace. Her eyes closed as he pulled her down over him, beside him. The old fear licked at her nerve endings, so that the barest touch of his fingers about her neck seemed to lacerate her skin.

Panicked by the invincibility of her opponent and by her own second thoughts, she stirred against his hold, but he lodged her more securely between him and the couch's back so that she lay pinioned. When his right hand slid down her shoulder to palm a breast covered only by the gown's silky material, she gasped out a smothered "No!"

She tried to pull its lacy edge up, and his hand stopped hers. Caught in his mesmeric gaze, she allowed his fingers to continue their sensual domination of her. She tried to disassociate her mind from her body, as she had done with Frank, but Wolf would not let her. "Look at me, Maggie," he commanded. "I won't have you hiding anything from me, not even your thoughts."

Her long lashes fluttered open to meet his dark gaze. Without relinquishing her gaze, he ran his fingers through her hair, drawing a handful of it forward over her shoulder. "I would keep you like this, Maggie. Here in my cabin. If I thought that I could keep you. But it would only be your body, wouldn't it?"

She nodded, afraid to speak, afraid he would hear the weakness in her voice. His fingers lovingly stroked her tumbled hair from her bare shoulders before moving down to slip inside her thigh where the gown had ridden up. Involuntarily she stiffened, and he said, "You've never known the pleasure, have you?"

She shook her head, her fear paralyzing her tongue, and he said, "There is a pleasure, but it's greatest only in the giving, only in the sharing. Touch me, Maggie. I'm not some ogre. I'm a man. A man who found his mate—almost too late."

The desire to know if the pleasure he spoke of actually existed conquered her fear, and her hand hesitantly slid down his chest. His body hair seemed to capture her fingers and tug them ever downward. She found that integral component of the male physique, held its throbbing hardness in her hand, and discovered the sudden want and need for her complement. It was no weapon of terror but an instrument of love, and she wanted to be impaled by that shaft.

She almost cried with disappointment when his hand closed about hers and pulled it up to his chest. "No more, Maggie. I'll not let you tease me, nor I you. You must give yourself to me completely or end it here." She looked up into his eyes, and he whispered, "Say it; say you're mine."

For the first time she smiled, a twisted travesty of a smile. "And are you mine, Wolf? Can you say the words 'I love you'?"

She glimpsed something in his eyes, what, she wasn't sure, then they shuttered over. "There have been many women in my life," he whispered, his voice raw with an indefinable quality, "but none of them has had the power to touch me inside as you do, Maggie."

"Then what we bring to each other will have to be enough."

Into the early hours of the morning when dawn's pink light mixed with the fire's rosier glow that played on their sweat-sheened bodies, they laid together, their limbs entwined as they discovered the wonder of each other. Maggie buried her head in the hollow of his shoulder. Now she knew what it felt like to be loved...

...the trembling of her body, the flesh that grew dry and feverish until she hungrily opened herself to his maleness, the lightness and the rising of her body as it was borne and swept away on currents of desire and anticipation of ecstasy...her hips moving effortlessly and irresisti-

ply . . . the throbbing, the pulsating, the convulsion . . . and
that final great spasm that racked her body, imparting an
iron rigidity and yet a weightlessness . . . and ultimately that
exhilarating and frightening geysering of unbelievable pleasure, followed by the warm glow of lassitude, as if she had
lain a long time in the sun and was sapped of all energy.

But not once had Wolf whispered a word of love.

He shifted his shoulder so that his thumb and forefinger
could catch her chin. He tilted it, but she was afraid to meet
his eyes, to see the triumph blazing there.

CHAPTER
thirty-two

⚜

*T*he Buffalo chapter of the Wyoming Women's Club was fifteen minutes late in ending, and when Peg opened the door, Maggie walked in to find her parlor rammed with men. "Reporters and photographers," Peg said, taking Maggie's cloche hat, kid gloves, and red fox coat from her.

"Thanks, Peg," she said quietly. "Where's Jamie? Shouldn't he be home from school by now?"

A guilty look crossed Peg's usually cheerful expression. "Benito—Mr. Bilbao—came by half an hour ago for Jamie." The woman added hurriedly, "'oo know how much fun Jamie had at La Conquista last summer, and, well, Mr. Bilbao invited him back for the weekend. She blushed and asked, "'oo don't mind, do you, Maggie me dear? Seeing as how you and Mr. Bilbao's son-in-law don't get along, I didn't know if I should be letting him go or not."

So that was how things were with Peg and Benito. It made Maggie glad. Those were two people who deserved to be happy. Or was there really such a thing as that kind of happiness?

Her gaze went past the double parlor doors to Frank who stood in the circle of men, smiling and gesturing expansively. He saw her and held out his hand, beckoning her to join him. "Sorry, I'm late," she said, casting a polite smile at the surrounding men before she held up her cheek for her husband's perfunctory kiss.

His kisses had grown more proprietary since the summer before when he returned with Wright and Crawford to Wolf's cabin. The look in her husband's eyes when he saw her sitting on the couch alone, calmly drinking coffee, told her that he knew that Wolf had been there, that he knew what had transpired between her and Wolf. She wasn't surprised for she felt sure the impassioned hours she had lived through the previous night had to have left their imprint on her face.

But what did surprise her was the look on Frank's face, one almost of triumph. And when the two of them were finally alone on the drive back to Buffalo, Frank's words shocked her even more.

"It's obvious you've been in Wolf's bed, Maggie. Oh, don't try to deny it. I'm glad."

"You're glad?" she echoed.

"Sure. Now that you see the sex act for what it is—a fun time in bed and nothing more—you can get the man out of your mind."

"You set us up!"

"Certain events conspired to help," he said grimly. He took his eyes from the road and glanced at her. "Maggie, I'm not as obtuse as you think. I need you, and if it means letting you fly free occasionally in order that you return to me, then I'll gladly open the cage's door."

Her laugh had been cynical. "Emma Goldman would have loved to have recruited you for the woman's movement."

Now, in their parlor, Frank put an arm about her waist and winked at her, saying, "I was just letting the press in on a scoop."

"Your husband has just announced his candidacy for the coming gubernatorial race," a female reporter said.

Maggie and Frank had argued all the points that would ve to be covered a hundred times since Governor Wilson d announced he was retiring from office the week before. ank thought he would be a shoo-in for office, but she felt other two years of campaigning would be needed. How- er, she smiled radiantly as one of the photographer's shbulbs exploded. While the man quickly changed the mera's plates, a reporter standing next to him asked, "If ur husband wins the election, Mrs. Van der Rhys, how you think you'll like living in the governor's mansion?"

Wolf had asked something similar that last hour they had ent together in his cabin, though his tone had been not spectful but scathing. They were dressing, or rather he as dressing her, buttoning her blouse.

His hands lingered on the top button, and he said, "Mag- e, come with me."

She turned away, unable to meet the passion that burned the heavy lidded eyes, and reached for the cigarette pack- e on the low stand. Her hand trembled as she shook out cigarette. "I can't."

His eyes narrowed. "You can't," he asked softly, "or on't?"

"There's Frank's career," she muttered.

He caught her wrist and jerked her up against him. "It's e governor's mansion you want for yourself, isn't it? Vi- ariously you're seeking to enjoy a sense of power over the ale sex."

"They've dominated politics for too long!" she retorted, lieved at channeling the argument in another direction. ut Wolf didn't buy it.

His fingers dug into her arms. "It's not politics we're lking about, Maggie. It's this."

He crushed her to him, his arms about her waist and ack, holding her immobile as his lips captured hers and his tongue ravaged the interior of her mouth. A weakne slithered through her and she was unable to pull free as h hands slid down to pin her hips against him. The kiss wa like a drug, slowly dulling her brain's messages of resi tance. Then, like a puppet, her hands slipped up over h chest to encircle his neck, and she gave over to the exhi aration that vibrated through her. As she relinquished th last vestige of self-control, her mouth opened to his.

At last, as if he sensed that final acquiescence of he body, he released her from the rapacious kiss. With an effo her eyes opened, to focus on his, that blazed with a fierc domination. She knew then the scales had tipped in h favor. He had completed his domination of her body. Hov long before her own free will would be subjugated to tha of his? She must break, once and for all, whatever cord was that bound them to each other.

She forced a brazen smile to her lips. "You were righ Sex is marvelous. You've been good for me, Wolf. I don think I shall ever be afraid of men again." She laughe flippantly and rubbed her fingertip down the groove in hi beard-stubbled chin. "Who knows, perhaps I shall turn th tables and use their sexual weakness to my advantage."

The force of his palm slashing across her face, knocke her backwards. She stumbled. Grabbing at the chair, sh kept herself from falling. Her fingers slid up to touch he throbbing cheek. She saw the powerful fury that smoke his eyes and the faint flicker in his jaws, and another typ of fear grabbed hold of her. But he made no move towar her.

"I don't know if you're worth the effort, but by God Maggie, I will yet break you to my will." He paused at th door and said with a contemptuous sneer, "Screwing yo was just the first step!"

She should have known that Wolf would never be a generous, as civilized, as Frank was in his concept of fre love. Wolf was too primitive to share something he con sidered his. Frank was exactly what she wanted in a man. He left her free to do what she wanted. He did not try to dominate her. So why were her thoughts ever meshed about Wolf?

Wolf had gone then, left her alone with his violent promise and the memory of those last intimate hours that she swore she would forget. But over the months she had not been able to forget; the vision of those fierce, predatory eyes still haunted her, even now as she smiled charmingly at the reporter and said, "I'm very much looking forward to living in the governor's mansion," adding the usual inanity every hopeful first lady must: "I think it would be marvelous to become involved in the redecorations."

There were many more questions tossed at Frank, questions she had prepared him for and answers she had coached him on over the preceding days. Her years of thoroughly reading a multitude of newspapers were paying off.

The famous, or infamous, Cheyenne Club was demolished now, making way for the capital's new Chamber of Commerce. Thus, that January, Wolf signed in at the Plains Hotel for the forty days of the legislation's session. Once in his room he stretched out on the bed that was, like all others, too short for him, and picked up The *Wyoming State Tribune*. As usual, Frank's photo was in it, this time on the second page. He was shaking hands with Cheyenne's mayor over a donation the Elks Club had just made to the city's children's home.

Wolf held the paper closer. Yes, in the background, smiling, stood Maggie. She hadn't changed. She was still just as beautiful, in that haughty way of some royal princess. His fingers itched to entangle themselves in that long, golden-spun hair; his mouth wanted to shatter that mask of cool control with ravaging kisses. He wadded the newspaper into a crumpled ball and hurled it against the room's far wall. Damn her!

He was still damning her two months later when, during the last days of the session, the Senate met to vote on the Travel, Recreation, and Wildlife Committee's recommendation on the dude ranch proposal. He watched Frank move among the members of his party, stopping at each desk to talk. Would the bastard be able to swing the bill's passage? Since the voting almost always followed party lines, Wolf had little hope that there would be a partisan division.

Normally, he would not have been so adamant against the bill's passage. The members of his party did not really care one way or another. But they looked to him as their floor leader for direction in the matter. He told himself that he was against the bill not only because it *was* harmful to Wyoming's future, but also because there had to be a halt put on legislators like Frank sponsoring bills that benefitted their own pocket. In reality, Wolf knew there was a much greater reason for his strong opposition to the Dude Ranch Bill.

His gaze swept up past the Senate's rectangular stained-glass ceiling to search the smattering of spectators in the gallery. But Maggie was not among them.

The President of the Senate was calling the meeting to order when the door off to one side of the Senate gallery opened, and Maggie slipped through. From his desk he saw her slide quietly into one of the many vacant seats near the front. It was difficult for him to realize that she must be twenty-eight, that for a dozen years or more she had held sway in his mind.

She wore a smartly tailored pearl-gray suit with a frothy apricot blouse. That, her peekaboo gray felt hat, and her heels were her only concession to her feminine gender. If she was aware of his scrutiny, she did not indicate it. Not once did she so much as glance down in his direction.

For a few moments he permitted himself the luxury of dwelling on her. He recalled the fiery passion that burned beneath the glacial exterior; he recalled the way her hair, hanging past the small of her back when unbound, had spread out like molten gold over his loins, setting them afire, and how when she moved the stray tendrils teased and feathered the taut sun-darkened skin of his stomach, contrasting so sharply with the coal black patch that apexed at the fork of his legs.

She shifted her legs, and his gaze was momentarily drawn to the shapely ankles encased in the flesh-colored hose. But as she leaned forward to watch the proceedings below, the intensity in her face drew his gaze back to the matters at hand. The Reading Clerk had just delivered the third reading of the legislation. Now came the roll call and the voting on the Dude Ranch Bill. For a moment he forgot her as his attention returned to the Senators who delivered their ayes and nays.

He knew even before the count was in that the bill would pass. Apparently Maggie did also, for she rose to leave, the fox fur coat draped over her arm. Only then did she glance in his direction, and he saw an expression of triumph before she turned away and walked toward the gallery doors.

He moved then, silently, quickly, exiting through the chamber's side door. He heard her heels click on the steps as she descended the staircase. He headed her off at the bottom. Two-thirds of the way down the flight, she looked up to see him waiting below. He took some satisfaction at the fear that flickered behind the lenses of her glasses. He took the five steps separating them and grabbed her elbow. "What do you want?" she demanded.

What was it about her, just looking at her, that made him want to mount her like some determined stallion? He hauled her down the stairs and thrust her through the Senate's cloak room door. He slammed the door behind him. She backed until she could go no farther and was enfolded by the hanging clusters of overcoats. "You won this round," he gritted, "but I want the consolation prize, Maggie."

The need to impose his will on her caused him to catch

her shoulders and press her against the wall. His mouth silenced her faint outcry; his lips conquered hers with a hard kiss. Her head twisted from one side to the other in an attempt to escape the domination of his kiss, but after a moment her fur coat slid to the floor at their feet. The hands pressed against his chest relaxed.

He pulled away and looked down at the upturned face. Behind the lenses, her thick sooty eyelashes fluttered tremulously before raising to reveal eyes glistening with tears. "You can play at being the First Lady of politics and fool Wyoming society into believing your subdued respectability," he said harshly. "But you and I both know it's a facade, Maggie. You'll be as restless as a wild horse corralled."

"And who be you to lecture me?" she bit back, slipping into her Irish brogue. "You, who married for land and money!"

He grinned then. "You don't know the first thing about me, Maggie. But you will. By the time I have finished with you—"

"You *are* finished with me! *We're* finished!"

"Oh, no," he snapped, his fingers biting into her shoulders. "I'm not finished with you yet." The commotion in the hall signaled the Senate had adjourned. He reached down and picked up her coat, thrusting it at her. "And I'm making you another promise: to run against your husband for governor."

"It was a rash thing to do, I know," Wolf said, as he knotted Benito's black bowtie for him. "But someone has to oppose Van der Rhys. He'll corrupt the government so badly that he'll make Wyoming's Teapot Dome Scandal four years ago seem like a nice little tea party!"

Benito turned away to look in the three-part, gold-flecked mirror. "I think you'll make an excellent governor, Wolf. But are you old enough to run for office? I thought there

was some state law about having to have thirty years of age
or something."

"You do, but only by the time the Oath of Office is
administered, which would come eight days after my thir-
tieth birthday."

Benito adjusted the bowtie slightly and sucked in his
stomach. "Do you think I'm too old to get married again,
Wolf?"

The habitual cynicism carved in the two grooves flanking
Wolf's mouth faded with his sincere smile. "Hardly. And
I think Peg will keep you young."

Benito turned back and faced his former son-in-law. "You
realize, of course, that Celina and Diego will be here today?"

Wolf nodded. Celina and Diego had run off to Cheyenne
to get married the day after their divorce had become final.
Benito told him that Diego had worked at several outfits
before drifting down to Texas the year before. Wolf felt
certain that Celina had a chance at happiness now. He smiled
ruefully, thinking that at least Diego would not be afraid to
tell his wife he loved her.

His thoughts turned to Maggie, knowing that she would
be present at Buffalo's Catholic church as Peg's matron of
honor. Even if he could admit to himself that he loved her,
how did he tell that to a woman who belonged to another
man? Their argument in the cloakroom the previous winter
had caused him to take stock in what he really wanted from
life. That night he had lain in his hotel bed and chain-smoked
while his mind reflected on the women he had known and
reviewed the affairs he had lightly gone through.

Now, as he drove Benito to Buffalo, he considered what
he was doing. He knew that for so long he had avoided
making any kind of commitment. Knowing this made him
that much more determined to stand by his decision to run
for the governor's office. And, of course, only in defeating
Frank, and thus Maggie, did he have that slim chance at

winning her. It was a last-ditch battle of wills, and his mal-
instinct knew that a nature as strong as hers would neve
allow her to give herself to a man whom she could in any
way dominate.

"Hey," Benito said, interrupting his morose thoughts
"you look like you're on your way to an execution, not to
my wedding."

He pulled his gaze from the newly oil-topped road and
quirked a smile in Benito's direction. "Sorry, Benito."

But the Basque was right, he thought. Soon he would
be facing Maggie. And he'd almost rather face a firing squad
than have to see Maggie, watch as Frank put a possessive
arm about her—not now, not after having her, after knowing her more intimately than any man ever would. It'd be
like ripping his guts out.

And yet he knew, despite it all, that his pulse was beating
as irregularly as the old Ford's engine in anticipation of
seeing her again, of just watching the sway of those sensuously curved hips, of watching the warm blush suffuse
her skin, contradicting the cool, controlled gaze.

"It's Maggie, isn't it?" Benito asked.

"It always has been," he replied, and was grateful that
Benito didn't pry further.

He turned off Buffalo's Main Street and wheeled into
the church parking lot, his narrowed gaze searching for
Frank's Lincoln. Benito and Peg had opted for a small
wedding. Only a few cars dotted the parking lot, and the
Lincoln was not among them.

From the chapel's archway, a tall boy stepped forward.
It appeared he was about to wrap his arms about Benito,
then recovered and held out his hand, first to his future
stepfather, then to Wolf. "How do you do, sir," Jamie said
politely to both with only the barest trace of brogue to color
his English.

Wolf rumpled the boy's unruly red-brown curls, and
Benito put an affectionate arm about the boy's shoulder.

ut both men were anxiously searching beyond for sight of
he particular woman. It was Benito who breathed a sigh
; Peg appeared, looking almost vibrantly beautiful in a
ale-green, street-length coat, her wild, gloriously red curls
nchored closely to her head by a green-feathered, shallow-
-immed hat.

Wolf's gaze moved behind the woman and came back
> meet her shadowed eyes. Despite his reslove, he asked,
Where's Maggie?"

Peg looked to Benito and back to Wolf. "There was an
:cident this morning."

His heart lurched like the sudden breaking of a runaway
igine. "What happened?"

Weeping, Peg turned into the shelter of the arm Benito
ut about her, and Wolf thought the blood vessels in his
:mples were going to burst.

CHAPTER
thirty-three

❧❦❧

*T*he stoop-shouldered doctor pulled the stethoscope from his ears and drew the sheets up over the lower half of the bandaged torso. He looked at Maggie, who stood on the other side of the hospital bed. "Your husband will eventually regain the use of his limbs, but it may take a long time, maybe as much as a year or more. And even then he'll probably walk with a limp."

Maggie nodded, unable to fully comprehend everything that had happened. That morning Frank had left as usual for the gunsmith to take care of some last-minute business before the wedding. Then there was the sudden screech of tires, followed by shouts, and a few seconds later, the neighbors at her door. Apparently whoever hit Frank as he stepped from the curb had panicked and immediately driven away from the scene.

There were more shocks to come. The next week, when she went by the bank to see about withdrawing some money to pay the hospital, she discovered there were no funds in their account.

There had to be a mistake! She hurried across the street to the accountant. The rubicund little man popped his suspenders nervously. "Well, you see, Mrs. Van der Rhys, sometimes there's a lot of money, and, well, sometimes your husbands draws out a lot."

She was getting nowhere. Years before, when she had turned over her ledgers to an accountant, she had grudgingly relinquished a portion of her knowledge of Frank's outside activities. But she had deemed the action necessary in order to assist Frank in his career. Now she questioned her wisdom.

Later that day, when she visited Frank at the hospital, he was a little improved, able to raise his head and drink from a glass, albeit somewhat shakily. But he seemed unwilling to talk, and answered her few questions in monosyllables. With Frank depressed, she decided that now was not the time to create any further stress by questioning him. She went home that evening and sat in the dark parlor, gathering her thoughts. Money was needed badly. And with Frank unable to work, a special election committee would have to be called immediately to fill his place as Senator, putting an end to that source of income. There seemed no recourse but for her to look for work as soon as possible.

She sighed, wishing Peg was there to talk to. But Peg and Jamie were at La Conquista now. The room was too dark and too lonely. The ring of the telephone shook her from her dismal reflections. Warily she picked up the earpiece. "Yes?"

"Maggie." Her breath sucked in. "It's Wolf."

"I know." How to explain she had almost sensed it was Wolf before she answered the telephone.

"Are you all right?" That soft, exciting drawl. She began trembling just at the mere sound of his voice. She must be possessed. "I want to come over. You need some—"

"No!" her voice almost croaked.

"Don't be childish, Maggie! I'll bring Peg, if it'll make
ou feel any better. She wants to come."

Maggie drew a deep breath and looked around the dark-
ned room for her cigarettes. "No," she said, forcing a
:almness to her voice. "I'm all right. And Peg needs to
pend her honeymoon with her husband. Please tell her I'm
orry I missed the wedding, and give her my love and best
vishes. Good-bye."

Closing her eyes, she replaced the earpiece with a sigh
of relief. The knocker thudded against the door. Damn! Was
here nowhere she could hide?

She opened the door to Weidemeyer and another gentle-
nan, whose age-wrinkled face was vaguely familiar; she
emembered seeing him at some of the committee meetings
she had attended. Weidemeyer twisted his bowler hat in his
nands and mumbled, "I know this is an inopportune moment, Maggie, but we'll only take a few minutes of your
time."

She invited the two men into the parlor and turned on
the lamps. Weidemeyer waited until she had seated herself
in the wingback chair, then introduced the elderly man with
him. "Mr. Rankin, the Chairman of the State Democratic
Committee; Mrs. Van der Rhys."

She turned her attention on the somberly dressed man,
and he began hesitantly but clearly. "Mrs. Van der Rhys,
after meeting with some of my committee members, we
have come to the conclusion that you are the one who must
become the candidate of our party to fill the place left vacant
by your husband."

With her gesture of dismay, he said gently, "Hear me
out. You have lived in an atmosphere of politics for close
to ten years now and have been vitally interested in the
problems and policies of the administration. And you have
the distinct advantage of familiarity with the general re-
quirements of the legislator and with the particular affairs

of the various senate committees. I can think of no one in our party better qualified to fill Frank's shoes. Do not answer me now, but give it your thought." Then, with assurances of loyalty and friendship, the two men left.

For the next few days she did think about it. She knew that if she were to run in the special election that would have to be held, many of the voters would question the ability of a woman in politics.

When, toward the end of the week she at last broached the subject to Frank, she was surprised to see the lightening of the new lines that had been taking their toll on his handsome face since the accident. He reached out and took her hands. "I couldn't be happier, Maggie. It's important to me you carry on my unfinished work."

Three days later, when the emergency convention announced its nominees for the special election, she was besieged by reporters. Calmly she posed for photographers on the front-door steps and fielded the questions.

"Mrs. Van der Rhys," one reporter queried, "do you think that, as a wife, you will be hampered in your new position?"

"Sir, as a husband, are you hampered in your profession?"

Applause broke out, and Maggie uttered an inward sigh. The first hurdle was over.

She decided it wiser to make practically no effort on her own behalf in campaigning. Her only utterance was a letter to the public, first, pledging that she would do everything in her power to complete her husband's term of office to the best of her ability, devoting herself heart and soul to public service so that never, through failure of hers, could it be truthfully said that a woman should not be entrusted with a high office.

Maggie remained at the bed beside Frank, who had at last been released from the hospital, while the State Canvassing Board compiled the official figures. "You must win this," Frank said, agitation edging his weakened voice.

The first inkling she had of her election came an hour later when a motion picture operator telephoned her from a distance of two hundred miles to make an appointment to film her engaged in some domestic activity, "such as making bread or sweeping." And when a little later reporters gathered outside her house, she stepped out onto the front porch and smiled for the photographers.

After she falteringly expressed her gratitude and her hope that she might justify the trust the people put in her, she was bombarded with questions. "Senator Van der Rhys," queried a reporter from the *Denver Post*, "do you plan to continue in your husband's footsteps and enter the campaign for governor against Congressman Nicholson?"

Maggie managed to smile. "Of course."

It may be chance or it may be destiny that Wyoming, first of all the states in the Union to extend equal suffrage to women, could also be first of all actually to have a woman inaugurated as governor!

Maggie put down the newspaper. She was getting used to seeing her name and picture in print. The cartoons she found most amusing. The *Chicago Tribune* pictured her in cowgirl costume riding into Cheyenne on a bucking bronco. Another cartoonist played on the traditional attitude of her sex and drew her as a stern mother shaking an admonishing finger at the small-boy legislature.

There was an immediate deluge of applications for offices, which by that time she knew to expect. And now that she was involved in the campaign for governor it became almost mandatory she attend the state functions, dinners, teas, and receptions for officials.

On the senate floor that next week she wondered what was worse, making her first motion, which practically gave her palpitation of the heart, or mixing with the all-male legislature, which she dryly judged would give her the black lung if she continued to smoke at the rate she was going.

But of course, the worst were those occasions she ran into Wolf, usually in the capitol corridors where there were spectators to watch the two opponents for the governor's office confront each other. She would nod her head, her expression polite and distant. Wolf would return the nod, his expression one of seeming insouciance. But in his eyes, the eyes of the beast, she saw lurking the devilish mockery.

The other legislators who made their not-so-subtle passes she could quail with one chilled glance, like pouring ice water over the desire in their faces. But not so Wolf. He alone was immune to the frigid contempt she turned on the male sex. Thus, it was all she could do to attend the reception for the visiting governor from Colorado, which was to be held at the executive mansion the last week of the legislative session.

As she donned the lavender-blue chiffon velvet evening dress, which with its simple lines contrasted sharply with the usual fringed and beaded bodices and uneven hems of the day, she murmured a silent prayer that this time Wolf would not be present. She slid into her fox fur and went into the parlor where Frank sat drinking a scotch and reading the sports page, his crutches propped against the chair's cushioned arm. His eyes raised above the page to gaze at her. He lowered the paper. "You're beautiful, Maggie."

His voice reminded her of their first months of marriage, when she really believed she could be the only woman in his life. She knelt by his side. "You'll be all right, won't you? I won't be gone long."

"I'll be fine." He took a sip of the scotch and said, "Crawford might drop by later to discuss a new venture he's interested in."

She frowned. She wished he would terminate his association with the man and some of the others who occasionally still stopped by the house. She always managed to find something else to do at those times. When she rose, Frank rabbed her hand. "Maggie, you won't ever leave me, will ou? I need you."

She saw the desperate entreaty in the blue eyes. Squeez-ıg his hand, she whispered, "No, Frank. I'll never leave ou."

The February wind wailed outside like an Irish banshee, nd Maggie, shivering in her car, knew with ominous cer-ainty she would see Wolf that night. The rising of the wind eemed to almost always presage Wolf's imminent ap-·earance; she nearly turned the car around. But the stubborn ighter in her refused to cower, not even when, fifteen ninutes later, she accepted a crystal leaded glass of the tandard fruit punch from a tray passed by a liveried butler nd looked across the crowded room to meet that deliberate ;aze.

She thought to escape it by mingling with the people, nostly politicians and their wives and the upper echelon of ames that graced The *Wyoming State Tribune*'s society)age. In the drawing room a black man sat at a Chickering :oncert grand piano and rhapsodized a melody beginning o catch on across the country, "Stardust." Beneath the)rismed light of the chandeliers, diamond necklaces spar-:led and genuine gold cuff links glittered. Maggie, barely ·asting the citrine punch she sipped, reflected that she had :ome a long way from the girl who had padded the insides)f her shoes with newspapers.

And soon, come November, she might finally achieve he fulfillment of all she wanted. And not by proxy through Frank, but on her own merit. The state of Wyoming and :ven the national press were taking notice of the first woman senator and were no longer shocked by the idea. And with woman suffrage becoming more and more a dominant factor n politics, Maggie found she had many backers suddenly anxious to campaign for her. The idea of a woman governor was not so far-fetched; the possibility of defeating her opposition was not so unrealistic.

Involuntarily her gaze shifted through the room of laughing faces to find the one face that never failed to arrest her. It was smiling sardonically at something murmured by one of Cheyenne's last season's debutantes, a pert strawberry blonde. Wolf looked wickedly handsome in the black dinner suit with the silk shirt's white ruffles at the cuffs accentuating just that much more his potent masculinity, primitive and out of place there in that civilized gathering.

Maggie decided she had stayed long enough. Besides, if the weather worsened any, she did not want to be driving home in it. She spent ten minutes longer in conversation with the Colorado governor, whose eyes kept straying to her breasts, sheathed by the clinging chiffon velvet, while he calmly talked about the severance tax on oil exploration he hoped his legislature would implement.

At the door Governor and Mrs. Wilson, a tiny woman in her fifties with a kindly face, bade her good-bye, and the Governor reminded her about the banking reform law he was sending over for her perusal the next day, saying, "That is, if you make it to your office. The weather may snowbound us all tomorrow if it gets any worse."

Mrs. Wilson looked out the door and exclaimed, "The snow's already piling in drifts."

Maggie moved to take the coat the butler brought her, but Wolf was suddenly there, taking the coat and sliding it over her shoulders. "It's too risky for Mrs. Van der Rhys to drive home alone. I'm on my way out. I'll see her home." He looked down at her and said, "You can send someone for your car tomorrow if the weather permits."

Maggie raged at his presumptiveness. What colossal arrogance! As if he had authority over her. But rather than create a scene, she slid into the fur, seething, and let him guide her out the door. While he started the engine, she huddled on the far side of the car in eloquent silence. Wolf said nothing as he guided the Packard out onto the snow-slickened streets. She cast a wary glance in his direction, noting the snowflakes that glistened in his dark brown hair.

"You don't have to sit over there trembling like you're about to face an execution squad, Maggie," he snapped. "You're safe enough with me."

"Am I?" she asked breathlessly.

His hands tightened on the steering wheel. "The campaign you're waging for the governor's office—it's more than a political race, isn't it?" He flung her a hard, penetrating look. "It's an all-out effort to break the final domination of the male sex."

Something inside her snapped. "And what about you? Aren't you afraid of the domination a woman might have on you? Aren't you afraid of committing yourself in loving?" She recalled Celina's hungry eyes and understood now. "I bet you never even once told your wife you loved her! Now I know why she took another lover!"

He kept his gaze on the demands of the treacherous road, but when he at last spoke his voice was as raw and bracing as the arctic wind that slammed against the car. "You already have your lover, don't you, Maggie? But a career makes a mighty cold bedpartner."

He pulled up before her house and turned to her. With a shock she saw the agony that burned in his dark eyes. "All these years I wanted you, for your love," he said in a low, terse voice. "But you could not spare me one breath of your life. Our paths have crossed once too often. Goodbye, Maggie."

"You *will* cast your vote in favor of the Railroad Right of Way?"

Maggie halted in drawing on her gloves. It was the second or third time Frank had brought up the subject that week. She turned to look at him. "I'm not so sure. It depends on the final testimony today. Some of the committee members feel further investigation is called for before they give their approval."

He limped toward her on the crutches, and she noticed again how thin he was, how dark the circles were beneath his eyes, more often than not red-rimmed by too much drinking. "You have to persuade them differently."

"It's not up to—" She broke off when she saw the intensity that rigidified his face.

"You have to."

Maggie slowly sank in the nearest chair. "Why?" she asked, praying that this time her instincts were wrong.

Frank gripped the crutches and hobbled over to the window. "Because I've been taking bribes," he said quietly.

"Frank! No, it—"

He whirled on her. "Where do you think that fur came from, and our house, and everything else I've given you over the years?"

He stood over her, glaring down at her. Her eyes widened as the import of what he was telling her hit her.

She took a deep breath. "Who all is involved in this?"

"Hell, Maggie, almost everyone is involved in the syndicate these days. It goes all the way to the White House. From politicians in the local precincts to presidential cabinet members. Fortunes have been made selling inside information, trading favors, using entrusted secrets."

Horrified, she shut her eyes, wanting to block from her sight the truth of the corruption. She began to shake her head.

"Maggie, Maggie," Frank implored, "just this once, vote for the Railroad Right of Way, and I promise I'll get out of the syndicate. I swear I'll never take another bribe."

She opened her eyes and met her husband's wild gaze. "I can't, Frank. It's unscrupulous."

He hurled one of his crutches at the wall, and a picture frame thudded to the floor, the glass shattering. He whirled n her. "Dammit! Don't you understand what I'm saying? The gambling has gotten me in over my head in debts. When I couldn't meet my commitments—Maggie, this accident was no accident! It was a warning! You've got to go through with this for me. If the Railroad Right of Way is cleared by the Senate, I'll receive the—" He broke off and said instead, "I can pay off my gambling debts. If not... Maggie, for God's sake, we lose everything!"

CHAPTER
thirty-four

"*Senator Van der Rhys?*"

There was a silence that almost echoed in the senate chambers. Wolf watched as Maggie, stately and regal, slowly rose to her feet to deliver her vote on the Railroad Right of Way Act. He felt the old want stir in him. He shifted to ease the hardening.

Maggie's eyes gazed coolly from behind the lenses that could not disguise her beauty. That square little chin was held high. Haughty as a queen—no, he thought, haughty as a governor. Though the elections were still more than six months away, she was virtually assured the governor's office due to the support of the various factions that were falling in behind the increasingly popular women's movement. It was an idea whose time had finally come.

He looked down at the typewritten letter on his desk. 'HAVE EVIDENCE YOU SOUGHT WHICH CONFIRMS FRANK VAN DER RHYS INVOLVEMENT IN RAILROAD PAYOFF. KRAUSLOW PRIVATE AGENCY."

For years Wolf had suspected Van der Rhys's illegal machinations. All he had to do was produce the evidence

against Van der Rhys. Not only would the election be his
but he would ultimately break Maggie's will. He woul
bend her indomitable will to his, which was what he wante
above all else: Maggie's surrender.

Maggie. He looked at her again. The want of her actuall
hurt, like some cancerous cell eating away at his guts. Hi
jaws clenched. For years she had been his every wakin
thought. For years he had both damned her and desired her

And loved her.

After all these lonely years he had finally learned to le
himself love. Somehow Maggie had broken down his fea
of loving, of giving.

Only the strongest of natures, only a woman like Maggie
would on the unfairest possible terms, with all the rule
made by the enemy, fight men on their own ground an
openly contend for the equality of the sexes. He believe
in her integrity and knew that in the governor's office sh
would carry out her duties honestly. And he would not b
the one to deny her that chance.

He wadded up the letter and tossed it into the trash ca
beside his desk. In losing—losing the election, losing Mag
gie Van der Rhys—he was ironically winning.

"Senator Van der Rhys?" the President of the Senat
repeated.

In the prolonged silence, heads began to turn in he
direction. All that was required of her was a simple aye.

Why then did her mouth feel like cotton and her knee
shake? Perspiration broke out on her forehead. In the galler
she saw Crawford, clutched to his chair like a slug an
watching her with malevolent intensity. If she voted agains
the proposal, she and Frank would lose everything. And sh
would lose what she had worked for all those years. Hardl
a choice.

*Dear God, no; not now! Don't force such a decision o
me!*

She opened her mouth . . . and closed it as her gaze fell
n the American flag draped on the wall behind the President
f the Senate's chair. The image of that flag on Kate De
alera's wall flashed through her mind. It was that flag that
ad enabled her to escape the horrors of Ireland and had
iven her the opportunities Ireland lacked. In that one mo-
ent, she took the only course of action she could live with.

"Gentlemen," she began her voice clear, steady, "rather
an cast a vote, I must use this moment to expose to you
e corruption that lurks behind this Railroad Right of Way
ill."

What she had to say did not take long. She named the
onspirators she knew, and in her peripheral vision was
ware that Crawford blanched a pasty white. His and Wright's
ays of wheeling and dealing were over. The gasps as she
evealed Frank's part in the bribery seemed to her to re-
erberate throughout the senate chambers. In the resulting
onfusion and bedlam, she left by the side door. She wanted
nly to hurry home to Frank and privacy.

She had hoped to have time to prepare Frank for what
he had done. But incredibly, the phone was ringing as soon
s she opened the door. "I'll get it," she told Frank, who
vas awkwardly wielding his crutches toward the telephone.
he picked up the receiver and answered, not surprised that
he caller was a reporter. "I've already made my statement,"
he said crisply and hung up.

"How did you vote?" Frank asked, his voice shaky.

She took a deep breath. "I told the Senate everything,
rank."

His face blanched. "How could you do that to me?" he
vhispered, his voice raw with fear.

"I did it *for* you!" She grabbed his shoulders. "Oh, Frank,
lon't you see? An end had to be put to the corruption
ometime. The next time you were unable to pay off your
ambling debts, it would maybe mean your life."

"You fool!" he shouted. His palm lashed out, and her

head jerked with the impact. She held the back of her har
against her stinging cheek and blinked back the tears th
threatened to spill over as Frank hobbled into the bedroo
and slammed the door.

Frank was right. She was a fool. And she knew she wa
She had forfeited her dream of being the first woman go
ernor. With the Van der Rhys name besmirched by scanda
she would lose the election by a landslide.

Her hands trembling, she lit up a cigarette and went
the window. A soft, gentle snow flurried to the ground wi
no wind to swirl it. No wind.

It was a peaceful scene, but there was no peace in h
mind as her agonizing thoughts raged against the futility
all her life's efforts. Then even the peaceful scene wa
shattered by the gunblast. Instantly she knew. She spun an
raced for the bedroom. At first she saw nothing but Frank
firearm case open on the bed. Then beyond the bed she sa
his feet. And the crimson-sprayed floor.

And she heard the screaming, her own.

CHAPTER
thirty-five

ᑲ᜶ᑲ᜶ᑲ᜶

"'Oo're getting some color back into those cheeks, me girl."

Maggie smiled lazily, a smile that did not really reach the shadowed eyes, and tipped her face back up to the sun, closing her eyes, feeling its warmth soak into her cold, lifeless interior. For two weeks now she had sought out the green striped lawn chair on the veranda to catch the afternoon sun, drowsing in its opiatic heat. "Thank you for letting me come, Peg. I had to get away from Buffalo for a while."

Peg plopped down beside her and laid her hands across her ample stomach, even larger now with the child she carried. "'oo don't have to go back. 'oo could stay at La Conquista as long as 'oo be wanting. Me jamie adores 'oo, and Benito couldn't be happier for me to have another woman around to talk to."

Maggie knew there was nothing in either Buffalo or Cheyenne to go back to. After Frank's funeral she had sold everything in both houses to try and pay off the debts that had mounted up. And she had withdrawn from the gover-

287

nor's race and withdrawn from the world. That part was easy, with winter to isolate her. But spring brought too many prying people to her doorstep. She had retreated to La Conquista, where Peg's unquestioning friendship was like a balm. Yet she could not hide away at La Conquista forever. Somehow she had to rebuild her life.

Aloud she said, "I have been thinking about returning to New York, Peg. Perhaps I can start over again there."

"'oo'd leave Wyoming—give up all this wild beauty?" Peg asked incredulously.

"There's nothing here left for me."

"Aunt Maggie," Jamie called. He pushed open the screen door and stuck his freckled face out. "Can I have a slice of that apple pie you baked?"

Maggie smiled fondly at the boy. "You'll have to ask your mom, sweat-pea."

Peg sighed and rose. "'oo be like a sheep, James Bilbao, eating everything in sight. Come along now, and I'll cut 'oo a piece."

Peg paused at the screen door before following her son inside. "Maggie, girl. Mayhap tis none of me business, but I know there's something a'tween 'oo and Wolf. Benito told me about the man, about how he watched his mother and sister die in one of those bloody revolutions. Mind 'oo, I knew I be meddling, but just maybe he loves 'oo more than 'oo be kening. Think on it," she said and stepped inside.

Maggie rose, too, but instead turned her footsteps in the direction of the outbuildings, hands jammed in the pockets of her trousers. A dragonfly fluttered ahead of her, and grasshoppers droned in the tall gray-green grass encroaching on either side of the dusty drive. The sweet scent of spring's wildflowers drifted up to envelope her, slowly awakening her to reality. Over the weeks at La Conquista she began to realize that she had looked upon the male sex as menace incarnate. But now it seemed that it was her fears and her

elf-doubt that was the villain. She had been her own op-
onent.

Yet she had also fought against fate, against being a
awn of circumstance. And she had won. She did have a
hoice, the choice of how she could live: courageously or
n cowardice, honorably or dishonorably, with purpose or
n drift.

And she had decided what was trivial and what was
mportant to her in life. But the one thing that was, Wolf's
ove, she had destroyed by her own willfulness. In the
nonths that had followed Frank's death she had been too
umb to cry. But now the tears brimmed over. Blindly she
:ontinued to walk down the drive, as one by one the tear-
lrops trickled down her cheeks.

She was not really sure what it was that caused her
ootsteps to slow. Vaguely she was aware that her tears
vere rapidly drying on her cheeks. Then she understood
vhy and what it was that caused her to halt: the wind. The
vind was rising, swirling the high grass about her, stirring
he dust into billowing eddies.

The wind beckoned her!

Wolf's dark head canted. There it was again. Above the
rustling of the wind through the trees he heard the hum of
a car motor. He closed the ranch's books on which he had
been working and crossed the room to throw open the rough-
hewn wooden door. At first he was not sure whether to
believe his eyes. But—yes, it *was* the Lincoln, and as the
car drew closer, he could make out Maggie.

Rarely in his lifetime could he remember being afraid—
not anxious as he had been during the Russian purge but
gut-wrenching scared. Yet now, as he watched the small,
slender woman come toward him, a fear knotted in him.
His blood vessels pounded at his temples, and his hands
clenched at his sides. Dear God in heaven, he had hoped

for more time before he would have to encounter that tantalizing face again. How could he control the hands that ached to catch her to him, when he could not even control his daily thoughts and nightly dreams about her?

And how she must hate him! She had lost all, and he stood to win what she wanted most. His lids narrowed as she came to stand before him. That stubborn little chin of hers tilted upwards. Her lips, curved so sensuously, quivered.

"Wolf," she said in a voice that was almost inaudible yet very brave, very courageous, "I was wrong. All my life I was fighting for the wrong thing. Is it too late for—'

He was unable to help himself. His arms swept about her waist and under her legs, and he cradled that small feminine body up against his chest. He felt the tears that smarted his eyes. "Maggie, love, we have the rest of time.'

He swung around and strode with her in his arms toward the bedroom, and a slight whisper of wind softly blew the door closed.

They watched from the heavens above, the venerable gods who amuse themselves with mankind's activities, as the young man and woman committed themselves to a lifetime of loving. Above the roar of the wind the old deities' ears strained to hear the words that passed between the two below. Slowly, almost reverently, the man withdrew the pins from the woman's tawny hair. When his lips finally released hers, he whispered, "I love you."

"I lost!" muttered the one old god, agitatedly stroking his long beard with gnarled fingers. "I lost after all!"

"Of course, you did, you old fool," gibed a god who was some millennium younger.

"But I had it all down, right to the last minute of their coinciding births," the old god wailed.

"Bah! How could you forget the Russians still used the

lian calendar at the date of the man's birth? The girl is
a days older."

The old god grabbed up the dice. "We shall bet on a
volution this time! A much safer wager than the course
love!"

About the Author

A favorite of romance readers everywhere, Parris Afton Bonds is the author of 9 books and mother of 5 sons. In addition, she teaches creative writing at a local community college. Her most recent Fawcett title, DEEP PURPLE, was a best-selling trade paperback. She is a co-founder and board member of Romance Writers of America, and was the recipient of the Best Novel of 1981 award given by the Texas Press Women for her novel, DUST DEVIL.